CASTON...
PAF...
A Regency Upsta...

**Survival of the fittest is fine, so long as you're the
one on top...but the family that has everything
is about to lose it all...**

The Montagues have found themselves at the centre of the
ton's rumour mill, with lords and ladies alike claiming the
family is not what it used to be.

The mysterious death of the heir to the Dukedom, and the
arrival of an unknown woman claiming he fathered her son,
is only the tip of the iceberg in a family where scandal
upstairs *and* downstairs threatens the very foundations
of their once powerful and revered dynasty...

August 2012
THE WICKED LORD MONTAGUE – Carole Mortimer

September 2012
THE HOUSEMAID'S SCANDALOUS SECRET – Helen Dickson

October 2012
THE LADY WHO BROKE THE RULES – Marguerite Kaye

November 2012
LADY OF SHAME – Ann Lethbridge

December 2012
THE ILLEGITIMATE MONTAGUE – Sarah Mallory

January 2013
UNBEFITTING A LADY – Bronwyn Scott

February 2013
REDEMPTION OF A FALLEN WOMAN – Joanna Fulford

March 2013
A STRANGER AT CASTONBURY – Amanda McCabe

Montague Family Tree

Hannah Stratton
Housekeeper
b.1766

Duchess of Rothermere
b.1767
d.1800

Duke of Rothermere
b.1758

Charles
b.1761
d.1797

Claire
b.1787

Adam
b.1784

Jamie
b.1786

Giles
b.1788

Henry
(Harry)
b.1791

Kate
b.1792

Edward
b.1796
d.1815

Phaedra
b.1796

Ross
b.1787

Araminta
b.1795

KEY:
↔ Legal Marriage
| Child
┆ Suspected illegitimate child
▬ Sibling
▬ Half sibling

Darling Kate,

I know you have had a turbulent time of late and that being part of the Montague family comes with its own pressures. Still, it is good to have you home, where I hasten to say I can keep an eye on you. Daughter, your fiery nature and past misdemeanours have not gone unnoticed by me or the rest of the household. Still, your reputation can be salvaged—and I do hope you'll take this time to find a most suitable husband.

Yours,

Father

First published in Great Britain 2012
Mills & Boon, an imprint of Harlequin (UK) Limited,
Eton House, 18-24 Paradise Road, Richmond, Surrey TW9 1SR

© Marguerite Kaye 2012

ISBN: 978 0 263 90187 0

52-1012

Harlequin (UK) policy is to use papers that are natural, renewable and recyclable products and made from wood grown in sustainable forests. The logging and manufacturing processes conform to the legal environmental regulations of the country of origin.

Printed and bound
by CPI Group (UK) Ltd, Croydon, CR0 4YY

The
Lady Who Broke
the Rules

❧ MARGUERITE KAYE ❧

To the strong women in my life, from my mother and sister to my friends and the authors who inspire and encourage me.
Annie

Prologue

Booth Plantation, Virginia, Fall 1805

It had been cold last night, the temperature dropping rapidly as dark fell. The initial pain of the whipping had passed. He was used to it, the searing heat of the lash as it ripped open his skin, the white-hot flashpoint as the salt water bit like acid into the open wounds, the sudden blackness which accompanied the soaking—which always accompanied it, no matter how hard he tried to remain conscious. Now the cycle of recovery would follow. He was inured to that, too, the throbbing which became a dull ache as his flesh began to heal, the stiffness in his shoulders and neck from holding himself upright.

Huddled into the corner of the tiny space of the cellar, Virgil was grateful for the cool air on the lacerations which crisscrossed his back. He must have leaned against the rough stone walls, for there was a raw pain tugging at the knitting flesh of his wounds this morning. It was almost impossible to avoid the walls in the confined space, which was not big enough for one his size to do anything other than crouch, not wide enough for him to lie down. He could only curl, foetus-like, on the hard-packed mud of the floor.

Tentatively, Virgil sought out the newly tender spot. His fingers came away wet. Unable to see anything in the pitch-black of what his fellow slaves called the hellhole, he sniffed. The iron tang of fresh blood reassured him. Once, when he was fifteen or sixteen, his wounds had become infected. He'd wondered, before then, whether death would be better than the life he was shackled to. No more after that, and now that there was Millie, what he wanted was not just any life but a better one.

Virgil winced, dropping his head onto his knees. He'd been so sure their strike would succeed this time. So damned certain! But even though the tobacco leaves ripened on the stalks, even though the clock was ticking mercilessly towards the arrival of the merchants' ships, Master Booth had held strong and the rebellion had been broken. He'd thought they would hang him for it, but he'd been festering so long in the dungeon now that Virgil had concluded he would be sold instead.

If it were not for Millie, this would be a victory of

sorts. What would she do without him? What would he do without her? The sweet, tender moments they shared were what kept him going. Lying together under the stars in the blissful aftermath of lovemaking, they wove their dreams. His insurrection hadn't come close to making them real.

Guilt, an agony much worse than any whipping, racked Virgil's soul and wrung his heart. Millie was everything to him. Everything! He clenched his fists tight, making the cords of his sinews stand out. He would keep their dreams alive. He would make them happen and that would be his revenge. The time for trying to right the system which kept them all in chains from within was over. Master Booth and his like would never bend. No point in bloodthirsty plans for taking revenge on them either, for bloodshed only led to more bloodshed. He would have his revenge, he would triumph over them all, and he would make his dreams happen, not by physical force but by force of will. His will. He was better than them. He was stronger. He would show them, he would prove to them all that he could be better, and he would do it on *his* terms. He would win his freedom. He would win their freedom, his and Millie's. He could read and write. He knew himself smart, for he'd seen that look, fear and confusion, on Master Booth's face when he'd presented his case before the strike. And he could work. He could certainly work. No one could work as hard as he. The interminable hours he'd worked for the larger part of his nineteen years on earth had honed his body into a powerful machine.

They'd most likely sell him in one of the northern markets, for everyone in Richmond would know him for a troublemaker. If he hit lucky, his new master would be a liberal. It was of no import. He would triumph, and no matter where he was sent to, no matter how long it took, he would win. Then he would come back for Millie. He would make sure and tell her that somehow, though she'd know—she knew him enough not to doubt that, surely? He'd come back for her. He'd tell her so. She just had to keep herself safe until then.

Deep in thought, he hadn't noticed the tiny fingers of light slanting through the hatch of the cellar. Only as the key grated in the trapdoor lock did Virgil realise they had come for him. He braced himself for the pain as he unfurled his large frame, shading his eyes against the light, taking his first stumbling step in five days.

The plantation square was headed by the master's residence, the other three sides formed by the huge drying rooms which housed the newly harvested tobacco leaves. His fellow slaves filled the space. As his eyes became accustomed to the light, fear made Virgil's skin clammy. All of them, field workers and indoor servants, were there in ranks. In front of the whipping post stood Master Booth himself. Was he to be beaten again? Anxiously, he scanned the row of house servants, looking for Millie, but she wasn't there. Fear turned to dread. The sweet, rotten smell of drying tobacco was overlaid with the sharp, tangy scent of sweat. He saw his dread reflected in the faces of his fellow slaves. A terrible premonition made him stand stock-still. Only a sharp nudge from one of the white servants urged him forward, the manacles on his ankles clanking, to stand in front of the master.

'You will be sold,' Master Booth said in that peculiar drawl which still held the faintest traces of his English ancestry. Beads of sweat dripped down his ruddy cheeks. His brown tied wig sat at its usual odd angle. 'I will not tolerate insubordination. It is time you learned your place in life, boy.'

Virgil straightened his shoulders and threw back his head, meeting Booth's gaze full-on. 'There is nothing you can teach me about my *place* in life,' he said, his voice raspy from lack of water.

In the past, such defiance had angered Booth. Today, he smiled. It was this which tightened the knot in Virgil's stomach. Following the direction of the master's gaze, he was aware of that smile broadening. His knees threatened to buckle as his stunned mind absorbed what he was seeing. Millie. Her hands tied with rope. Her eyes fastened on him. Pleading. Terrified. And beside her, Harlow. The overseer.

Virgil lunged, but the white men holding him strengthened their grip. Even so, he had all but escaped when his manacles were yanked, dropping him to his knees. Millie was crying now, loud, racking sobs that pierced his heart. Not this. Not Millie. Not this. The pride which had kept him silent all his life meant nothing in the face of this new horror. 'Please,' he yelled to Booth, 'please.'

But the master simply scowled. 'Too late.' He nodded at his overseer. Millie was struggling desperately. Regina, the cook, took a step towards her, but she was pulled away by one of the housemaids. They all knew from bitter experience that interference would only result in a more brutal assault. Virgil knew it, too, but it made no difference. He continued to struggle, his muscles straining with every last ounce of their power to free himself, to reach her.

He called her name over and over. Their eyes met across the dusty courtyard. The overseer readied himself, unbuttoning his breeches. His white buttocks would have looked absurd under any other circumstances. Millie screamed. One almighty surge of energy and Virgil was back on his feet.

The two blows fell at once.

The overseer smacked Millie hard across the mouth.

Silenced but still conscious, she fell onto her back and Harlow made short work of rucking up her brown sackcloth skirts.

The cosh hit Virgil hard across the back of the head. He fell, his face biting into the hot dust, into an oblivion denied Millie as the overseer set about the brief and brutal business of punishing her for her lover's crimes.

Chapter One

Maer Hall, Staffordshire, 1816

'Kate! So glad you could make it.' Sarah Wedgwood pushed her way through the crowd to greet her friend. 'I was afraid you were still in the Lake District.'

Lady Katherine Montague grimaced. 'No, I returned a couple of weeks ago, just in time for my cousin Araminta's wedding.'

'I heard that your other cousin, Ross, ran off with a ladies' maid,' Sarah said sotto voce, eyes agog as she led Kate to a quiet corner of the room. 'Surely that cannot be true?'

'We don't actually know what happened. When my Aunt Wilhelmina discovered that Ross's intentions towards the girl were honourable, she rather lost the rag with the poor soul and sent her packing. Ross was furious—he headed hotfoot after her, and frankly we have no idea where they are now. Wherever it is, I do most sincerely hope they are married, for it seemed to me that Ross was quite besotted, and of course,' Kate said with a mischievous smile, 'to discover that her meddling has had the exact opposite effect of what she intended will make my dear aunt furious. She can talk of nothing but nourishing vipers in her bosom, and my father—actually, I'm not sure that Papa takes in anything much these days, since Edward and Jamie...'

Kate broke off, the familiar lump in her throat preventing her from continuing. Though it had been more than a year since Ned died at Waterloo, longer since Jamie had disappeared, the loss of her brothers still felt unreal. Both were buried in the distant lands where they fell. She wondered sometimes if that was it—with nothing to mark their passing, she could believe that they were still abroad, fighting. At times, she could wholly understand her father's desire to live in the past. Though Jamie had always been too much the duke-in-waiting for her to do anything other than spar with him, she had loved Ned.

'Sorry,' she said to Sarah. 'Things at home have become rather horribly complicated. I won't bore you with the details, but suffice to say that your invitation for tonight was most welcome, though my aunt was furious at my accepting it. But I could not deny myself *such* an opportunity. Where is your guest of honour, I do not see him here?'

'That is my fault, I fear,' Josiah Wedgwood, son of the famous potter and the owner of Maer Hall, interrupted. 'Mr Jackson was with me at the Etruria works, and I did not notice the time. He is changing for dinner, but he should not be long. How are you, Lady Katherine? It is very good to see you.' Josiah bent low over Kate's hand. 'Our Mr Jackson made his fortune in American stoneware, you know, and we plan to do some business together, but I will not bore you with the details, my dear. Tell me how the duke does?'

'Bearing up. He sends his regards,' Kate said, a bare-faced lie, for her ailing father was not even aware that she was here in Staffordshire, and would never have thought of sending his regards to a man he would con-sider to be a tradesman. 'Never mind Papa, tell me about Mr Jackson. I cannot tell you how excited I am about meeting him. What is he like?'

'See for yourself,' Sarah replied, nudging her arm in a most unladylike manner. 'Here he is now.'

As the double doors at the end of the Great Hall were closed by the Wedgwoods' head footman, a ripple of excitement fluttered through the assembled guests. All eyes turned towards the man making his way down the room. Whispers, like the ruffle of a spring breeze playing on new leaves, rose to a murmur of anticipation. Silks rustled as the ladies of the company vied surreptitiously to be the first to greet him. Gentlemen edged closer to their host with the same intention.

The focus of all this attention seemed oblivious. He was tall, which was the first thing which struck Kate. And he was exceedingly well-built too, with muscles straining at the cloth of his coat, though he carried himself with the grace of a predator. There was about him something fierce, an aura of power, of sheer masculine force which should have repelled her but which Kate recognised, with a frisson of awareness, was actually fatally attractive. In every sense, Mr Jackson was different from any man she had ever met.

As his host stepped forward to greet him, Virgil Jackson resisted the urge to pull his coat more closely around him. A huge fire blazed at the end of the long gallery, but the heat it emitted radiated out to a distance of a few feet only, before disappearing into the chilly air. The copious renovations which Josiah had explained to him in detail during the tour of the hall the day before had not extended to this great gallery, which was part of the original Jacobean building. Despite the tapestries and hangings, a permanent breeze seemed to flutter around the cavernous space. The English didn't seem to notice the cold, however. The ladies were all bare-shouldered, the rich silks and lace of their evening gowns low-cut, showing an expanse of bosom that in Boston would have been deemed shocking.

The starched collar of his shirt was chafing Virgil's neck. The gathering, which his host had described to him earlier as 'a few choice friends,' seemed to consist of at least thirty people dressed in their finest. He smiled and made his bow to a stream of faces it was not worth his while remembering, relieved that he'd had the sense to visit a London tailor upon arriving in England.

Though he had nothing to be ashamed of in the quality of his Boston-made clothes, there was no denying that they were behind the times compared to English fashions. The dark blue superfine tailcoat he wore tonight was fitted so tightly across his shoulders and chest that it was frankly a struggle to put on, but the tailor had assured him that this was how it should be. His knitted grey pantaloons seemed indecently tight, and a far stretch from the formal black silk breeches and stockings worn on such an occasion back home, but the valet he'd hired—much against his own inclinations—had assured him that in the country evening dress was reserved for balls. The man had been right. He had been damned finicky, fussing over the perfect placing of a pearl pin in the cravat Virgil had been forced to allow him to tie after his own third attempt ended in a crumpled heap with the others, but he'd been right, and though it irked him that it should be so, Virgil was grateful for this small mercy. In attire, at least, he was the same as every other male guest in the room.

Of course, in virtually every other sense he was quite different. Virgil suppressed a sigh. He was grateful for the effort that Josiah and his wife had made to welcome him into their home, but with business concluded, he would much rather have avoided this soirée and the collection of influential people Josiah had invited for the sole purpose of demonstrating their support for what they perceived to be a shared cause. So many variations of that famous abolitionist medallion created by Josiah's father were being brandished under his nose— the manacled slave cast in gold and silver worn as a bracelet, a necklace, a fob or a hair ornament—that he could be in no doubt of their goodwill. But the people of Old England were as ignorant of one salient fact as those in New England. It was one thing to cut the chains of slavery, quite another to be free. No one in this room knew that better than he.

He was the only black person at the gathering. Since leaving London, Virgil felt as if he was the only black man in England. Being so distinctively different nibbled away at the edges of his hard-earned confidence. He felt as if he were constantly teetering on the precipice of some irrecoverable *faux pas*, for though his success made him accustomed to mix with the highest of Boston society, and the people in this room were rather politicians and businessmen than aristocrats, the rules seemed to be quite different. It was disconcerting, though he was damned if he'd allow anyone to see he found it so!

'Virgil, I would like you to meet our most esteemed neighbour and my sister Sarah's dear friend.'

'Surely not *most* esteemed, Josiah. That honour must go first to my father, and I have four older brothers who—I mean, two. I have just two older brothers now.'

The voice, slightly husky, lost its lightly ironic tone as the woman's smile faded. Josiah patted her bare shoulder. She flinched and tightened her jaw in response. 'Lady Katherine's youngest brother died fighting for his country at Waterloo,' Josiah said, oblivious of the fact that the sympathy he exuded was making his guest squirm, 'and her eldest brother—the heir, you know—also died fighting in Spain. It is quite tragic.'

'It is, however, of no interest to Mr Jackson, I am sure.'

Virgil, who had been about to offer his condolences, was rather taken aback by this brusque tone. Was she simply a very private person, or was she in some very English way slapping him down? Before he could make up his mind, a slim, gloved hand was held out towards him, confusing him even further, for ladies, whether old world or new, did not shake hands.

'I am Lady Katherine Montague. How do you do?'

His first impression of her was that she was rather severe. His next, that she had a clever face, with a wide brow, sharp cheekbones and a decided chin. Her eyes were her best feature. Neither blue nor grey, fringed with curling lashes, they seemed to tilt up at the corners like a cat's. Virgil took the proffered hand in his own, noting the way her gaze fell to the contrast of his dark skin on the white kid of her glove. 'My lady,' he said.

'Lady Katherine is the daughter of the Duke of Rothermere,' Josiah Wedgwood said. 'Castonbury is the biggest estate in Derbyshire, and the Montagues are the oldest family in the county. You have heard of them, I'm sure. The duke...' He broke off in response to a summons from his wife. 'Ah, you will excuse me, I must go and see—dinner, you know. Virgil, if you will escort Lady Katherine?'

A forbidding duke's daughter, who would cast her eagle aristocratic eye over his table manners. No doubt she expected him to eat with his fingers or, at the very least, use the wrong cutlery. As Josiah hurried over to join his wife, Virgil repressed another sigh. It was going to be a long night.

'Are you enjoying your visit to the Midlands, Mr Jackson?' Kate asked politely, wondering at the harassed look which flitted across his handsome face. 'Josiah was telling me that you are to go into business together.'

'Imported Wedgwood pottery will be subject to the new Protective Tariff which our government is introducing, putting it well beyond the means of your average American. We plan to introduce a new range, manufactured in my factories, which can fill a gap in the market for affordable luxury. Josiah's people are working on the design at the moment.'

Virgil Jackson's voice was a slow drawl, neither ironic nor lazy, certainly not languorous, but mesmerising. Though she was, like all the Montagues, above average height, Kate had to look up to meet his eyes. Almond-shaped and deep-set, they were an indefinable colour between tawny brown and gold. His hair was close-cropped, revealing a broad, intelligent brow. His lips were full, a sort of browny pink tone which she found herself wanting to touch. His skin was not really black, but closer to…bronze? Chestnut? Coffee? None of those did it justice. Bitter chocolate, maybe?

Realising that she had been silent far too long, Kate rushed into speech. 'You will forgive me if I tell you that I find you far more interesting than tea sets,' she blurted out. 'I cannot tell you how thrilled I am at having the opportunity to meet you. I braved the wrath of my brother and my aunt to do so, you know, and my aunt is a *most* formidable woman.'

'To brave an aunt and a brother, your desire to meet me must have been strong indeed. I'm flattered, Lady Katherine.'

His teeth gleamed an impossible white. She supposed it must be the contrast with his skin. Despite his smile, his expression had a shuttered look, as if he had seen too much. Or perhaps it was simply that the habit of always being on his guard was so ingrained as to be impossible to overcome. Virgil Jackson was not a man who would trust easily. Or at all, Kate thought. She wondered what there was in his history to have made him so.

The fullness of his lips were a stark contrast to the hard planes of his face. She had not seen such sensual lips on a man before. The thought made her colour rise. She was not in the habit of having such thoughts. 'It is Kate, if you please—I hate Katherine. And as to being flattered—why, you must be perfectly well aware what an honour it is to meet you. Your achievements are little short of miraculous.'

All traces of his smile disappeared. 'For a black slave, you mean?'

Kate flinched. 'For any man, but perhaps especially for a black slave, though that is not how I would have put it.' She met his hard look with a measuring one. 'Every man and woman in this room is in awe of you.'

It was the truth, but he seemed quite unmoved by it. 'As they would be a performing bear, I suspect,' he replied.

Was he trying to intimidate her? On consideration, Kate thought the opposite. Unlikely as it seemed, given the kind of man he must be to have achieved so much, it appeared to her that he was actually trying *not* to be intimidated. 'We are all staring, I know, and it is very rude of us, but I doubt any of us has ever met an African before, let alone one with such an impressive story to tell. Our fascination is surely quite natural. Is it so very different in Boston?'

Virgil Jackson shrugged. 'Back home, it is not so much my colour as my success that makes people stare.'

'Unless the ladies of Boston are blind one and all, I doubt very much it is that alone,' Kate retorted. 'You must be perfectly well aware that you are an exceptionally good-looking man. Why, even my friend Sarah is sending you languishing looks, and believe me, Sarah is not a woman who is prone to languishing.'

She was laughing, not at him, but in a way that seemed to include him in a private joke. Virgil couldn't help smiling in return, even while he wondered whether her words contained a hint of the irony for which the English were so famous. 'And yet I do not see you languishing, Lady Kate. I suppose you will tell me that you are the exception which proves the rule?'

'I am afraid languishing, along with every other feminine wile, is anathema to my nature. Which is just as well, since I am hardly endowed with the feminine graces which make such wiles effective.'

The laughter faded from her eyes, which was a shame for it had quite transformed her, softening her expression, making her bottom lip look more kissable than prim. Even that white skin of hers above the creamy froth of lace on the décolleté of her gown had turned from winter snow to warm magnolia. Was she fishing for a compliment? Virgil studied the tiny frown which puckered her brows and decided most definitely not. 'That is a very disparaging remark,' he said.

She shrugged. 'Realistic, merely. My mirror tells me the limitations of my attractions whenever I look in it, Mr Jackson. I bear rather more resemblance to a greyhound than I would like.'

Her words were a challenge, but in the short space of this conversation Virgil already knew her well enough not to fall into the trap of flattery or polite contradiction. 'Yes, I can see that,' he said coolly, 'there is about you a kind of sleek gracefulness in the way you carry yourself, and your bone structure, too, has that delicate, well-bred look.'

For a fraction of a second, she looked as if she would slap him, before she laughed again, a low, smoky sound, intimate and sensual. Once more he was struck by the transformation it wrought, as if a curtain had been thrown back, allowing him a very private glimpse of the person behind the severe facade. Why would such a privileged woman require such a disguise?

Before he could pursue this question, the butler announced dinner. Virgil offered his arm, and he and the duke's daughter followed their hosts through a succession of chilly corridors to the dining room which was, thankfully, in the renovated part of the house. The petticoats of Lady Kate's gown rustled seductively as she walked. The claret velvet of her dress lent a lustre to her skin, and brought out golden highlights in her brown hair. As Virgil held her chair out for her, catching an illicit glimpse of very feminine curves as he did so, the first stirrings of attraction took him by surprise. It had been so long, he hardly recognised them.

Lady Kate sat down, leaving the faintest trace of her scent in the air, flowery and elusive. Despite the relative heat of the dining room compared to the gallery, it was not particularly warm. Another quirk of the English, Virgil had discovered, to serve their food tepid—or perhaps it simply travelled so far from the kitchens that it could not help being cool. Warming dishes were a rarity here, though kitchens built in the most inconvenient place possible were sadly common. 'Aren't you cold?' he asked abruptly, taking his place on Lady Kate's right-hand side.

She took a sip of her wine. 'A little. I forgot my wrap. It was my own fault. Polly, my maid, was offended by something the butler said to her, and for almost the entire dressing hour I had to listen to her wax lyrical about servants who were no better than they ought to be, who wouldn't know a hard day's graft if it bit them on the ankle, who lived a cosseted life wrapped in cotton, and who had no right at all to look down their noses at a working woman. My dresser used to be a working woman of a very particular kind, you see.'

Virgil replaced his glass on the table, slopping a drop of red wine onto the immaculate damask. His eyes narrowed. 'You can't mean you have a—a courtesan for your maid?'

'Streetwalker. I don't think Polly ever rose to anything so lofty as a courtesan,' Kate replied candidly.

She was expecting him to be shocked, Virgil realised.

There was a defiant look in those blue-grey eyes. He recognised it, and he liked it. She was no insipid English rose. 'Did you take her on to annoy your aunt or your brother?'

'Let us not forget my father, the duke. And no, I did not. Well, only partly,' Kate admitted ruefully. 'I took Polly as my maid because she used to work the streets around Covent Garden, and since her protector was rather eager for her to continue to do so, I thought it best to remove her from the city.'

'And does she like being your maid, this reformed streetwalker—I take it she *is* reformed?' Virgil asked, torn between amusement and shock.

'Oh, I'm pretty certain of that. There is Mrs Taylor's Gentlemen's Parlour in Buxton, of course, but I really don't think Polly is refined enough for Mrs Taylor, and besides, I feel sure that I would have heard if my maid had been practicing her arts so close at hand, for it is a mere two or three miles from Castonbury you know, and we are a very tight-knit community,' Kate said, smiling once again. 'Though Polly is an extremely loyal maid, she's a little like a vicious dog, liable to savage anyone else who tries to pat her. Her taste in clothes, however, is exquisite. I can see from your face that you're thinking I am one of those English eccentrics you have read about.'

'I'm thinking that you are about as far from a typical Englishwoman as I am likely to meet,' Virgil said bluntly.

'I shall take that as a compliment. My father would agree with you, though he views my eccentricities in a rather less positive light. He would much prefer me to be what you call a typical Englishwoman, though to be fair, since I put myself beyond the pale, his efforts to make me conform have been rather half-hearted.'

Though she had not put the shutters up completely, she had definitely begun to retreat from him. There was an edge to her words. Virgil was intrigued, and a little at a loss. 'You must have committed a heinous crime indeed,' he said, careful to keep his tone light. 'And here was I thinking myself privileged to have such a blue-blooded dinner companion. Should I have shunned you? No, I have that wrong—given you the cut direct?'

'You are mocking me, but believe me, in what is termed the *ton*, I am very much a social pariah.'

She was turning a heavy silver knife over and over, not quite looking at him, not quite avoiding his eye. Hurt and determined not to show it, Virgil guessed. 'Then that makes two of us,' he said, covering the back of her hand with his. 'I know all about being an outcast.'

Kate was not used to sympathy, even less used to understanding, but she *was* accustomed to insulating herself with her flippant tongue. 'You are very kind, but I know perfectly well the circumstances are not the same at all.' The words were out before she could consider their effect.

Rebuffed, Virgil snatched his hand back. 'Temerity indeed, to compare myself to a duke's daughter.'

'I didn't mean that!' Kate exclaimed, aghast. 'I merely meant that...' But Virgil Jackson shrugged and looked the other way, and they were clearing the plates, and Kate's other neighbour was patiently waiting to claim her attention. She was almost grateful for the interruption, despite the fact that the subject would inevitably be her family, and could not be anything other than painful, given the recent developments at Castonbury.

Sure enough Sir Merkland, an old hunting friend of her father's, and one of the few who seemed either oblivious or uncaring of her tarnished reputation, asked after the duke with that mixture of morbid curiosity and smugness which the healthy reserve for the decrepit, especially when the decrepit person in question was overly proud of his superior rank. Kate abandoned her soup. The consommé was good, but the Wedgwoods' chef was an amateur compared to the genius currently running the Castonbury kitchens. Not that Monsieur André was likely to remain with them for much longer, for her father's taste, since the loss of his sons, ran largely to milk puddings and gruel.

She provided Sir Merkland with a much more optimistic account of her sire's health than Papa's frail appearance the day before merited, then listened with half an ear to the squire praise her sister Phaedra's prowess on a horse, smiling and nodding with practiced skill as he proceeded on to one of his interminable hunting anecdotes. On her other side, Virgil Jackson was discussing American politics with the wife of one of Josiah's business partners, patiently explaining the differences between the federal system and the British Parliament. That slow drawl of his was mesmerising.

The arrival of a haunch of beef and various side dishes distracted Sir Merkland, who was almost as dedicated a trencherman as he was a huntsman, tempting Kate into leaning a little closer to her right. Virgil Jackson was a very solid man. There was a presence about him, a very distinct aura of power which drew one into his orbit. He was certainly different, and undeniably the most innately charismatic man she'd ever met, and it was nothing to do with his colour either, she decided, taking the opportunity to study his profile while his attention was fixed elsewhere. There was just something about him.

She could not imagine him ever being subservient, which must have made him a rather unusual slave. Had he courted danger? She did not doubt it. Was the skin of that broad back covered in a fretwork of scars? She shuddered, for the answer to that question was almost certainly affirmative. What other scars were there, hidden deep inside that attractive exterior? For she did find him attractive, a fact which was somewhat confounding, given that she had been quite convinced that she was immune to such feelings. Was it that Virgil Jackson was in almost every way the antithesis of Anthony? Or was it, she wondered wryly, the fact that he was in every possible way ineligible, which tempted her wayward streak? Imagine Papa's reaction if she introduced him to the family. Or better still, Aunt Wilhelmina's. Oh, if only!

Finally released from his neighbour's earnest interrogation, Virgil stared down with distaste at the slice of bloody beef on his plate and decided to confine himself to the accompaniments. He was hungry, but the food seemed more designed for display than satisfying a healthy appetite. The goose in the middle of the table looked good, but it was out of bounds. Why it was that he must serve himself only from those dishes within reach he did not know, but he had no wish to repeat the shocked silence which had greeted him at the last formal dinner, when he had asked his neighbour to pass the peas.

He helped himself disconsolately to some mushroom fritters. On his other side, Lady Kate was moving her food around without making any attempt to eat. A smile played at the corners of her mouth. Her eyes were unfocused, her attention obviously far from the dining room of Maer Hall. Her skirts brushed against his leg. He could smell her scent over the rich aroma of beef. The delicate diamond and ruby drops she wore in her ears drew attention to the slender line of her neck. At her nape, wispy tendrils of hair clung. Such a tender spot. What would it be like to breathe her in, to taste her? The muscles in his stomach clenched. It had been a long time since such thoughts had occupied him. Eleven years.

Lady Kate looked up, perhaps conscious of the intensity of his gaze. Their eyes snagged. A trickle of sweat ran down between Virgil's shoulder blades. He couldn't understand how he'd ever thought her severe. He couldn't take his eyes off her plump lower lip. Moist. Pink. 'Aren't you hungry?' he asked a little desperately.

Kate gazed down at her untouched plate and shook her head. Around them the scraping of china, the clatter of silver being dropped into the clearing baskets, made it clear that she'd been wool-gathering for some time. 'You don't like the beef, Mr Jackson,' she said, looking at the slab of meat sitting untouched in front of him.

He grimaced. 'Blood. You will call me heathenish, but it puts me off.'

'Monsieur André, our very superior French chef at

Castonbury, would call you heathenish. He thinks beef
is overcooked if the animal's heart has ceased to beat,'
Kate replied, 'but I prefer it properly dead and what he
would call burnt to a crisp. Not that I would dare say
so to his face. Monsieur André has a very Gallic tem-
perament and would likely beat me with his rolling pin.'

Virgil laughed. 'I would like to see him try.'

'I wish you could—come to Castonbury with me, that
is,' Kate said impulsively.

'Well, I… That's very nice of you, but—'

'It's not nice, it's selfish. I have to leave first thing tomorrow, you see, and I haven't had the chance to talk to
you properly. There is so much I would love to discuss
with you, I have so many questions, but there are matters—family matters—oh, why is it that family matters
always arise at the most inconvenient of times?'

'I wouldn't know, since I have no family,' Virgil said.

'Lucky you!' Kate exclaimed, then was immediately
contrite. 'Oh, I am so dreadfully sorry, I did not think.
Have you indeed no family at all? Your parents—?'

'I was separated from my mother as soon as I was
weaned,' Virgil said tersely.

'So, too, was I. Mama was not much interested in any
of her children, and as a female of course, I was…' Kate
broke off, covering her mouth in horror. 'Do you mean
you were *sold*?'

'Family ties are very much discouraged in the plantations. It was—still is—common practice to separate mothers and children.'

'And your father?'

Virgil shrugged. 'I never knew him.' He took a draught of claret. 'As I said, family ties were discouraged. You should be grateful for yours, whatever your relationship with them.'

'I am quite humbled.'

'That was not my intention.'

'You need not concern yourself. To be honest, what I meant was that I *ought* to be humbled. If you knew my family, you would understand why it's very difficult to be grateful for them—some of them, at least.'

He liked that hint of wickedness in her smile. She was not only unconventional but irrepressible. It was a pity their acquaintance was doomed to be of such short duration, Virgil thought. 'You are not, then, in the habit of doing as you ought?'

Her smile disappeared abruptly. 'My aunt would tell you that I am rather in the habit of never doing so. Tell me, Mr Jackson, did Weston make that coat?'

He would have taken the change of subject for a deliberate snub had it come from anyone else, but he was pretty sure that a snub from Lady Kate would be much more direct. He had obviously quite inadvertently touched upon a sore point. 'My tailor *was* Weston, though how you knew I have no idea.'

To Virgil's relief, Lady Kate laughed. 'My brothers go to Scott, being military men, so I knew it was not one of his, and I confess that I know only one other tailor. It was an educated guess, that's all. You will have the Bostonian ladies sighing into their teacups at your style, Mr Jackson. Though perhaps you are interested in the sighs of just one particular lady?'

'I am not married, and nor do I have any particular lady in my life,' Virgil replied curtly. 'As to my coat—I doubt it will see the light of day when I get home. It took that valet I hired several minutes to get me into it, and I feel as if every time I breathe the shoulders will burst at the seams. Back home, I dress for comfort.'

'I'd like to hear more about back home,' Kate said, telling herself that the fact that Mr Jackson was unattached was neither here nor there. 'May I ask how long you expect business to keep you here in Staffordshire?'

'Actually, I'm planning on heading north tomorrow while Josiah's men work on the samples for our wares. We'll meet up in London to conclude our business before I return to America, but I have other business in Glasgow to see to in the meantime, and there is a model village not far from that city which I have arranged to visit.'

'Do you mean Mr Owen's New Lanark?' Kate ex-

claimed. 'How I would love to see it. I am a great admirer of Mr Owen, I have read all his works, and in
fact our own little school in Castonbury was established
along similar lines—or at least that is what I would like
to believe.'

'Your school—you mean *you* have set up a village
school?'

'Do not look so astonished. Not all English ladies confine themselves to playing the pianoforte and painting
watercolours for amusement, Mr Jackson. Some of us
prefer to utilise our time to more effect,' Kate said stiffly.

'So you rescue streetwalkers and educate the village
children. I did not mean to offend you, but you'll admit
it is something out of the common way, to meet a duke's
daughter who is a revolutionary.'

'You are far too modest. Rare as we revolutionary
aristocrats may be, a freed slave who has made himself into one of the richest men in New England must
be rarer. I wish you would tell me more about how you
became so.'

Virgil shook his head. 'I am much more interested in
your school. Do you teach there yourself?'

'I help out when I can, but we have an excellent mistress in the form of Miss Thomson. I rescue governesses
in addition to streetwalkers,' Kate said with a smile.
'Miss Thomson tries to follow the principles which Mr

Owen set down, but to see them in practice would be so much better than reading about them. I wish *I* could visit New Lanark. How I envy you. Were you serious about establishing a similar place?'

'Serious about testing its merits. Very serious about the school. Without education, it is not possible to make the most of freedom. I believe that education is power.'

'With that I wholeheartedly agree. My own education did not amount to much, which goes some way to explaining why even setting up a simple school has taken an enormous amount of effort.' Kate pulled a face. 'That, and the fact that as a mere woman I am not considered worthy of having an opinion on the subject. Being female does rather shackle one.'

Virgil bit back a smile. 'You don't strike me as being someone constrained by her position in society.'

'I know perfectly well that there is no real comparison between myself and a female slave,' she replied, disconcerting him by reading his thoughts, 'but it is nevertheless how I feel sometimes. Perception and reality are not always the same thing.'

'*That* is most certainly true.'

How had *he* come by his education? Kate was about to ask when a footman leaned over her shoulder, a huge lemon syllabub trembling on the platter in his hands. She shook her head impatiently. Sir Merkland was clearing his throat. The change of course dictated a turn in the conversation. Port and cigars and business would detain the gentlemen until tea. She would be obliged to surrender her monopoly of Virgil Jackson to the other guests when she had barely scratched the surface of what she wanted to know about him.

'You could do a lot worse than come to Castonbury with me,' she said impulsively. 'Then you could see our school for yourself and it would give you something to compare with Mr Owen's. You know, the more I think about it, the more I am sure it is the perfect solution.'

'To what?' Virgil asked, confused by the sudden change in the conversation.

Kate had been thinking only of her desire to know him better, so his question threw her, for though of course it was because she wished to know him better, to say so would imply something much more personal. And though it was personal in a way, it was not *that* sort of personal because she wasn't the type of female with whom men wished to be *that* sort of personal. 'The solution of your travelling all the way to Scotland without having seen anything of our true English countryside,' she said mendaciously. 'Derbyshire is the most beautiful of the counties, and though I admit to being rather biased, Castonbury is one of the most beautiful houses.'

'Are you serious?'

Determined, more like, now that the idea was in her head, but Kate thought better, at the last minute, of saying so, for Virgil Jackson looked like a man who would resist any attempt to force his will. 'Perfectly,' she said instead. 'I would love to show you our school, and I would welcome your opinion on the plans I have to extend it.'

Virgil frowned. He was tempted. A school established on the Owen model would certainly merit a break in his journey, and he had not yet confirmed the precise dates of his visit with New Lanark's proprietor. Besides, there could be no denying that a visit to a real stately pile held its own subversive pleasure. He shook his head reluctantly. 'Much as I appreciate the honour, I very much doubt your family would be as welcoming as you,' he said.

Which was, as far as her father and Aunt Wilhelmina were concerned, the truth, but that only made Kate more determined. Since those same two relatives had taken such pains to collaborate in her ruin, she would have no compunction in flaunting that ruin in their faces. 'Actually, it is rather your birth than the colour of your skin which will concern my father. According to him, there are less than a dozen other families in the country with blood so blue as the Montagues. Though since he chooses to confine himself to his own quarters, his opinions do not particularly matter. My brother Giles is acting head of the family at present and he is not at all prejudiced.'

'Nevertheless,' Virgil said, 'I do not think...'

She could see she was losing the battle, but Kate, now quite set on winning, switched tactics. 'Are you afraid you will be put under the spyglass, Mr Jackson?' She could see from the way he stilled, that she had hit home. 'How can you expect to break down barriers if you do not face them?'

'I hope, Lady Kate, that you are not thinking of using me as a weapon in some sort of private war. Are you perhaps eager to prove your reputation for being a revolutionary to your father and your aunt?'

He spoke softly, but there was an underlying air of menace which made Kate's skin prickle. Virgil Jackson was obviously not a man who could be threatened. She threw up her hands in a gesture of surrender. 'I admit, there is a part of me which relishes the notion of introducing you to Aunt Wilhelmina, but I promise you, it is only a small part. What I really want is to get to know you better.'

Her frankness disarmed him. He *was* tempted. Who would not be, by such an argument put forward by such a— He could not think of a word to describe Lady Kate

Montague. Not that her personal attractions had anything to do with his decision. 'I will think about it,' Virgil said.

'With a view to saying yes?'

'I'll think about it,' he repeated, telling himself he would, though he had already more than half decided.

Chapter Two

His valet brought the note with his shaving water, proffering the folded sheet of thick paper on a sliver tray. Virgil knew who it was from the moment he saw it, though he couldn't have said how. Had he been expecting it? Hoping for it? His name was written in a clear hand utterly bereft of flourishes, starkly legible. A man's hand, he would have taken it for, under other circumstances. His valet was not taken in either though, judging from the curious looks he was casting at him via the mirror over the dressing stand.

'I'll shave myself, Watson,' Virgil said, deliberately catching the man's eye. Though he would have preferred to break the seal in private, he would not lower himself to the subterfuge of sending the valet away, nor indeed would he grant the note the importance such an act would imply.

I was perfectly serious. I wish you would do me the honour of paying a visit to Castonbury. We have much in common, and I am most eager to further our acquaintance. I leave at ten. I have sent a note ahead warning them to expect us, and arranged for your man to travel separately with my maid and the baggage. From what Polly has told me of him, he will have an entertaining journey! K.

Virgil smiled. Practical, blunt and wry, and leaving him with very little option but to accept. It was as well he had already resolved to go, for he made a point of never allowing himself to be coerced. Reading it again, he could picture the sparkle in her eyes as she wrote that last sentence.

'A change of plan, sir?'

From the supercilious look on his face, Watson already knew the contents of the letter. How the hell? In the way that all servants knew, Virgil supposed. It had been the same on the plantation. Knowledge was power; he shouldn't judge the man for that. He folded the note and placed it in the pocket of his silk dressing gown. 'I take it you've been speaking to Lady Kate's maid?'

Lathering his face, Virgil watched out of the corner of his eye as his valet debated between honesty and what seemed to be the English servant's custom of pretended ignorance. He was relieved when the man plumped for the truth. 'Miss Fisher did mention that Her Ladyship had invited you to Castonbury,' the man admitted grudgingly.

'And did Miss Fisher happen to share her views as to my likely reception there?'

Watson blanched. 'Miss Fisher had a— She was— The truth is, sir, that Miss Fisher is not short of opinions,' he said grimly. 'I cannot imagine how Lady Katherine came by such a female, nor indeed how such a female survives in a ducal household.'

'Like her mistress, I believe she is rather unconventional,' Virgil replied. 'Prepare yourself, Watson, for you will be sharing the baggage coach with her.'

'You mean we are going to Castonbury? You wish me to accompany you? I was under the impression that you were journeying north alone.'

Judging from the look in his valet's eye, the invitation was even more of an honour than Virgil had surmised. 'Do you wish to return to London?'

'No indeed, sir. I would not dream of leaving you to the ministrations of another,' Watson declared.

'Nothing better to do with your time, eh?'

Watson drew himself up. 'If I have fallen short of your expectations…'

'Don't be an idiot, you know perfectly well that you've

been keeping me right. I don't like to be waited on, but it seems I must be, and you do it very well, so if you wish to continue with me in the short term…'

'I do indeed, sir.'

'Then get packing. I must make my farewells to my host.'

Kate swept down the stairs with her gloves and whip in her hand, trying to ignore the fact that her heart was fluttering in a quite ridiculous manner for one of her age. It was simply that she was *interested* in Virgil Jackson, that was all. There was a lot to find interesting in him. It was nothing, nothing at all, to do with the fact that he was an attractive man.

Just as the fact that she had spent much longer than usual dressing had nothing to do with wanting to look her best. As she very well knew, even at her best, she could never aspire to beauty, though it had to be said that this particular shade of blue was becoming, and the rather military cut of her riding habit, with its silver braiding and snugly fitting jacket, draped well on her slim form. Kate made a face, chastising herself. What mattered was that *she* was pleased with her appearance, she reminded herself. What did *not* matter was what Virgil Jackson thought.

Except, as she turned the corner to the last flight of

stairs and saw that he was waiting for her in the tiled
hall, dressed in a plain black coat with a grey waistcoat,
buckskins and top boots polished to a gleam, and she noticed that his eyes lingered on her as she made her way
towards him, she found that she did care. Chiding herself for it, she couldn't help the tiniest flush of pleasure
at seeing that he liked what he saw any more than she
could deny that she liked what she saw too. Very much.

She held out her hand. To her surprise, he bent low
over it, pressing a kiss on her knuckles. His lips were
warm. The touch was fleeting, but it was enough to set
her pulses skittering. In the bright light of the early-
autumn sunshine streaming through the fanlight above
the door, his skin gleamed. His eyes were more amber
than brown. The way he looked at her warmed her, as if
he saw something in her that no one else could see. 'I'm
so glad you decided to accept my invitation,' she said
brusquely, for it was embarrassing enough, this girlish
reaction, without letting him see it.

'I could not pass up the opportunity to visit this school
of yours.'

It was most foolish of her to be disappointed, for what
else was there between them save such business? Kate
smiled brightly. 'I'm glad.'

Virgil frowned. 'Yes, but I'm not so sure that your
family will be as enthusiastic. It is one thing to test bar-

riers, as you said last night, but another to force an un-invited guest on people who, frankly, may not be very happy to receive me.'

'You *are* invited, for I invited you.'

'Did you tell them— The note you sent—how did you describe me?'

'As a man of great wealth and extraordinary influence, a business associate of Josiah with a fascinating history.'

She had not mentioned the one salient fact that he was sure would have been the first to occur to almost anyone else. 'You don't think,' Virgil asked tentatively, 'that it would have been safer to warn them about my heritage?'

'Why should I? I look at you and I see a man who has achieved what very few others have. You are rich and powerful and you have succeeded against overwhelming odds which also makes you fascinating. Why should I tell them the colour of your skin any more than I should inform them the colour of your hair, or whether you are fat or scrawny.' Or attractive. Really extraordinarily attractive. Which, she should remember, was quite irrelevant. 'Besides,' Kate said disparagingly, 'why encourage them to judge you before they have even met you?'

Virgil drew himself up. 'I don't give a damn—begging your pardon—about what your family think of me. I was more concerned about what they'd think of you.'

'My family can think no worse of me than they already do. They are perfectly well aware of my support for the abolition laws, and I am perfectly capable of defending myself, if that is what you are concerned about,' Kate said with a toss of her head. 'I've had practice enough, God knows.'

'I don't doubt that. I suspect you take pride in being a rule-breaker.'

'Not at all,' Kate said, 'you misunderstand me. Breaking rules, even unjust rules, is far more painful than unquestioning obedience. I wish I did not have to be a rule-breaker, as you call me. Life would be so much more pleasant if what one believed and what was expected of one coincided more often.'

She looked quite wistful and Virgil found himself at a loss, for it seemed that they were speaking about two different things. He could, however, agree with the sentiment. 'I know exactly what you mean.'

Kate nodded, touching his sleeve in a gesture of sympathy he was already beginning to associate with her. 'Our cases are hardly comparable. There are a good deal of rules which ought to be broken, no matter how painful.'

She would not have said so if she knew the price he had paid for his disobedience. No matter how unconventional she was, she would likely condemn him for it, and quite rightly so. Virgil rolled his shoulders as if the familiar burden of guilt were a tangible weight he carried. 'I play by my own rules,' he answered, more to remind himself of that fact than in response to what she had said. He could see his remark confused her, but the crump of carriage wheels on the gravel kept him from saying more, and then the Wedgwoods' groom appeared at the front door and informed them that the gig awaited Her Ladyship's convenience.

Kate pulled on her driving gloves. 'I hope you don't mind the cold, but I drive myself. I hate to be cooped up in a carriage.'

'That's fine by me.' Virgil pulled on the greatcoat his valet had insisted that he would require, having been forewarned that Her Ladyship scorned the closed carriage in which any other lady of her rank would have been expected to travel. With extreme reluctance, he donned the beaver tricorn hat which Watson had also insisted upon. Hats and gloves were items of gentleman's apparel to which Virgil had never managed to become accustomed.

Kate leapt nimbly into the carriage in a flutter of lacy petticoats at odds with the masculine cut of her dress, and took up the reins. The gig rocked under Virgil's weight as he climbed in beside her. His knee brushed her skirts. The caped shoulder of his driving coat fluttered against the braiding on her jacket. The air smelt of leaves and moss, with that sharpness to it that was distinctively English. As she urged the horse into a trot, she smiled. 'I'm glad you're here,' she said impulsively.

Virgil laughed, and for once spoke his mind without thinking. 'That makes two of us,' he said.

They had left Maer village behind, and were heading eastwards along a country lane at a steady pace. The morning was bright but cool, the sun shining weakly in the pale blue sky. The blackberries which grew so prolifically in the hedgerows were past their best now. The leaves on the trees had turned from gold and amber to brown, curled and crisped by the change in the temperature, ready to float down at the merest hint of a breeze. In the distance, a bell clanged as a herd of sheep made their way across a field.

'I was about to ask you last night, before the lemon syllabub separated us, how you came by your education,' Kate said. 'I realised later that I must have sounded quite the malcontent, complaining about my lack of formal schooling when it was likely that you'd had none at all—as a child, I mean.'

'I never went to school, not when I was a slave, nor when Malcolm Jackson freed me either.'

'Jackson is the man who brought you to Boston?'

'Bought me at auction, and brought me to Boston.

There's no need to dance around the subject. I was a slave. I was sold. Malcolm Jackson paid for me in gold and set me free.'

'You took his name.'

'That man placed a lot of trust in me, it was the least I could do. Besides, the only other name I had belonged to the man who sold me. It was no hardship to give that up.'

'And this Jackson, he gave you an education?'

Virgil smiled. 'I gave myself an education. Malcolm Jackson gave me a job at his factory and a place to live. He let me have books, and when I was done with his, I found more, and plenty of ideas, too, at the African Meeting House in the city. I studied hard every night and I worked hard every day so that within a year there wasn't a job at that factory I couldn't turn my hand to. Sometimes I had just two or three hours' sleep, but I didn't need any more. I discovered I had a head for figures. I found I had a mind for business, too, which is more than poor Malcolm Jackson had. He was leaking money, he was being taken for a ride by just about everyone he did a deal with, and he was missing so many opportunities that it was criminal to watch.'

Virgil had shifted in his seat as he talked, so that his knee brushed against her skirt. He was more animated than she had yet seen him. His eyes glowed. He had cast his hat onto the floor, and tugged repeatedly at his neck cloth as he spoke. The finicky valet he had mentioned had obviously tied it tighter than he was used to. He had already admitted that he could not tie such a fancy knot himself. It was endearing, though Kate took care not to let him know she thought so, judging quite rightly that he would have been horrified. 'I assume there came a time when you could no longer stand by and watch things going wrong,' she said.

'I would have interfered eventually, but I didn't have to. Malcolm Jackson didn't have the hardest business head but he wasn't a fool. He could see what was happening, and he could see I knew what to do about it. He was getting old, and he was getting tired and he had learned to trust me. In a year I'd doubled our turnover and he made me a partner. Another year, and we had just about cornered the new market for cheap, practical stoneware.'

'Was that your idea?'

'One of them.'

'And not too many more years later you are one of the wealthiest men in America. This deal with Josiah, is that going to allow you to corner another new market?'

'I wouldn't be doing it otherwise,' Virgil said with a grin.

'But you have other businesses than—what do you call it, stoneware?'

'I sure do. I have real estate—that's property, to you English. Homes to rent to the freed men coming north that are fit for human habitation. Rooming houses that aren't flea pits. I have some interest in retail—shops to sell what we make at the factories. And some other investments too. As I said, I have a head for business.'

'It must be a very ruthless one, to have achieved so much in such a relatively short time, with the odds stacked against you to boot. Your ambition knows no bounds. Tell me, do you still exist on two or three hours' sleep a night?'

'I prefer not to waste time sleeping if there's something better I can be doing.'

Kate pursed her lips, her brows drawing together in a deep frown. 'But why? Why not enjoy your success? Forgive me, but you sound almost like a man obsessed. What more can you possibly want? Aren't you wealthy enough?'

'I don't care about being rich.'

Alerted by the change in his tone, Kate glanced sideways. The light had gone from his eyes. What had she said? 'You're so used to working twenty hours a day that you can't stop, is that it?' she ventured, trying to make a joke of it.

'I'm not interested in money, Lady Kate. I'm interested in what money can buy.'

He had shifted in his seat again, to look straight ahead. His expression seemed to have hardened.

Kate's brow cleared. 'Oh, you mean schools? Your model village?'

He meant reparation, but it was the same thing. 'Power,' Virgil said. 'The power to change.'

Kate nodded. 'Yes. If I felt I could have that, I think I'd manage on two or three hours' sleep a night too. Do you ever wish you could go back? To the plantation, I mean, to show them what you have become.'

He realised, from the casual way she slipped the question in, that this was the subject which interested her most. 'No.' It was baldly stated, making it clear, Virgil trusted, that neither did he ever discuss it. He could sense her eyeing him, calculating whether to press him or not.

'I'm surprised,' she said cautiously. 'Were I in your position, I think I'd want to rub their noses in it a bit.'

'There's other ways of payback.' This time, Virgil was relieved to see that she recognised the note of finality in his voice. He never talked about that part of his past, never consciously thought about it, for to do so would be to admit the tide of guilt he had spent the past eleven years holding back. It was one thing to talk around his history, quite another to paint its picture and admit to the pain which he had worked so hard to ignore. Yet there could be no denying that her choice of silence made him contrarily wish she had questioned him more.

The miles wore on. At the border between Staffordshire and Derbyshire they stopped at a village tavern, taking bread and the crumbling white local cheese on a bench outside. It was chilly, but there was no private parlour, and neither Kate nor Virgil wished to endure the curious eyes of the locals in the tap room who had greeted their appearance with a stunned silence.

As they continued on into Derbyshire the scenery changed. The land became softly undulating, the higher, rolling hills of the Peaks casting shadows over the valleys through which they drove. It seemed wetter and greener here. The limestone villages huddled into the creases and folds of the hills, or stretched out along the banks of the fast-flowing rivers such as the Dove, which they followed for some time, where the water mills turned.

It was beautiful, though incredibly isolated, each hamlet seeming to exist in its own world, unconnected and self-contained, Virgil thought. 'Why aren't you married, Lady Kate?'

The question startled her, for her hands jerked on the reins, pulling the horse to a walk. 'Why do you ask?'

Why? He hadn't realised, but now he thought about it

he saw that her remarks over dinner last night had been niggling at him. He could not reconcile what she'd said of herself with the little he knew of her. 'You said you were a social pariah, though I saw no evidence of it.'

'Josiah's guests are my friends but they are not what my father would consider high society. Were you to see me in that milieu you would have evidence aplenty.'

The horse took advantage of her lapse in attention to stop and crop at the grass verge. Virgil took the reins and looped them round the brake. 'Why? I know I joked about you being a revolutionary, but...'

'Oh, it is naught to do with that. I have always been outspoken, but the daughter of the influential Duke of Rothermere, you understand, is given rather more latitude than, say, a mere Miss Montague.' Her voice dripped sarcasm. She threw her head back and glared at him, her eyes dark and bleak, the colour of a winter sea. 'The fact is, I am a jilt.'

Virgil searched her face for some sign that she was joking, but could find no trace in her stern expression. 'That's it? You changed your mind about getting married?'

'A mere two weeks before the ceremony, and the engagement was of very long standing. I had known Anthony all my life. I did not quite leave him at the altar, but I may as well have, according to my aunt.'

The husky tones of her voice were clipped. There was hurt buried deep there. Had she loved this Anthony? Virgil didn't like to think so. 'What made you change your mind so late in the day?'

'We didn't suit.'

'But…'

'I know what you're going to say, if I knew him so well why did it take me so long to change my mind? I knew him as a friend of the family. I thought we would suit, and when I tried to think of him as a husband I found I could not.'

The anger in her voice was raw, fresh. 'How long ago did this happen?' Virgil asked.

'Five years.'

'Did you love him?' He should not have asked such a deeply personal question. He could not understand why he had done so, for he was usually at pains to keep any conversation, especially with a woman, in neutral channels. But he knew all about the pain of loss.

He covered her tightly clasped hands with one of his own, but Kate shook him off. 'Don't feel sorry for me, there is no need. I am not wearing the willow for Lord Anthony Featherstone.'

Rebuffed and baffled, Virgil said nothing. All his instincts told him to drop the subject, which was obviously extremely sensitive and extremely painful, but there was something in her voice, in the way she had closed herself off, that he recognised and could not ignore. She was hurt and determined not to show it. He gently unfolded her fingers and took one of her hands between his. 'Then tell me,' he said. 'What happened?'

She hesitated. He could see the words of refusal forming, but for some reason she swallowed them. 'Do you really want to know?'

When he nodded, she took a deep breath. 'Anthony was—is—the son of one of my father's close friends. His family has a bloodline which can be traced back to the Norman Conquest, according to my father. Our betrothal was the result of a bargain struck by our parents when I was still in my cradle. What you have to understand is that as far as my father is concerned, my only value is in making the best marriage which can be arranged. I knew from a very early age that I was destined to marry Anthony, and since I had not met any other man I preferred after almost two full Seasons, I agreed. Anthony was far from repulsive,' Kate said, determined to be scrupulously fair. 'In fact, he was considered to be something of a beau.'

'But you were not in love with him?'

'I have never been in love with anyone. I doubt it is in my nature to feel so strongly, and in any case, love has nothing at all to do with marriage. At least, not for a Montague. People of our sort make alliances, not love matches,' she said bitterly.

Falling in love was the one thing Virgil had been free to do. He had loved Millie. He would have married Millie. Were there other forms of chains he didn't understand? Duty had weighed heavily with Lady Kate. It was not a comparison she would dream of making, but he made it. 'So you agreed to the marriage because it was what your family wished, even though you were not sure?'

'I wasn't unsure, it would be unfair to say that. I was resigned. No, it was not even that. I simply didn't question it, I suppose.'

Virgil smiled. 'I find that hard to believe. You seem to question everything.'

'As I said, life would be less painful if I did not. Would that I had questioned this match earlier. Or had the strength of will to say no when I knew what—knew my own mind better.'

'What about your mother?'

'Mama died when I was a child. My Aunt Wilhelmina is her sister, and she was most—most anxious for the match to take place. Even more so than my father, in the end. When I tried to discuss my reservations about Anthony she—she did not— She said that I…'

Her hand curled into a fist within his clasp. Her jaw

clenched, her eyes were bright with tears. This was obviously the source of her hurt, or one of them. Virgil felt a momentary spasm of anger at the unknown aunt. 'And the duke?'

Kate laughed bitterly. 'My father's word is law. He made the match. As far as he was concerned, there was no question of my changing my mind, whatever the circumstances.'

'And yet you did change your mind?'

'I had to.'

I had to. It was a curious choice of phrase, Virgil thought, but the tightness in her voice, the way she held herself, as if she was afraid she might shatter, and the sheen of tears which he was fairly certain she would be mortified to shed, made him cautious. 'So you called it off?'

She nodded. 'My aunt said that I would be ruined, and she was right. Papa refused to put the notice in the paper. He left it to Anthony to do so. *"Lord Anthony Featherstone wishes it to be known that his betrothal to the Honourable Lady Katherine..."* You can imagine how that looked.'

What Virgil found extraordinary was that such an act could have led society to ostracise her, but he had discovered that there was much he found inexplicable about the English. He supposed it was something to do with her family's status, and the fact of the date having been set. 'But your father, your aunt, they are surely reconciled to your decision now, after five years?'

Kate gave another of those bitter little laughs. 'You'd think so, but you see, I have refused to do penance in the only possible way by making any other sort of match. Though, of course, my situation must have reduced my expectations significantly,' she said in a voice which left Virgil in no doubt she was quoting her aunt, 'my blood and my dowry were still sufficient to tempt a few ambitious suitors. However, I may be foolish but I am not stupid. I have no intention of repeating my mistake. I am resolved never to marry.'

'That is what you meant when you said you have put yourself beyond the pale?'

'Did I?' She smiled faintly. 'Yes, that is what I meant. So you see, as far as His Grace and my aunt are concerned, I am a failure.'

She had said more than enough to make Virgil despise the duke, though it was the aunt, who had signally failed to support her as a mother should, towards whom he directed his anger. All his reservations about the effect of his presence in the ducal residence fled. He very much hoped he *would* throw them all into disarray. He could now perfectly understand Lady Kate's desire to defy them. 'I don't think you are a failure, far from it,' Virgil

said. 'To stand up for yourself in the face of such opposition took real courage. I think you are extraordinary.'

'Do you?'

She had been staring down at her feet, but his words
made her look up, and the vulnerability he saw there
pierced Virgil's defences. 'Yes, I do,' he said softly.
Pushing back the leather cuff of her driving glove, he
pressed a kiss on the inside of her wrist. 'You really are
quite extraordinary.'

He meant merely to show her that he understood. That
he admired her. That he had not judged her as her family had. A token gesture of solidarity, that's what he intended. But when his lips touched the delicate skin his
intentions changed. Her scent, the taste of her, turned
his empathy into desire.

She stilled, her eyes fixed on his when he looked up,
wide, startled, but she made no move to pull away. A
pulse fluttered at her neck. Entranced, Virgil could not
resist touching it. The diamond drops in her ears glinted
in the sunlight. He pressed his lips to her skin. It was
cold and smooth. She breathed in sharply, but did not
pull away. 'Extraordinary,' Virgil repeated softly. The
air was still, save for the contented sound of the horse
champing on the grass by the wayside. There was no
one else in sight. He shifted on the narrow bench, his
knees pressing into her thigh. Still she didn't move. Her

scent, flowery and already imprinted on his mind, made him think of summer meadows. His heart was beating in time to that fluttering pulse of hers. 'Kate,' he said, thinking that her name suited her precisely.

Admiration leached into wanting. He covered her mouth with his own, pausing just a second lest she protest. She did not. Her lips were so soft. She tasted of peaches or apricots or strawberries, sweet and lush. He slipped his arm around her back and pulled her closer. So long it had been since he had kissed a woman. His other hand he used to push back her hat and his mouth shaped hers so easily, so naturally, that he forgot to think about whether he could remember what to do, and sank into her kiss as if he had been waiting to do so from the moment they met.

Kate closed her eyes. Such a gentle touch he had. And the look in his eyes, as if he could see the feelings she kept parcelled up deep inside her. His mouth was warm. His kiss made her feel as if the sun had strengthened. His lips moved over hers slowly, tasting her, seeming to want nothing but to savour her. It made her skin tingle. It made her want. Just want. The purity of it gave her a pang. The simplicity of it, the ease of it, as if their mouths were made for each other, made her wonder. The gentleness made her want to cry.

But as she reached up to touch his hair, as she nestled closer, as she sank into the sensual haze of his kiss, Virgil pulled away. 'I guess I should apologise for that.'

Kate blinked and touched her fingers to her lips. He sounded singularly unrepentant. She ought to be insulted, but in fact this realisation was pleasing. 'Mr Jackson...'

'I wish you would call me Virgil. Hardly anyone does.'

It was a relief to see that he looked slightly dazed, because that was exactly how Kate felt. Or was it dazzled? Were kisses supposed to make you feel like that? Not in her experience. 'Virgil,' she said. 'I like it. Your name, I mean. I like your name.' And his kisses. She didn't want him to think she didn't like his kisses, but she couldn't very well tell him that. She fanned her cheeks.

Virgil took her hand, stroking the pulse at her wrist with his thumb. 'I haven't wanted to kiss anyone in a long time.'

'Then that makes two of us,' Kate said with a husky little laugh. His touch was making her even hotter.

'How long?'

'Not since Anthony.' Had she ever wanted to kiss Anthony? She must have done, else she would not have... 'What about you?'

Virgil shrugged. 'A while.'

'Days? Weeks? Months?' Kate persisted. 'Years?' she squeaked, disbelievingly.

'A while.'

He dropped her hand, moving away from her, as far as the gig's limited seating allowed. She wanted to probe, but she knew better than to do so. Whatever *a while* was, it was surprising. Astonishing that a man as attractive, as assured, as Virgil had kissed no one. Though not as astounding as the fact that he had kissed *her*! She wanted to know why. Or did she? Perhaps ignorance in this case truly was bliss. Kate untangled the reins from the brake. 'I hope it was worth the wait,' she said, resorting to her customary glibness.

'Have we much further to go?' Virgil asked some time later.

Kate shook her head. 'We've been on Montague land for the past couple of miles. The farmers here are all my father's tenants.'

'Good God, I didn't realise he owned so much.'

'Well, it's not really my father but the dukedom. The land is all entailed, so he can't sell it, and he can't bequeath it to anyone other than Jam—I mean, Giles. Giles is the heir. Or at least he is at the moment. That may well all be about to change.'

'How so?'

Kate grimaced. 'It's complicated. I should have told you. I've invited you into a hornet's nest, but I so wanted you to come with me. I didn't really think about it last night, but—oh, God, the truth is that we're actually in a bit of a mess,' she said. 'Are you angry?'

'How can I be, when I don't know what you're talking about?'

'Yes. Of course. Sorry. Well, it seems that my brother Jamie took a wife in Spain just before he—he died. We knew nothing about it until a few months ago, when my father received a letter from the woman demanding that we do right by her son who is, she claims, Jamie's heir. You can imagine the uproar that caused. My brother Giles suspects the whole thing is an elaborate fraud but Ross—he is my cousin—met the woman, and seemed fairly convinced by her. So now Giles, who is the heir at the moment but might not really be the heir, has sent my brother Harry—who is the next in line to Giles but of course is further out if this child…well, anyway, Harry is off to Spain to see what he can discover, and in the meantime my father, who is most anxious to detach his grandson from what he has called the scheming wretch, has insisted that they both come to Castonbury.' Kate drew a breath and laughed at Virgil's expression. 'I told you, it's complicated.'

'Extremely,' Virgil said, amused by her method of re-counting the tale, dismayed by its content.

'The reason I had to come home today is because Giles has demanded a sort of family counsel of war.'

'And knowing all this, you still insisted I accompany you! Surely your time will be quite taken up with these matters, and my presence in the midst of it all can only be an inconvenience at best.'

Kate slowed the horse down as they rounded a bend in the lane, pulling the gig to a halt at a large wooden gate. 'You *are* angry. I'm sorry, I ought to have told you sooner, but I so wanted you to come to Castonbury and I was afraid that you would not, and that is the truth.' She transferred the reins to one hand, placing her other on Virgil's sleeve. 'I'm glad that you're here.'

He covered her hand with his, and smiled crookedly down at her. 'Thank you, but I think perhaps I should not make it such a long visit.'

'We'll see,' Kate said, deciding wisely not to push her luck. 'Now, look over there.' She pointed her whip. 'That is Castonbury Park.'

The field by which they had stopped was on a rise, looking down on the house. Behind them, the trees which bordered the lane through which they had been driving would provide a pleasant perspective. The house itself was perfectly symmetrical with matching wings set to the east and west. In the centre of the building, a domed roof gave it a distinctive appearance, more like a classical Roman villa or place of worship than a family home. Though it was difficult to see the detail at this distance, it looked as if the architect had been an admirer of the classical style, for there were pediments and pillars, the rustic stonework of the ground floor giving way to the smooth finish on the *piano nobile*, from which a grand staircase curved down to the neatly manicured lawns. He had expected something flamboyantly grand, but the perfect proportions were so beautiful that he could not but admire them.

'What do you think?' Kate asked.

'It's not what I thought it would be. I thought the home of a duke would be more…showy.'

She gave a gurgle of laughter. 'Just wait. There is gilt and gold aplenty in the state rooms.' She urged the tired horse into motion once more. 'The prettiest part of the grounds is to the north, which is where the main lodge is. The smaller one you can see leads to the Dower House. And through those woods there is a path to the village, where Lily, Giles's betrothed, lives in the vicarage.'

'Let me make sure I have this right. Giles is your eldest brother now, and you are next in age?'

'No, I come after Harry. Ned was next after me,' Kate said, ignoring the familiar lurch in her stomach as she spoke Ned's name, 'and then there is my sister, Phaedra, who is twenty, four years younger than me. Since my spectacular failure to make a good marriage, all my father's hopes are pinned on Phaedra making her debut next Season but I suspect they are misplaced, for though my sister has the potential to be quite danger- ously attractive, she has very little interest in anything but horses, and none at all in either parties or clothes, much to my aunt's despair. My Aunt Wilhelmina,' Kate explained, seeing Virgil's puzzled look, 'is a widow, my mother's sister and has been at Castonbury since Mama died. Oh, and then there is my cousin Colonel Ross Montague, the one who has met Jamie's wife. He also grew up at Castonbury with his sister, Araminta, but she is lately married. And Ross has returned to India… and very possibly ran off with his sister's maid! And that,' Kate said, laughing, 'concludes the current his- tory of the Montagues. I can see from your face that we have signally failed to live up to your expectations, and I haven't told you half the skeletons we have in our closet, believe me. Why Papa thinks himself superior, I have no idea.'

'Nor indeed have I,' Virgil replied, wondering what the devil he'd let himself in for, but unable to resist re- turning her smile, all the same.

Chapter Three

It was late afternoon by the time they turned into the main entrance to Castonbury Park. Virgil watched with increasing unease as Kate tooled the gig through the iron gates, waving her whip at the gatekeeper. She continued at a smart trot along a well-kept carriageway through pretty parklands where two lakes, the larger with an island in the middle, were divided by a rustic bridge, before coming to a halt in front of the main entrance of the house.

Close up, the building looked far more imposing, the central structure fronted by a colonnaded portico worthy of the Roman senate, flanked by two curved galleries sweeping out to an east and west wing. Rows of windows gazed watchfully down. As he leapt lightly onto the gravel and held out his hand to assist Kate, Virgil told himself that it was purely fancy to think that they looked disapproving.

Inside, a rather gloomy hall dominated by a number of stone pillars and four huge empty fireplaces.

'Lumsden, I trust you received word that I was bringing a guest,' Kate said to a superior-looking grey-haired man.

'Indeed, Lady Kate, I have prepared the Blue Room.'

'Excellent. Mr Jackson's man is travelling with Polly. I don't expect they will be too far behind us. This is Mr Jackson, Lumsden. Virgil, this is Lumsden, our butler, who has been at Castonbury longer than any of us care to remember.'

'Pleased to meet you....'

The butler stopped in the act of executing a bow.

'Mr Jackson is an American,' Kate explained.

The butler made a huge effort to pull himself together, but his protuberant eyes remained fixed on Virgil.

'From Boston,' Virgil corroborated, more amused than offended, for the man was looking at him as if he were about to pounce.

'Boston,' the butler repeated.

'In Massachusetts. That's New England. Though obviously I'm not originally from there,' Virgil said helpfully.

'Indeed, sir, I had gathered not.'

'Oh, do stop staring,' Kate said impatiently. 'Mr Jackson is not going to bite you.'

'Well, not yet, at any rate,' Virgil said. 'I've just been fed.'

Taken aback, for she had not thought him a man given to teasing, Kate suppressed a chuckle and cast Virgil a reproving look before turning back to Lumsden. 'I take it you know about this counsel of war that Giles has called?'

'Indeed.' The butler looked as if he himself bore the burden of the Montagues' woes. 'A difficult business, my lady. Lord Giles wishes to discuss the matter in the drawing room before dinner. If I may suggest, perhaps Mr Jackson could take sherry in the library, since it is a family matter. We have the London papers there.'

'That will suit me fine,' Virgil said, smiling reassuringly at Kate, who was looking troubled.

'If you're sure? Then I shall see you in a couple of hours. Lumsden will show you to your bedchamber.'

Kate disappeared into the gloom of the vast hall, leaving Virgil alone with the old retainer, who made more stately progress in her wake. The guest rooms were in one of the wings which adjoined the main body of the house, connected by a curved corridor lined with ancestral portraits, where Lumsden slowed to a crawl, intoning: 'the fourth earl who became the first duke'; 'his first duchess'; 'his second duchess'; 'her second son'—as if he were introducing them at a party. Virgil wondered if he was expected to make his bow to each one. Their eyes followed him as he passed. He was pretty certain he could hear their affronted muttering.

Alone at last, staring out the window of the Blue Room at the lakes, he felt a wave of homesickness. This house was steeped in the kind of history he could not begin to comprehend. Though the current building was less than a hundred years old, Kate's ancestors had lived on this land for centuries. A direct line, as Lumsden had informed him, fluffing his feathers like a proud cockerel, going back to the first earl, who had been raised from a mere baronetcy by Queen Elizabeth. The Montagues had roots so deep they were entrenched in the very soil of England. Their customs and traditions, their blood-line and heritage, hung around Castonbury like a protective cloak.

Virgil had not thought of himself as rootless until now. Gazing around the Blue Room, at the tapestry depicting a naked woman bathing surrounded by nymphs and exotic creatures, at the Chinese porcelain on the carved mantel, at the rich silks of the bed hangings and the thick oils of the paintings in their heavy gilt frames which hung on the walls, and the soft pile of the rug which covered the polished wooden boards, he felt as if all of it was conspiring to remind him that he had no

place here. The antiques screamed of wealth and position, of traditions so well established as to be inviolable.

He ran his hand over the embroidered coverlet. Black
skin on celestial blue silk. His being here was a violation
of something entrenched. Though Kate did not think so.
She had welcomed his touch. The contrast of his skin
against hers seemed to fascinate her. In another world,
the differences in their skin colour would not matter.
Virgil stared at his image in the long mirror which stood
by the nightstand. 'Not another world, another planet,'
he muttered.

A gentle tap on the door made him snap to. He was
here now, and he was damned if he would allow these
blue-blooded aristocrats and their haughty servants to
look down on him!

'Ah, Katherine. So good of you to join us. Finally.'
The Honourable Mrs Landes-Fraser swept into the drawing room, the puce feathers in her turban waving ma-
jestically, the demi-train of her evening gown swishing
violently, while the fringes of her shawl caught on the
crook of a Dresden shepherdess perched atop a card
table, causing the maiden to skitter across the polished
rosewood before coming to rest just short of the edge.

Deigning to accept her customary glass of very dry
sherry, a libation ideally suited to her extremely dry hu-

mour, Mrs Landes-Fraser disposed her wraith-like person upon one of the large blue damask sofas. The sofas, ornately scrolled and gilded, were adorned by a blatantly naked sea creature on each arm, a feature at which Mrs Landes-Fraser took personal affront each time she sat upon them. With a flair born of practice, she flicked her shawl expertly over the exposed bosom of a mermaid. 'I am sure,' she said, looking down her Roman nose at her niece and speaking in a tone which made it clear she was no such thing, 'that your hasty visit to Staffordshire was necessary, but it was most ill-timed. Though I am aware you do not think so, I believe that your family have first claim on your time, particularly in a crisis. I cannot quite believe that you have, under the circumstances, inflicted a guest upon us. Really, Katherine, it is most thoughtless of you. You must get rid of the person as soon as possible. Giles will agree with me, I know.'

Her nephew, who was leaning his tall frame against the mantel, shrugged impatiently and sipped on his Madeira. 'This is Kate's home—she's perfectly entitled to invite guests.'

'But this man is apparently an American,' Kate's aunt said with a shudder. 'Bad enough we have to put up with one outsider...'

'If this woman's claim proves to be true, then she is not an outsider but family,' Giles said shortly.

'Well, I, for one, have no intention of treating her as such until her claim *is* proved,' Mrs Landes-Fraser declared.

Giles shrugged. 'I expect she'll find a friend in Kate. Aside from her tendency to support the underdog, my sister will most likely form an alliance, if for no reason other than to oppose our father,' he said, casting his sister a sardonic glance.

'You do me an injustice, brother dear,' Kate retorted. 'I would support any downtrodden female. As to Papa—I believe my refusal to consider that old goat Sir Nathan Samuelson as a husband set me well and truly beyond the pale.'

Giles gave a harsh crack of laughter. 'I told him it was a bloody stupid idea. I'm glad you gave it short shrift.'

Kate smiled. She and Giles were almost always at outs, since he would never deign to explain or discuss anything and she regarded his reticence as arrogance, but they shared a dark sense of humour. 'I gave him shrift so short it was barely detectable,' she replied.

'And you will rue the day, Katherine,' her aunt said witheringly, 'for you have now quite firmly confined yourself to the shelf of spinsterhood.'

'Oh, for goodness' sake, Aunt, the man is a buffoon,'

Giles said, throwing back the remains of his Madeira and thumping the glass onto the marble mantelpiece. 'We have far more important matters to discuss than Kate's matrimonial prospects.'

'My niece has no matrimonial prospects, thanks to her imprudence,' Mrs Landes-Fraser intoned, always determined to have the final say. 'Were it not for her lineage, even Sir Nathan would carp at taking on soiled goods.'

'Aunt Wilhelmina! Whatever do you mean?' Phaedra, who had been sprawling on the opposite sofa, flicking through a stud book, looked up. Seeing her aunt's pursed lips, her brother's scowl and her sister's blush, her interest, normally reserved solely for horses, perked up. 'Kate? What does Aunt Wilhelmina—'

'Damn it! This is no time to go raking over *that* matter.' Giles glowered at his aunt. 'Lumsden will be ringing the bell for dinner before we know it. Just for once, can we discuss something in a civilised manner without squabbling like cats?'

'Civilised, Giles? That will be a first for you,' Kate said softly.

Her brother had the grace to smile, but as he threw himself onto the sofa beside Phaedra, his expression darkened once more. 'This is serious. Our father is—to be frank, I fear our father has become slightly deranged.'

'Giles! His Grace—'

'Aunt Wilhelmina, His Grace has more or less suggested that we separate his purported grandson from his mother by force if necessary,' Giles interrupted in clipped tones. 'He is willing to bring the full weight of the law to bear in order to do so, and if that fails, he talks of kidnap.'

Mrs Landes-Fraser clutched at her meagre breast. 'I feel sure you exaggerate.'

'And I feel sure he does not,' Kate said tersely. 'Behind that feeble front he uses to his own advantage, our dear papa has a will of iron. This woman—what are we to call her, Giles?'

'Until proved otherwise, I suppose she is the Dowager Marchioness of Hatherton,' her brother responded with a shrug.

'Lord, we can't call her that,' Phaedra piped in, 'she's no older than you, Kate. Her name is Alicia. Ross says she's very pretty.'

'I fail to see what that has to do with anything,' Mrs Landes-Fraser said acerbically.

'Knowing Jamie, it has everything to do with it,' Kate retorted. 'If she were fubsy-faced and plump, we could at least be certain that she was a fraud.'

'True,' Giles agreed, 'but quite beside the point.'

'No, the point is that our father seems to believe his

title puts him above the law of the land,' Kate agreed. 'What is to be done, Giles?'

'She's agreed to visit, though of course I didn't invite her on the terms our father suggested, which was that she deposit the child into the hands of a nanny and disappear.'

'There is no nanny,' Phaedra interjected.

'Because I won't be party to my father's ridiculous conniving. He's had the old nursery redecorated in preparation, can you believe it? Yet he won't contemplate having a room prepared for the mother—though what he thinks we are to do with her, I don't know. Suggest she sleep in the stable block, I suppose.'

'There is no room there, unless she shares a bed with old Tom Anderson, and I don't think he'd be best pleased by that,' Phaedra exclaimed. 'In fact, I don't think it's a good idea at all. I don't want to upset him because that would upset the horses and—'

'And of course there is nothing so important as keeping the horses happy,' Kate said, laughing. 'He was joking, Phaedra.' She turned back to Giles with a frown remarkably like her brother's. 'It seems to me that we ought to do nothing precipitate until we can prove the claim—or disprove it. Assuming what this Alicia says is true...'

'Which seems more likely than not,' Giles interjected.

'Then we must act accordingly and offer them a home. There can be no question of separating them.'

'I don't see why not.' Faced with three disapproving faces, Mrs Landes-Fraser twitched at the fringe of her shawl. 'Provided she knows that her son is being cared for, what possible objection can the woman have?'

'You don't perhaps think that the child—who is a mere two years old—would prefer his mother to a complete stranger?' Giles asked incredulously.

'Aunt Wilhelmina, how can you say that to us?' Phaedra said indignantly. 'Do you think we would wish the poor little boy to be raised as we were?'

'What can you mean?' her aunt asked, bristling. 'Your mother was no absent parent.'

'She was to me. She died before I could even remember her.'

'Well, I remember her,' Kate said. 'Mama may have been a presence at Castonbury, but she was not a presence in any of our childhoods. Were it not for the fact that we were no longer paraded in front of her in the drawing room once a week, I doubt very much that we'd even have noticed she was gone.'

'Katherine! How dare you slander my sister in such a way? Your mother—'

'For goodness' sake, Kate, leave it,' Giles interjected. 'Not but what she ain't right,' he added, looking pointedly at his aunt, 'but we have once more strayed from the point and we are no further forward. I should have known better than to try to get some sort of consensus. Let us just forget it, I shall think of something. I always do.'

Struck by the weariness in her brother's tone, Kate felt a pang of guilt. With their father living in cloud cuckoo land half the time, the weight of managing the estate fell on Giles's shoulders, a burden he was very far from welcoming despite what Papa and Aunt Wilhelmina might think. She cast her mind around desperately for something to help him out, and it came to her that she had actually pointed out the solution to Virgil that very afternoon. 'I have it,' she exclaimed, 'the Dower House. It's been empty since old Cousin Frederica died, save for the dratted cats she left behind.'

Giles's brow cleared. 'Do you think it will suffice?'

'It's perfect. It will give the poor woman independence, and it will bring her into the bosom of the family without suffocating her. She may bring the child to visit Papa, but her living separately will ensure that he doesn't become too attached, should matters prove— well, we shall have to wait and see how matters prove once Harry has done some digging.'

'It will be a considerable amount of work to get the

place fit for habitation. I am not sure how I am to find the time, with all my other duties.'

'You may leave the detail of it up to me, Aunt Wilhelmina,' Kate said. 'I will look over the place tomorrow.'

'And His Grace?' Mrs Landes-Fraser demanded. 'Am I to tell His Grace that his arrangements have been overset?'

'You may leave our father up to me,' Giles said brusquely.

'And you may leave the ordering of a pony for the boy up to me,' Phaedra said, bestowing one of her naughty smiles upon her aunt.

'The child is but two years old,' Mrs Landes-Fraser blustered.

'If he is a Montague, that is long past the age of throwing him onto a saddle,' Phaedra retorted.

Her aunt's opinion of this was lost, as the butler made his stately entrance. 'Dinner will be served in fifteen minutes, my lord.'

'Excellent timing as ever, Lumsden.' Giles beamed. 'Best fetch my sister's guest now.' He poured himself another Madeira, and turned to Kate. 'An American businessman, eh? What on earth does he hope to find of interest here at Castonbury?'

'You know what these New Worlders are like.' Though

Mrs Landes-Fraser had never, in fact, met anyone from
the New World, American or otherwise, her complete
ignorance did not prevent her from holding an opinion—it never did. 'More than likely he wishes to boast
to all his friends of his rubbing shoulders with a duke's
family. They have no aristocracy over there, you know.
It is one of the many things which makes them an in-
ferior country.'

'Actually, Aunt, I believe that America is likely to
prove a most superior country in the very near future,'
Giles said. 'You only have to look at the way the cotton
trade is going to see—'

'Trade!' Mrs Landes-Fraser wrinkled her nose.
'Money cannot buy rank.'

'Yes, well, if we don't sort out our family finances
soon, we will be living in genteel poverty, and frankly
I'd rather be wealthy than well-born,' Giles muttered.

'Actually, Mr Jackson is more interested in our village
school than our family tree,' Kate chipped in brightly.
Looking around the room at her relatives, she felt the
first flicker of serious doubt. Lumsden had obviously
said nothing. Perhaps she should have mentioned it,
after all, but then that would have implied that it mattered to her and it did not, save that she liked the way
Virgil looked. What must he be feeling? Had she allowed
her determination to shock to overrule her judgement?

Jumping to her feet, she was at the door of the drawing room just as Lumsden threw it open. Virgil stood on the threshold, his tall, well-built figure immaculate in evening dress, quite dwarfing the butler.

'Mr Jackson.'

Lumsden's tone was funereal. Thinking that Virgil must be feeling horribly like a gladiator cast into the lion's den, Kate stepped towards him as if to shield him, but he shook his head, tilted his head back proudly and stepped into the drawing room.

The effect of his entrance was almost comical.

'I thought you were magnificent. I confess, when you walked into the drawing room last night, I felt dreadfully guilty for putting you through the agony of a family dinner, but you were wonderful.'

It was not yet nine of the clock the following morning, but having decided, after the endurance test which had been last night's repast, to spare Virgil—and, if she was honest, herself—the ordeal of breakfast *en famille*, Kate had used the need to investigate the Dower House as an excuse for an early start. It was a pleasant day, the air crisp with autumn, the grass mossy and soft underfoot as they made their way along the lower lakeside.

'It was hardly an ordeal. Your sister doesn't care

who she talks to as long as it's about horses, and your brother...'

'Yes, what were you talking to Giles about? You sat forever over the port.'

'Business.'

'My father's investments, you mean. Don't worry, you are not breaking a confidence. I know his imprudence has left the family coffers sadly empty. Were you able to advise Giles?'

'I need to understand more about the situation first. In my experience, there are always loopholes if you know where to look. If that doesn't suffice, your brother has a number of other ideas for raising funds. The problem is,' Virgil said with a grin, 'that they are all too safe. Low risk is what Giles calls them, and I can understand why—it's not his money. If it were down to me—anyway, I said I'd take a closer look and let him know what I think.'

'That is very generous of you.'

'Business of any sort interests me.'

They stepped onto the rustic bridge whose three arches spanned the cascade between the two lakes, and which Kate claimed gave one of the best views back to the house. They stopped at the centre, leaning side by side on the lichen-covered parapet. A silver fish leapt dramatically in pursuit of a fly, landing with a loud splash which sent ripples eddying out over the greenish-brown water. Blades of grass stuck with the dew to Virgil's top boots. The skirts of his coat brushed against Kate's gown. She wore a dark green habit today, with another of those tight little jackets which clung to her slim form. Her hair was gathered into a heavy chignon at the base of her neck. She wore neither hat nor gloves.

'Giles strikes me as most unhappy with his situation as heir apparent,' Virgil said. 'I got the impression that he would much rather be back in the army than here.'

'He's a dark horse, my brother. There are depths to him which I confess I did not realise until recently. Lily, his betrothed, is of Romany origin, you know—though Giles has been at pains to keep *that* fact from our father. Romany blood is no blood for a future duchess in our father's eyes. And you're right, he would much rather be back in the army. Giles never had any expectations of inheriting this place.'

'It is quite a place.' Virgil gazed back at the house across the parkland; it seemed to nestle in the line of trees to the south. The symmetry of the building was most pleasing from this angle. 'It looks as if the landscape has been designed for it.'

'It was,' Kate said with a brief smile. 'None of this perspective is natural—it was all designed by Robert Adam, the man who built the house. Even the lakes have been dammed to give a more pleasing prospect. Nothing here is as nature made it, though I'll admit it has been very well done.'

'Very well indeed,' Virgil exclaimed, 'it all looks as if it has been here forever.'

'Yes, that is rather the intention, to make it seem perfectly natural. In order to reflect the perfectly natural right of centuries of Montagues to exploit Castonbury villagers,' Kate replied caustically. 'If my father had his way, none of it would change. Educating the serfs, you must know, is in his eyes nothing short of anarchy, for it will only give them aspirations beyond their proper place in life.'

'It is a view I am unfortunately extremely familiar with,' Virgil said.

Kate turned to face him, leaning back against the stonework of the bridge. 'You mean my father shares his outlook with the plantation owners. I shall make a point of telling him that.'

'Do you enjoy being at outs with him?'

Her smile faded into a small frown which spoiled the smooth arch of her brows. 'It's not that I do it deliberately, but we have so little in common. He doesn't really know me. I don't think he knows any of his children very well. We are not exactly a close family, nor have we been raised to expect affection from one another. I used to think it would have been different if Mama had lived, but actually I don't think it would have been. I don't recall her being in the least bit maternal. Of course, I care for my father in a dutiful way, but I don't like him any more than he likes me.'

There was hurt there, behind that fierce expression that made her eyes more slate-grey than blue. It was there, too, in the way she crossed her arms over her chest, in the defiant tilt of her chin. 'Shall I meet him while I am here?'

Kate chuckled. 'I hope so, and if you do, I beg you do not let the fact that he is nominally your host constrain you. He is bound to be just as offensive as Aunt Wilhelmina, so you need have no qualms. She was quite crushed by the end of dinner last night. I could have kissed you.'

Immediately the words were out, Kate wished them back. 'I mean, I thought you put Aunt Wilhelmina down beautifully. I did not mean I actually wanted to kiss you. Not in the dining room.'

She could feel the hot flush prickling up her back and prayed it would not reach her cheeks. Why had she mentioned kissing? She had been trying so hard not to think of kissing Virgil ever since he had kissed her and now... Much too late, Kate bit her tongue.

'Not in the dining room,' Virgil mused. The pulse was

there again, just below her ear. He touched it. He could not resist touching it, feeling it flutter under his finger-tip, fascinated by the soft warmth of her skin, by the contrast of his skin on hers. 'If not in the dining room, then where? I wonder.'

He hadn't meant to touch her. He hadn't meant to kiss her again, but he could not resist her. Eleven years, and he had never had any real trouble in repressing his de-sire, but there was something about Kate. He forgot to be on his guard with her. 'What about here?'

Virgil curled his fingers into the thick bundle of her hair and covered her body with his. She was pliable as a willow. Her thighs brushed his. His blood stirred and heated. His desire for her unfurled sleepily, slowly, but surely all the same. He knew he was playing with fire, but still he leaned closer to her. Her breath clouded the air between them. 'Will you kiss me on the bridge, Kate?'

'Virgil, I'm not very good at this sort of thing.' Her heart was hammering in her breast. Her body was tin-gling where it met his, and aching where it did not. She wasn't the type of woman who even wanted this sort of thing, whatever it was. Except that she did want it.

Virgil pulled her towards him, bracing one hand on the parapet, the other sliding down from her hair to the small of her back. He smiled, a slow smile, as if that, too, was unfurling from a long hibernation, stretching sensuously, sinuously. 'You're not good at this sort of thing, and I'm out of practice, and yet we managed well enough yesterday.' He nibbled at the lobe of her ear, then tasted the skin behind it, the fluttering pulse. Sweet and heady. His hand settled on the curve of her bottom. He had forgotten what curves could do to him.

'Virgil.' Kate touched his face. She ran her fingers over the springy crop of his hair. His head was beautifully shaped. His body was so solid. So very different from hers. So very different from…

She closed her mind on that thought. The scent of him was so different too. She leaned in to him, nipping his ear in imitation of what he had done to her. He shuddered in response. She wanted more. She wanted to know more too. Why was he out of practice? How long had it been? Why her? She opened her mouth to ask him, but something stopped her. A warning in his eyes? His hold on her slackened. Unable to bear it, Kate stood on tiptoe and kissed him.

He was startled into stillness. His lips were cool with the morning air. He tasted of the coffee he'd had at breakfast. It was not so much his intriguing abstinence or her own far from satisfactory experience, but a simple desire to merge and to mingle with another, to be no longer alone, which made Kate move her lips more insistently against his. His body was so big compared to hers, so powerful, yet it was a potent contrast, exciting and reassuring rather than intimidating. She felt infinitely female against his blatant maleness, then he gave a little groan and his arms went round her like a cooper's hoops around a barrel, yanking her almost off her feet, and she stopped thinking about anything at all.

He was not gentle. His kiss was neither untutored nor timid. It was a harsh kiss, his mouth hungry, ravaging hers in a way completely unlike their kiss of yesterday. Heat flared between them. Kate felt as if she could not breathe and did not want to breathe, squeezed tight and breathless, lightheaded with it. His lips pressed against hers, his tongue licking its way inside her mouth in a shockingly intimate way, his teeth nipping and biting, the pressure too much and yet not nearly enough.

Her back was pressed against the stone of the bridge. Her breasts were pressed against Virgil's chest. Her nipples were tingling. The solid length of his manhood pressed between her thighs. She had forgotten. She had not quite forgotten, though she did not remember this… this urgent need, ache and throb. Her hands clutched at his head, his shoulders, his coat. A strange guttural sound came from deep in her throat.

And then she was free, panting, staring up at Virgil,

who was staring out across the bridge towards the house, his eyes narrowed. 'What...?'

'I don't know. A gardener. A groom, perhaps,' Virgil said, moving away from her.

Kate peered across the lake. The figure was some distance away. She could just about make out that it was male. 'Do you think he saw?'

Virgil shook his head. 'I doubt it.' He blinked and looked down at Kate. She was flushed. Her lips looked like crushed berries. He was uncomfortably aware of his erection, and was relieved that he was wearing buckskins and not those ridiculously tight-knitted pantaloons. Though Kate must be perfectly aware—he swore under his breath.

'You must have very keen hearing. Or eyesight.' Kate's own eyes had been closed. Hadn't Virgil, then, been as carried away as she? 'Which was it?' she asked, striving and completely failing to sound light, as if kissing a man on Robert Adam's bridge was an everyday occurrence for her.

'Both. Neither. I don't know.' Virgil realised he was rubbing his forearm, caught himself and self-consciously tugged the starched cuff of his shirt. 'Instinct, I suppose,' he said. 'It was a stupid thing to do.' Here, he meant. Or anywhere, he should have meant, though he was too coiled, tense, wound up with the soaring heat of that kiss, to wish it had not happened, quite yet.

'Yes, it was,' Kate said, mortified.

Her eyes were overbright and Virgil, who had made his own opaqueness of character a trademark over the past eleven years, found he did not wish this particular woman to misunderstand him. 'Kate, I don't care who sees us, but you ought to. This is your country, your home. People will talk.'

'I doubt it,' Kate said drily. 'They will think they have imagined it, it is so very unlikely. It doesn't even seem real to me.'

'That a duke's daughter should kiss a freed slave, you mean?'

She shook her head impatiently. 'That someone like you would find someone like me even remotely kissable. I am not the type of woman men want to kiss, I know that. Besides, what can I ever be to you? Your life is so different from mine you may as well come from another world. You are here to see our village school. Castonbury is but a stopover on your route north. It is known that I have an interest in abolition. Why should people put any other construction on our being together? It is ridiculous, that is what I meant.' Kate nodded, quite satisfied with this explanation, now she came to think of it.

'Ridiculous,' Virgil repeated slowly. 'Ridiculous that

we could possibly mean anything to each other, is that what you mean?'

'Well, I suppose so.'

'Though that doesn't stop me finding you extremely kissable.'

'But that's probably why you do. Because it's so un-likely.'

'You have a very low opinion of yourself, Kate.'

'A very accurate one, Virgil.'

'No. You are quite unique.' He caught her hand and pressed a kiss on her palm. 'But you are quite right too,' he said, smiling down at her. 'It is so impossible that it is almost laughable. You think that's why we are attracted to each other?'

Was that relief in his voice? Was he, then, just as confused as her? It was true, Virgil being the antithesis of everything her family would deem eligible added a frisson to their kisses, but it wasn't all there was. 'Each other,' she said with relief, only just realising what he had admitted. 'It's not just me?'

'I thought that was pretty obvious.'

She was going to blush again. She was twenty-four years old, and quite beyond blushing. Kate consulted the little gold watch which she wore on a fob at her waist. 'We must get on. I promised Giles I'd set whatever must be done to the Dower House in motion this afternoon.

Our new sister-in-law—if that is indeed what she is—is expected within the week.'

She was right, again. It was just a kiss. An aberration for both of them, and they now had a perfectly reasonable explanation. No point in discussing it further. It couldn't mean anything. It was just a kiss. Virgil nodded to himself and made haste to follow Kate off the bridge.

Chapter Four

The path they were following went round the side of the house, joining another, wider but overgrown, which led in one direction back to the disused gatehouse where they had stopped yesterday, in the other to a copse of trees, behind which the mellow sandstone of a building could be glimpsed. They made their way through the copse of oak trees, and onto the approach to the Dower House. Kate walked quickly, her arms swinging out by her sides, easily keeping pace with Virgil's long-legged stride, the skirts of her habit flying out over the weed-strewn gravel.

The Dower House was built of mellow sandstone, with a pillared portico, two stories under a very low roof and very long windows in the old French style reaching almost to the ground. It was shuttered, and had about it an air of neglect, with weeds clogging the approach and a fretwork of ivy working its way along one of the side walls up into the eaves. Several large shrubs were so overgrown as to make the path which wound round to the north-facing garden impenetrable.

'These will need to be cut back,' Kate said, producing a large iron key from the pocket of her habit. Though it fitted easily enough into the lock, it would not move. Kate swore under her breath as she wrestled with it in vain. 'I don't think anyone has been here since Cousin Frederica died.'

'Let me try.'

'It needs oiling,' Kate said stubbornly.

Nudging her aside, Virgil turned the key easily. She glowered, caught his eye and was forced to laugh. 'Very impressive,' she said sarcastically, though, in fact, she *was* impressed, and shamefully excited by his strength. She wondered what he would be like naked, and gave a little shiver which she quickly covered up, pushing the door back on its protesting hinges. A sensible woman would conclude that kissing Virgil again would be extremely foolish. Dangerous, even. So why was she thinking that the very impossibility of kissing Virgil again was what made it—well, possible. Safe? Not that, but…

Like swimming naked, as she sometimes did under cover of the night. It gave her a vicarious thrill to know how appalled her aunt would be, how outraged everyone would be, a thrill she could savour all the more for knowing she was highly unlikely to be caught. Kissing Virgil would be that kind of safe and a whole lot more exciting. Too exciting. She had to stop thinking about it and concentrate on the task in hand.

Shafts of sunlight pierced the gloom through the fanlight above the door. Their boots rang out on the chequered marble of the reception hall. Dust motes danced, stirred up by the sweep of Kate's skirts. The place smelled musty, though there was an acrid undertone. 'Cats,' she said, wrinkling her nose. 'Cousin Frederica had at least a dozen of them. They get in and out through the stillroom window. At least it should mean that there won't be any mice.' She stirred the pile of leaves and twigs which filled the hearth of the large fireplace with her boot, disturbing the remnants of a bird's nest. 'We'll need to have all the chimneys swept. And if this is anything to go by,' she said, gazing up at the cobwebs which swung in silver threads from the wrought iron chandelier, 'it will take an army to clean.'

The room to the right was the drawing room. Virgil threw open the creaking shutters which guarded the window, flooding it with light. The furniture was draped in Holland covers, the carpets rolled in one corner, but the room was pleasantly proportioned, the plain wall panelling and cornicing painted in pale shades of green. 'At least it doesn't smell damp.' A cloud of dust flew out of the window hangings when Kate shook them, making her sneeze.

Across the hall again there was a dining room and a small music room. To the rear of the ground floor, the windows of the study, another salon and the breakfast parlour, which opened out onto the wilderness of the garden. Virgil opened the catches and walked out into the late-morning sunshine. The fountain was clogged with ivy. A mangy brindled cat eyed him malignantly from the muddy basin. Another was washing itself perched atop a stone lion which guarded the entrance to what had once been a rose garden. 'I hope your new relative likes felines,' Virgil said, as yet another of the furry creatures twined itself around his legs.

'They seem friendly enough,' Kate said, 'and she's going to need some friends. Should I arrange to have the guttering cleaned, do you think?'

'You're going to a lot of bother for this woman. I thought you said she was just coming for a visit.'

'If her claim is proved, her son is my father's heir. Castonbury Park will be her home.'

'Unless she marries again.'

'Well, I suppose—I hadn't considered that.' Kate looked thoughtful. 'She is only just widowed, but I believe she is quite young, and according to my cousin

Ross she's pretty so—Lord, that really would set the cat amongst the pigeons.'

'How so?'

'My father wants his heir here at Castonbury. He certainly won't tolerate the child being raised by another man. Giles says he's already set his lawyers onto sorting out a legal guardianship for the boy. If his mother is not careful, she will find that she has signed away her rights to her child.'

'Surely she would not be so foolish?'

Kate shrugged. 'Since Jamie did not see fit to inform the family that he was married, there was no settlement made for her. She is wholly dependant upon my father's goodwill, and he can be very ruthless when he wants to be. I intend to ensure she has her own legal advisors. It's the least I can do.'

'So she will have at least one friend who is not feline,' Virgil said with a faint smile.

'I sincerely hope that she does not have cause to have to rely on me, however,' Kate replied. 'I would not like to wager on her success should the might of the Montagues be brought down upon her head.'

They made their way back into the Dower House and ascended to the first floor. It was darker here, with only the light from the landing window to guide them. Kate's arm brushed against Virgil's coat sleeve as they turned into the long corridor, where doors stood closed on either side. The largest of the six bedrooms contained a fantastically carved bed, the four posts a mishmash of gryphons and dragons and other strange fairy-tale beasts.

'It was meant for the main house,' Kate said, laughing at Virgil's expression, which was a mixture of astonishment and horror as he traced the form of a voluptuous siren-like creature, 'but even for my grandfather, it was a step too far. Cousin Frederica thought it profane and would not sleep in it, despite the fact that this is the best bedroom.'

'What are the carvings supposed to represent?'

'A confused mind?' Kate replied flippantly. 'Actually, the key is in the central carving up there in the support for the canopy.'

She leant over the mattress to peer up, explaining the various myths which the artist had chosen to entwine. The bed was high. Though he tried not to notice, Virgil couldn't take his eyes off the way her bending over brought attention to the roundness of Kate's rear, the indent of her waist, the length of her legs. She wore riding boots. Did they stop at her calves, or were they longer? Perhaps the leather fitted snugly all the way up to her thighs. Though the skirts of her habit were full, he had already noted that her long, graceful stride seemed to be unimpeded by layers of petticoats. He realised he had no idea what ladies such as Kate wore for undergarments. It hadn't occurred to him to wonder, until now. Lace and silk? Practical cotton?

He was hard again. He had already, in his imagination, taken the short leap from underwear to skin, from looking at her curves to imagining his shaft sinking into the pink, moist heat of her. He had taken a step towards her in the process, ready to cup and to mould and to stroke. So long it had been since he had shared such intimacies. He thought he had forgotten, but looking at Kate, he discovered he knew in astoundingly lurid detail exactly what and where and how he wanted to touch her. She had stopped talking, was looking at him, lips parted. Just looking at him, as if she could read the turn his mind had taken.

She was not shocked, that was what he thought first. There was something, a heat in her eyes, a recognition or a reflection of what he was thinking. That was his second thought. That it was wish fulfilment was his third. Just because no one else would ever guess, just because it was so outrageous it could not be anything other than fleeting, did not mean that he planned to indulge in this attraction which sparked between them.

Virgil stepped to one side of the tempting display of curves, careful to keep a distance between them, and leaned over on the mattress, looking up at the carving as if that, and not touching her, stroking her, sheathing himself in her, had been his intention all along. 'Charybdis, the daughter of Poseidon, you were saying,' he said.

'You *were* listening?'

'"Zeus turned her into a monster because she ate some sheep she stole,"' Virgil repeated, relieved to discover that he had, on some other level, been taking in what she'd said, after all. He wasn't touching her, but he was a breath away from doing so. They were on a mattress. On a bed. His body was very well aware of this, though Virgil tried not to be. He could smell her scent. Lavender? No, more complex than that. More female.

'Charybdis made whirlpools to wreck ships,' Kate said. 'There is her accomplice, Scylla, on the post there.'

Virgil had the impression that what she was saying and what she was thinking were quite different. He thought this because it was the same for him. Kate pointed at the post on the left side of the bed at the top, though she continued to hold eye contact with him. The movement made her wobble, but she steadied herself before he could help her. He adjusted his weight so that he was propped on his side. 'So the bed does tell a story,' he said.

'Several, all tangled up.'

She was not whispering, but her voice was low, husky,

sensual. Did she know it? Did she mean it? There was a speck of dust on her cheekbone. Virgil brushed it away with his thumb. The pulse was there, just discernable, under her ear. He ran his hand down the length of her spine, into the dip at the base, over the swell of her bottom. He hadn't meant to do that. He couldn't stop himself. 'All tangled up,' Virgil repeated, imagining just that.

Kate made that strange little noise he remembered from earlier on the bridge, a breathy growl which seemed to connect directly with his groin. She leaned over and repeated his own action, her hand trailing down his back, to the base of his spine, to his buttocks. His muscles tightened under her fingers. His coat, the silk back of his waistcoat, the fine lawn of his shirt, the leather of his buckskins—he resented every stitch of expensive, fashionable clothing he wore.

He was so unaccustomed to a woman's touch he had thought himself immune. The agony of loss had established a physical shield long ago. Celibacy gave him strength. In eleven years, he had never had the slightest problem in maintaining it, but Kate broke through all his defences with just this whispering touch. Virgil rolled onto his side. 'Turn around,' he whispered.

On her back beside him on the bed, her eyes wide, her skin delicately flushed, her mouth soft, she watched him. He touched her, traced her shape through her clothes, enthralled, fascinated by the shallow rise and fall of her breasts, by the fluttering of the pulse below her ear. When he flattened his palm over her belly she pulled it tight. When he cupped the slope of her breasts, she gave a tiny moan. Her eyes never left his face. When he tugged up the hem of her skirt, she made no move to help or to hinder. Her riding boots were almost as long as her legs. Like the boots worn in ancient times. Like the boots in one of her family portraits. He wondered if that was where she'd taken her inspiration from. He could hardly breathe, running his hands up the soft leather to her narrow flanks.

He ached to have her touch him, but it would be too much. Far too much. What had happened to his self-restraint? Think. Think! His scars. No one had seen those. Not since—and not even Millie…

Too late, he wished he had not invoked her ghost. Why had he needed to? It was done now. It had worked, that was the important thing. Virgil rolled over and got to his feet, turning his back on temptation in a pretence of examining the post where Scylla was carved. The silence, a few moments only, seemed to stretch and stretch. 'Unless you wish to give your new relative nightmares, I think you should have a different room prepared for her,' he said.

Kate got up, slanting him a puzzled look. He knew

before she spoke that she was not going to follow his lead. 'What happened?'

'Nothing. I'm sorry.'

She straightened her jacket and gazed out of the ivy-clad window at the carriageway below. 'Sorry you touched me or sorry that you stopped?' Which was she? She didn't know. Both. Kate rested her hot cheek against the thick glass. The panes were diamond-shaped, crisscrossed with lead. Some of them were loose. She would have to get someone to re-solder them. William Everett, the estate manager, he would know who. She must make a note to speak to him. He would deal with the chimney sweep too. And a gardener. And she'd have to get some help from the village to do the cleaning. Three women? Maybe four, with—

'Both,' Virgil said, making her jump. 'Sorry that I touched you. Sorry that I stopped.'

Having her own thoughts so exactly articulated confused her. He confused her. What he made her feel confused her. This whole situation confused her. Anthony had put an end to her nascent desire—or so she had thought. Anthony had said it was her fault, her lack, and she had believed him. But what she felt for Virgil, it was so different. Did that mean that Anthony was wrong? Or she had changed? Or Virgil was different? She had no idea, and he was waiting for her to speak and she could not think straight enough to prevaricate. 'I don't know what to say. I'm not like this. I thought I wasn't like this—wasn't capable of being like this.'

'Not capable!' Virgil exclaimed, quite taken aback. 'Kate, you can't possibly mean…'

'I don't know what I mean,' she said wretchedly. 'You confuse me.'

Another thing they shared, but Virgil was too much in the habit of keeping his own counsel to say so. He ought to say they should forget it, but could not bring himself to do so. Did Kate really believe she was frigid? The idea was preposterous. He was struggling to find a way of saying so, when a movement in the carriageway below caught his eye. 'Who is that?'

'Oh, it's Charlie!' Kate declared. 'The boot boy, you know. I wonder what he wants. I must go and see.'

She was already heading for the door, obviously relieved. He ought to feel the same. Virgil eyed the bed resentfully, wishing he could blame its confused mythology for what had happened. But it wasn't the bed or the bridge or the carriage.

He sat down on the edge of the mattress and stared sightlessly down at his boots. He had come so far in eleven years. He had the means to put his past to rights now, thanks to a decade's worth of single-minded, sheer bloody hard work. The relentless pursuit of success, the need to be better, stronger, sharper, quicker than anyone else had been exhausting, but he had never tired. He had reached the pinnacle, just as he'd always known he would. He couldn't help but see Malcolm Jackson's death as symbolic. The passing of the old. That his patron's dying request had coincided with the opportunity to do business with Josiah Wedgwood, Virgil could not help but interpret as an omen. When he returned he would finally make a start on paying his debt to Millie.

He would make his new world, and in it he would finally be free. Virgil got to his feet and looked out of the window, where Kate was talking to a small boy. That she had come into his life at such a crossroads perhaps explained, even more than the impossibility of it, why he had let down his defences. She was the apex, the turning point, nothing more.

Satisfied now that he understood himself, Virgil turned from the window. How could someone who kissed like Kate imagine herself cold? As he made his way downstairs, he couldn't help wishing for the opportunity to prove her wrong.

'Polly sent me.' Charlie, an irrepressible twelve-year-old, stood at the bottom of the shallow flight of steps clutching a large wicker basket to his chest. 'She said as how you would be busy and would more'n likely forget to eat and even if you was hungry she wouldn't blame you for not coming back to eat with the old tartar Mrs Landes-Fraser 'cause one look at that face would put anyone off their grub.' Remembering too late that Polly had also threatened him with a clip round the ear if he repeated her remarks, Charlie employed his most winsome smile. 'There's game pie and cheese and bread and chicken. And wine. And apples. Polly said you might give me an apple if I didn't drop anything and I didn't, so I ate it on the way 'cause the basket was awful heavy.'

Kate couldn't help laughing as she took the picnic from him. 'Very sensible.'

Charlie lowered his voice to a whisper. 'Polly says you've got a gentleman friend here what's come all the way from Africa.'

'It's America, Charlie.'

The boy's face fell. 'So it's not true, then? What they said, Mr Lumsden and Mrs Stratton and Joe and Daisy and all?'

Kate, who had been rummaging through the basket for another apple to give to the boy, instead gave him a sharp look. '*What* have they been saying?'

Charlie took a quick step back. Everyone in the big house knew that Lady Kate was one of the better ones, even if she was always banging on to him about practicing his letters, but he didn't like that look in her eye.

It was the same look his mum had when she was thinking about clouting him. Not that Lady Kate would actually hit him, but he'd been on the receiving end of one of her set downs before, and even if he didn't know half the words she used, he got her drift all right. 'Nothing,' he said, taking another defensive step away from her.

'Charlie, what did they say?'

Her tone made it clear that he would be better to come clean than make something up. Besides, she always knew when he was fibbing. 'They said he had skin the colour of coal, if you please, my lady. And Agnes, she said that it would make the sheets black. And Mr Lumsden, he said that he most likely wouldn't have been allowed to stay if His Grace wasn't ill and wouldn't have cared if the devil himself was visiting. Then Mrs Stratton, she said we oughter remember that whatever else he might be, Mr Jackson was your guest and so he must be a gentleman. I dunno what Daisy said but Polly clipped her ear. And that's when Joe said—Joe said...'

Virgil appeared in the doorway and Charlie let out a squawk, his mouth falling open in astonishment. 'Well? What did Joe say about me?'

'He said you had a tail.'

'Charlie!'

But Virgil gave a shout of laughter. 'What do you think?' he demanded, moving with impressive speed to catch the boot boy as he made to run, and spinning round in front of him.

'I think I'll plant a facer on Joe Coyle for making game of me,' Charlie muttered.

'Fancy yourself in the ring, eh?'

Realising that he had not, in fact, brought the wrath of the muscular giant down on his head, Charlie's spirits quickly recovered. He put up two very small and grimy fists.

Virgil tutted, and repositioned the child's arms. 'Like this,' he said, 'unless you want a bloody nose. And those feet, do you want to trip over them? Look at me. See. It's as much about balance as punching.'

'I reckon you'd strip down mighty fine,' Charlie said, staring with new respect at Virgil. 'Do you box, sir?'

'No. No, never.'

'You must have, else how would you know how to stand. I bet you were good. Were you good, sir?' Charlie asked, too excited to notice that his questions were making his new-found hero extremely uncomfortable.

'I told you, I don't,' Virgil said shortly.

'Did you fight anyone famous? What about that one, you know, my dad told me all about it. Molly—something. He was like you.'

'He means Tom Molineaux,' Kate said, giving Charlie a reproving look.

'I know who he means.'

'Good grief, *do* you know him?'

'Do you, sir?'

Virgil dug his hands deep into the pockets of his coat. 'I met him.'

'Did you—did you *fight* him?'

Charlie's eyes were wide as saucers. Kate's expression was more...arrested. Inside his pockets, Virgil's fists were clenched painfully tight. Inside his head, he could hear them. The shouting. The jeering. The smell of blood and dust and sweat. Baying at them, just as they did at the dogs they set to scrap, at the cockerels they put at each other in the pit.

'Did you fight him? Molly—Molineaux. Did you, sir?'

'No! I told you...'

'Charlie, that's enough.'

Kate's voice was sharp, enough to silence the boy instantly. Virgil blinked. She cast him a look, equally sharp, but it was one of concern, not reprimand. And though she couldn't possibly understand, he knew that she'd sensed enough. He wasn't sure whether to be angry or relieved. She was chastising the boy gently for his questions, and at the same time slipping him an apple. Charlie was looking sullen as he made for the path back to the main house. It wasn't the boy's fault, those memories, but how could he explain? He could not.

Charlie ran off down the carriageway. Virgil picked up the hamper. 'This looks good. I'm hungry. Where shall we go? I noticed a little arbour with some benches in the garden.' Without waiting on a reply, he set off with the basket, pushing his way through the overgrown bushes.

'Virgil!' Kate called.

'The sun isn't exactly warm, but it will be nicer than sitting in that dusty dining room.'

'Virgil!'

He whirled round on her so suddenly that she stumbled. His face was set, his jaw clenched. 'I don't discuss that part of my life. Ever. It's over.'

It was not the threat in his voice, nor even the frightening stillness of him, but the coiled-up pain, the bleakness which dulled his almond-shaped eyes, that made her back down. His expression had closed over completely earlier, at the mention of the prizefighter's name. He had retreated, to somewhere dark, frightening. Though she desperately wanted to know because she desperately wanted to help, Kate suspected that whatever part of his past Virgil was remembering, it was something quite beyond her ken. 'Yes,' she said. 'I'm sorry.' She reached for him, meaning only to touch his arm in a gesture of—what?—pity, sorrow, understanding, empathy?

She wanted only to comfort him, but he flinched, and then so, too, did she. He made to speak, but seemed to be at a loss for words. Instead he took her hand, and led her silently through the wilderness of the garden to the arbour. She sat down abruptly. Her hands were shaking. Her legs too. She couldn't understand it. Such a strong reaction, but she wasn't quite sure what it was she was reacting to. She clasped her hands together, watching her knuckles tighten.

'Kate.'

He was sitting beside her. He seemed to have the ability to move silently. She smiled wanly.

'I hope you're hungry,' Virgil said. 'Polly's packed enough to feed an army.'

They spent the rest of the day examining the house in more detail, from attics to cellar, taking pains to stick to the task in hand, taking even more pains not to touch as they did so. As they made their way back to the main house, the sun was already sinking.

'A cook, a butler, two footmen, say three maidservants, a scullery maid,' Kate muttered, biting the end of her pencil, frowning in concentration as she looked at the close-written pages of her notebook. 'The nursery maid and her own lady's maid I'm sure she will wish to manage herself, but I think we'll need two—or do you think three other menservants besides whatever occasional help she needs if she chooses to entertain, of course?'

She looked enquiringly at him. Virgil's own house, while not the grandest in Boston, was by no means one of the smallest, and was run by one housekeeper, one maid and one manservant. Wealth was power, power was what he needed to pay for his sins, but he had never felt the need to flaunt success with the trappings of wealth. He preferred to speak for himself. 'It's just one woman and a child,' he said.

'She is the Dowager Marchioness of Hatherton—or at least she will be, if her claim is validated.'

'Does a dowager marchioness, then, take more looking after than a mere miss?'

'That's not the point. It's not about her needs but her consequence.'

In the short space of time he had known her, Virgil had come to think of Kate's views as similar to his own. He had forgotten that she belonged in this other world, where consequence must be evidenced in the quantity and quality of servants, amongst other things. 'I don't even have a valet.' He was suddenly bone-weary. 'The man I brought with me, I hired him in London. He was offended that I wouldn't let him shave me. What does that make me, in your world?'

'Self-sufficient. Crotchety, for some reason.' Kate sighed. 'Don't you see, you carry your consequence with you, Virgil. There is an authority in the way you walk, the way you look, the way you talk. It's not about how many servants are necessary to run a household—were it mine I would certainly do with considerably less—but it is not mine. My father is dead set upon wresting this woman's child from her at any cost. Giles doesn't want to believe her claim, despite the fact that it would relieve him of the burden of this stately pile, because it would mean admitting that Jamie is dead. My aunt—well, I don't have to tell you what my aunt thinks. This woman, Alicia, she has no one to speak up for her. She has no idea what she's risking, coming here. She most likely thinks we're giving her sanctuary, when, in fact—oh, heavens, I don't know what will happen. Surrounding her with just a little of the pomp due to her position may not be much, but it's all I can do. Do you see?'

'I guess.'

Kate wrinkled her brow. 'What does that mean?'

'I reckon so. Would you really do things differently if it were your household?'

Kate shrugged. 'I guess,' she said, smiling faintly at the way the phrase sounded in her English accent. 'It's a moot point, since I'm never likely to have a household of my own.'

'Can't you just move out?'

She laughed, but not pleasantly. 'Apart from the fact that it would give both my father and my aunt an apoplexy, I don't have any money.' Seeing the look of disbelief on his face, she laughed, this time with genuine amusement. 'Don't let all this fool you.' Her sweeping gesture encompassed the house, the parklands, the Dower House. 'It has nothing to do with me, a mere daughter. All I have, save whatever pin money Papa allows me, is my dowry. And if I don't marry...'

'I know your father has financial troubles, but he has more than enough to set you up if he wished.'

'But he doesn't wish, because it's not the way things are done here in England.'

'In America, it is not exactly common, but it's not frowned upon for a woman of independent means to have her own establishment.'

'Had I independent means, then America is where I'd go.'

'You'd like it there.'

'I don't doubt it, but I'll have to take your word for that.'

Kate spoke lightly, but he knew her better now. That was just her way. 'It's our loss,' Virgil said, and realised as he did that he meant it.

With a date set for the arrival of Jamie's widow at Castonbury, and Aunt Wilhelmina declining to have any part in the overseeing of the mountain of work required to make the Dower House habitable for a confidence trickster, Kate found herself without any time to call her own. As she suspected he would, Virgil suggested that he cut short his visit and continue north to New Lanark. Utterly frustrated by her family commitments, furious at Aunt Wilhelmina, who, she was certain, had made herself unavailable precisely to achieve this very outcome, Kate was relieved and astonished when her brother Giles came to her rescue.

'I'd be happy to take Virgil out and about a bit, show him some of the countryside,' he said. 'To be honest, I'd be happy for any excuse to get me out of here for a while. I'm sick of this whole damned mess, what with our father carping on about taking sole guardianship of his grandchild as if the boy does not already have a mother, and hiding his head in the sand over the mess he's got us into with his investments. There's not been a word from Harry for weeks, and I still have no idea where Ross is, and—in short, Kate, I'm in need of some uncomplicated male company and your Virgil seems like a most interesting chap.'

Though she was delighted with the solution, for over a week Kate met Virgil only at dinner, when they were separated by the expanse of the dining table and Aunt Wilhelmina's determined efforts to keep her nieces from any personal conversation with 'the American,' as she called him.

Wishing to consult the housekeeper on the details of some of her arrangements for the Dower House one afternoon, and having no desire at all to take the chance on her aunt sticking her oar in, Kate decided it would be safer to seek Mrs Stratton out in the servants' hall. As she opened the heavy green baize door at the end of the kitchen corridor and stepped through onto the gallery from which Lumsden and Mrs Stratton were accustomed to keep a beady eye on the staff working below, she was surprised by a loud burst of laughter.

The huge Castonbury kitchen ran the full length of the house, with windows facing to the north and south. Heat emanated from the massive black range. On the long, well-scrubbed table was an orderly line of basins and bowls and kitchen utensils whose use was a complete mystery to Kate, but the main kitchen itself was empty. She made her way down the stairs and headed for the servants' hall, which was on the opposite side of the room from the warren of pantries and stillrooms over which Lumsden presided. Another burst of laughter greeted her, and made her pause. Surely the servants would not be so noisy in the presence of Lumsden or Mrs Stratton? Perhaps those two were taking tea elsewhere.

She was on the verge of heading for the butler's pantry

when a slow drawl stopped her in her tracks. Kate crept towards the open door and peered into the servants' hall. The table was set for tea, with bread and butter, a large fruitcake and several pots of jam, but the tea in the cups was half drunk, the bread on the plates half eaten, the majority of the wooden chairs pushed back and abandoned. Virgil sat in the middle of the table, shuffling a pack of cards. Lumsden was on one side of him, Mrs Stratton on the other, a smile crinkling her normally austere face. Clustered behind Virgil were Daisy the chambermaid, Polly, and Agnes the scullery maid, of all people. In all the years she had been working in the Castonbury kitchens, Kate had never once managed to elicit a smile from the dour maid and here she was, not just smiling but giggling.

Across the table, young Charlie was squirming in his seat, straining to get a better view. Beside him, Joe Coyle was looking decidedly out of sorts, while Watson, Virgil's valet, was by contrast looking decidedly smug. Of the senior servants, only Smithins, her father's valet, and Monsieur André, the chef, were absent.

'Do another one,' Charlie implored, his eyes fixed adoringly on Virgil.

'Haven't you seen enough yet?'

She hadn't heard that teasing note in Virgil's voice before. He looked completely at ease as he shuffled the deck expertly, his neck cloth loosened, his coat unbuttoned, sprawling back in his chair and seemingly quite at home. When Kate took tea in the servants' hall, which she tried to make a point of doing once a month, she was always horribly conscious that they were all on their best behaviour. Teaspoons tinkled against the cups. Conversation was muted. Only Polly ever laughed freely at her jokes, and even then, it was a kind of defiant laughter.

'Go on, Mr Jackson, just one more,' Mrs Stratton said, and to Kate's astonishment the housekeeper actually tapped Virgil on the hand.

The plea was taken up by all around the table save Joe Coyle, and Virgil laughed, a much more carefree laugh than Kate had ever heard; it was almost boyish. He spread the cards into a fan. 'Take a card, Mr Lumsden. And you, Agnes. I'll close my eyes while you let everyone see what you've chosen.'

'No cheating now,' Polly said, and outrageously leaned over to put her hands over Virgil's eyes, flicking a knowing look towards the open door as she did so, making it clear that she, if no one else, was aware of Kate's presence.

'Right, put them back in the deck, anywhere you like,' Virgil said. 'You done? If the lovely Miss Polly will free me from her clutches?'

- Kate caught her breath at his smile, and noticed she wasn't the only one. Agnes and Daisy, blushing and nudging each other, were obviously quite smitten, and she couldn't blame them. She longed to join them; she felt quite excluded and, yes, if she was honest, the tiniest bit jealous, hovering here in the doorway. But she knew that one step forward would have them all jumping awkwardly to their feet.

'Now, then.' Virgil made a show of shuffling the deck and frowning, selecting first one card, consulting it, shaking his head and putting it back. His audience craned their necks, anticipation and excitement writ large on their faces. They wanted him to succeed, Kate could see. All except Joe Coyle, that is. Charlie was kneeling on his chair, sprawled across the tea table in a way that would normally have earned him a sound box around the ears, but Lumsden and Mrs Strattton were far too engrossed in watching Virgil to chastise him.

'Well, I don't know. I think you have me beat this time. I just can't find either of the cards in this deck. Won't you check for me, Mr Lumsden?'

The butler took the cards and began to look through them, shaking his head. By the time he had finished, his face was a picture of bewilderment. 'But I put my card in myself,' he said plaintively, 'you all saw me.'

'And me,' Agnes agreed breathlessly.

'I wonder.' Virgil reached into the pocket of Daisy's apron and pulled out one card. He reached behind the housekeeper and seemed to retrieve another from her cap. Holding them up, he received a spontaneous burst of applause.

'But how…?' Lumsden spluttered.

'It's magic,' Charlie breathed, his eyes glowing in admiration.

'It's a trick,' Joe Coyle said sullenly. 'Go on, show us how you did it.'

Virgil grinned and shook his head, pushing back his chair. 'It's easy enough. Even a monkey could do it, if he knew how,' he said pointedly.

The footman turned a dull red and glared furiously at Charlie, but the boy was too intent upon begging Virgil for just *one* more trick to notice.

'No more,' Virgil said, ruffling the boy's hair. 'Your tea is quite cold, and we've kept Lady Kate waiting long enough.'

All eyes turned towards the doorway, and exactly as she had predicted, there was a scramble to push back chairs and straighten aprons and make curtsies and bows. 'Please, I didn't mean to disturb you,' she said. 'Finish your tea. I merely wanted to ask Mrs Stratton—but it can wait.'

Chapter Five

'Kate, what's wrong?' Virgil caught up with her as she started to climb the stairs to the kitchen gallery. 'I know it's not exactly the done thing for guests to take tea with the servants, but I'm not exactly a typical guest. If I've offended you somehow, I'm sorry. After the way young Charlie described the reaction in the servants' hall towards me, I wanted to meet them for myself. I didn't think you'd mind.'

'Of course I don't mind.' Kate hurried on through the baize door and back along the dim kitchen corridor.

'Then what is it?'

She stopped, leaning against the cool of the tiled wall, embarrassed. 'You'll think I'm being foolish.'

'Try me.'

'You're supposed to say that you could never think me foolish.'

'I never lie.'

Kate was obliged to laugh. 'You seemed so at home there and I felt like an intruder. I've never seen Lumsden so—so *unbent*! And Agnes! I thought that woman didn't know *how* to smile. It *was* foolish of me, I know it was, but I was jealous,' she confessed. 'I try, you see, to make friends with them, and though they are always polite enough, they are always on edge too.'

'You are their master's daughter. You cannot blame them for being concerned lest they offend you. They have their positions to worry about.'

'They should know I would never threaten those without cause. Besides, it's not that. I have not your ease with them, nor your ability to put them at ease.'

'I was a servant once. I understand them.'

Kate nodded. 'Yes, but it's more than that. You have a way of making most people feel understood, regardless of their status. People warm to you. Look at Giles.'

'Look at your Aunt Wilhelmina.'

'That is different. My aunt has never warmed to anyone.'

'And your father, you surely do not think he will warm to me either? If I ever have the pleasure of making his acquaintance, that is.'

'You need not indulge me, Virgil. I was only a very little jealous,' Kate said. 'In truth, I admire you for it. I

wish that I had a lighter touch with people. I make them
nervous.'

'Perhaps you try too hard.'

'My father would say I do not try hard enough.'

'But why should you set any store by what your father says, when by your own admission he knows you
so little?'

'I was not aware that I did,' Kate said stiffly after a
short silence.

Virgil raised a sceptical brow. 'I wonder how *he* would
be received, were he to choose to take tea in the servants' hall?'

Once again, she was forced to laugh. 'Thank you,
I shall now consider my conscience salved.' The corridor was narrow, the only light coming from the wall
sconces which were lit at long intervals. She did not
know how it was, but suddenly Kate was very much
aware of Virgil standing beside her, was conscious, too,
of the odd intimacy of the space, a no-man's land between upstairs and downstairs. She fought her own battles, and if challenged would have said unequivocally
that she was not just more than capable but quite content to do so. Nothing had changed, but it was pleasant,
just this once, to have someone on her side. She smiled
up at him. 'Thank you.'

'Kate.'

He was standing close enough for her to feel this breath on her cheek. Her heart was beating too fast again. Her skin felt too tight, straining for his touch. 'Yes?'

Virgil touched the pulse below her ear. He seemed fascinated by the spot. His fingers trailed down her neck to her collarbone. 'Giles told me that there is to be an assembly in Buxton in a couple of weeks. I thought I might take you.'

Kate gave a start. 'Oh, no. I cannot.'

His fingers stilled. 'Why not?'

'I told you, Virgil, I am not acceptable in certain company. Surely Giles told you so?'

'I was not aware that I was expected to ask Giles for permission to take you to a dance. You are four-and-twenty, even in this country that is well beyond the age of consent.'

'Virgil, I can't. You don't understand.'

'Surely you're not afraid, Kate? Or is it that you're worried I can't dance?' Virgil slipped his hand around her waist and pulled her close against him. His cheek brushed hers as he bent to whisper in her ear. 'Wouldn't you like to dance with me?'

She could think of nothing she would like more. Save perhaps a kiss, which she would not think about. 'Yes,' Kate said, 'but, Virgil, you would be my only partner.'

His hand tightened on her waist. 'If that's your way of trying to dissuade me, it's not working. It's been five years, Kate. I think you'll find that it's not nearly as bad as you imagine. Say yes.'

She wished she could believe him. She wished she did not care. But more than anything, what she wished was to dance with him. 'Yes.'

He smiled. He pulled her tight against him. She tilted her head towards him, but his lips had barely grazed hers when the baize door to the kitchen swung back on its hinges. Mrs Stratton, carrying a large tray, all but collided with them.

'Lady Kate, I was coming to fetch Mrs Landes-Fraser's tea things in the hope I'd find you, but I see you have pre-empted me. And, Mr Jackson. I expect you were looking for these.' She produced a pack of cards from her apron pocket. It didn't seem to occur to her that their presence in the kitchen corridor was in any way strange.

Impossible, Virgil had called their attraction, and it seemed he was right, Kate thought, as he took the cards with a polite thank-you and turned towards the main part of the house. Impossible, she reminded herself as she followed in the housekeeper's wake, wondering what that so-staid woman would have said if she had stumbled upon them a few seconds later.

* * *

In her bedchamber a few days later, as Polly put away her evening dress and jewels, Kate prowled restlessly. She wore her favourite dressing gown of heavy scarlet silk lined with quilting in the style of a Japanese kimono, the sleeves trailing almost to the ground. Ornately embroidered with wildly improbable flowers and tied with a long sash, it was both exotic and sultry, a garment quite contrary to Kate's practical, prosaic self.

Or so it would have appeared to any who saw her clad in it. But the truth was, Kate had a liking for fripperies and feminine folderols. Since she knew perfectly well that such indulgences ought to be despised, and furthermore, that they were quite at odds with her looks, she kept her gowns plainly cut and, contrary to the current fashion, free from beading, ruching and tucking, confining her love of such things to her undergarments.

In these items of apparel, however, Kate indulged her sybaritic tastes to the full. Her stockings were black, clocked and held up by extravagant garters. Lace and ribbons made frivolous her chemises and even her pantaloons. Thanks to Polly's connections with a specialised milliner, Kate had recently acquired a selection of decadent corsets in poppy red, sapphire blue, vibrant pink and even rich black velvet. Had she wished, Polly had informed her mistress, she could have had stays made of the softest of leather, but here Kate drew the line. It was one thing to wear, under her gowns, the undergarments of the doxy her father believed her to be, but quite another to wear something which she was pretty certain belonged to more specialised, if unimaginable, tastes.

It was late, past midnight. Outside, the night was clear, the moon half full, casting an eerie glow over the grounds. She wondered what Virgil was doing. Still closeted with Giles discussing politics? Perhaps he had retired for the night. Was he sleeping? Lying awake? Was he thinking of her?

Kate gave herself a little shake. They would go to the school tomorrow, no matter that there were still a hundred things to be done at the Dower House. She sat down at the inlaid escritoire which faced the sashed window embrasure to write a note to the schoolmistress. Picking up a quill, she trailed the feather over her lips. He would have kissed her the other day. She could have cursed poor Mrs Stratton for her untimely arrival. Kate knew she wasn't a *femme fatale*. She was not even a *femme* a-little-bit-intriguing, but for some reason Virgil found her attractive. He had said so. He had shown her so. She was not imagining it.

She tried to remember how it had been with Anthony. She'd been curious, she'd even expected to find it enjoyable, and Anthony, as he had never tired of telling her, was a man with lusty appetites, so she'd been persuaded. It was the threat of those appetites being slaked elsewhere which had won her over. But she hadn't ever been particularly moved by Anthony's kisses, which even at the time had seemed perfunctory, something he felt obliged to do, but which were merely a precursor to the main event, like sitting through the farce before the play. Virgil's touch had made her tingle in a way that Anthony's never had. Virgil's kisses were complete in themselves, not a means to an end. If she had not known herself better, she would almost have been able to convince herself that she would have enjoyed whatever Virgil decided to do next. Though she did know herself better.

'If I didn't know you better, I'd say the last thing you were thinking about doing with that feather was writing with it.' Kate jumped. Polly was leaning against the window seat with that look in her eye which preceded something outrageous. 'There's men will pay good money to have a woman stroke them with a feather like that—or stroke themselves, depending. On the lips. Though not them lips,' she added with a smirk.

Usually Kate found such insights embarrassing as well as incomprehensible, a fact which she was certain contributed to Polly's persistence in sharing them with her. Not wishing to seem naive, she was wont to pass them off with a knowing laugh and change the subject, but tonight her curiosity got the better of her. 'Why would they do that?'

'Why? What do you mean, why?'

'Tickle themselves. Why would that be—you know, why would a man pay to see that?'

Her previous pretences of understanding had obviously been too convincing. Her maid was looking at her in disbelief. 'Well, you know.'

'I really don't,' Kate said.

'Lord Almighty!' Polly plonked herself down on the window seat. 'You mean you and that Lord whatshisname—him that you were going to marry— But I thought—I heard— They told me downstairs that he ruined you. Isn't it true? What was his name?'

'Lord Featherstone,' Kate said.

Polly tittered. 'That's a bit of a coincidence,' she said, looking meaningfully at the quill. 'Isn't it true, then? Didn't you and him—*you* know!'

Kate blushed painfully. 'There weren't any feathers involved.'

Polly rolled her eyes. 'Usually there aren't. And it's not tickling so much as— Do you mean to tell me you haven't ever? Not with him? Not even by yourself? Never?'

If Polly was astonished, Kate was now utterly lost. 'By myself? Without a man, you mean?'

'For the Lord's sake, Lady Kate, you don't need a man to bring yourself off. Do you mean to tell me you haven't ever? And that lord of yours, he didn't do it for you either?' Seeing her mistress's blank face, Polly tutted extravagantly, sat down beside her and began to whisper.

By the time her maid had finished her explanation, Kate was fiery red and still not entirely sure what was being described, though she was certain it was something she'd never experienced. 'Do you mean that *every* woman can—can...'

'Well, not all the time,' Polly said, drawing her an odd look. 'If the man doesn't—I mean, some men, they just don't know their way around a woman. Listen...'

But as her maid, now she had recovered from her incredulity, determined to initiate Kate into what she obviously believed was some sort of natural rite, began to explain using even more graphic terminology, Kate stopped her. 'I understand, really,' she protested.

Polly shook her head. 'Do you? Sounds to me as if that lord of yours is the one who didn't understand. That Mr Jackson now,' she said.

'What about him?'

'I bet he knows what's what. Fine figure of a man, he is. And don't say you haven't noticed, because I know you have. I saw you looking at him the other day in the

servants' hall and I don't blame you. I'd look myself if
I thought it would do any good, but he's not interested
in me. Or Daisy—and that flighty piece has done her
best to get his attention, thrust that chest of hers practically in his face, and he didn't even notice. I bet if Virgil
Jackson stripped down for you, it would, um, tickle you,'
Polly said with a leer. 'I know it would tickle me. He's
got muscles on his muscles, your American. I'd like to
see him work up a sweat. There's something about a man
working up a sweat, isn't there?'

Was there? Kate decided not to answer this, but she
thought most likely Polly was right. The candles on the
mantel started to gutter, and she took the opportunity to
cover her high colour by snuffing them out and telling
her maid it was much too late to talk any more.

After Polly left, Kate, forgetting all about her note
to the schoolmistress, discarded her kimono and pulled
back the bed covers. The warming pan was cold. She
hauled it out and placed it on the hearth. Jumping into
bed, she blew out the last candle. In the all-encompassing
dark, she snuggled down under the bedclothes and
pressed her hands between her legs, and thought of
Virgil, sweat, muscles and tickling.

Kate's opportunity to discover for herself whether
there really was, as Polly said, something about a man

working up a sweat, came quite unexpectedly the next morning. Though she made a point of being down to breakfast early, Giles informed her that Virgil had already eaten.

'Said he had business of his own he needed to take care of today,' he told her.

'What business?'

Giles shrugged. 'I didn't ask him.'

Kate's hand hovered over the bread basket. The temptation to throw a roll at her brother was almost irresistible, but if Giles was teasing her, then he'd know he'd hit home, and if he was not, he'd wonder why she was so upset. She picked up the roll, but only to put it down on her own plate. 'He didn't give you any idea where he was going, then?' she asked with studied indifference.

'Why should it matter, you're going to be tied up at the Dower House all day. That woman arrives soon—you don't have much longer to get the place shipshape, and you certainly don't want Aunt Wilhelmina saying that you weren't up to the job, now do you?'

She knew he was trying not to smile, which meant he knew perfectly well where Virgil was and was determined to make her beg for the information. Her whole life, she had made a point of never begging for anything from any of her brothers, but she had never been so tempted as now. Though *damn it*, Giles was right.

She didn't want Aunt-bloody-Wilhelmina saying that she could have done a better job. Kate swallowed a cup of very hot coffee far too quickly and pushed back her chair. 'You are, as ever, quite right, Giles. I have a lot to attend to,' she said, smiling sweetly, picking up the roll from her plate and aiming it as his head as she quit the dining room.

Storming off, muttering under her breath about infuriating brothers, managing at the same time to mentally review her still horribly long list of tasks while wondering where on earth Virgil could be and wondering if she was ever going to be able to spend time with him before he took himself north, Kate got to the front door of the Dower House in record time.

Since it was not yet eight o'clock, the servants had not arrived from the village. Inside, the house was taking shape, but it was the garden which concerned Kate most. Cornelius Wright, the head gardener at Castonbury Park, was a tyrant who would not tolerate temporary labour in the grounds, and though he had promised three days in a row to send two of his lads round to start cutting back the bushes, as yet he had failed to do so. Not even Giles had been able to persuade the stubborn old man to do as Kate asked. She suspected the gardener resented the implied criticism of having let the place go in the first place.

Cursing the man under her breath as she made her way through the house making notes on her list, Kate wondered if Aunt Wilhelmina was at the root of Wright's claim that the orangery must take precedence. As she opened the French doors to take a closer look at the wilderness outside, it was the smell which she noticed at first. Wood shavings. Then the sound, the regular whack of an axe. Casting a glance to the right, she saw immediately that the best part of the overgrown bushes had been pruned ruthlessly. The side path was now clear. Giles's quiet word with Wright must have done the trick, after all. Smiling broadly, Kate made her way through the stone archway which bordered the rose garden, and over to the small huddle of outbuildings in the far corner.

Virgil had his back to her. A broad back, covered by a white lawn shirt. His coat and waistcoat hung on the door handle of the wash house. His movements were graceful, perfectly synchronised, his whole body caught up in perfect rhythm as he hefted the axe above his head, then swung it down to the branch, cutting through it neatly, sending chips of wood flying, before shifting on the balls of his feet readying for the next blow as his arms swung the axe high again. His movements were precise and ruthless. Each cut was made in one movement. When he was done with one branch, he moved forward to the next in line.

Kate was mesmerised. By the way the soft leather of his buckskins clung lovingly to his form, knees slightly bent, strong thighs, tightly rounded buttocks. By the way sweat made his shirt stick to his back. By the bunching of his powerful shoulders, the flexing ripple of the muscles on his arms. His movements were fluid and lethal. Each blow of axe on wood seemed to emanate not from his shoulders but from much lower, powered from the taut band of his abdomen. She recalled the first time she'd seen him at Maer Hall, the way he'd moved down the long gallery like a predator. Watching him now, she shivered, excitement tinged with fear. He was beautifully lethal.

He stopped suddenly mid-blow, sensing her presence, though she was still some yards away and had not moved. He looked straight at her, but for a moment she felt as if he were looking straight through her. His expression was remote and quite blank, frighteningly so. The mask a man would wear when he would show nothing, behind which he suffered torments.

'You don't need to do this,' Kate said, taking a few tentative steps forward. Despite the fact that he quite clearly wanted to be alone, she was impelled towards him, fascinated.

'You said last night that you were worried the gardener—Wright?—wouldn't turn up.'

A flash of his impossibly white teeth, but it wasn't a smile. Kate took another few steps. His shirt was open, showing an expanse of chest. Smooth, save for a few woodchips which stuck to his skin. He had pushed the sleeves of the shirt up. Sweat gave his forearms a sheen. In the bright sunlight, his skin seemed darker. She wanted to touch him. 'Did you tell Giles what you were planning on doing? Surely he discouraged you?'

Virgil shrugged. 'I knew how much it meant to you, to have the house ready, not to give your aunt the opportunity to criticise your efforts.'

This time his smile, though fleeting, was real enough. Encouraged, Kate covered the last few yards which separated them. Virgil smelled of wood sap and salty sweat. Without his modish coat and waistcoat, he seemed bigger. Not so much less civilised as more powerful. She looked around the small yard at the stack of wood, smaller branches and clippings which Virgil had placed ready to burn. 'You must have started very early.'

'I never sleep past dawn. What are *you* doing here so betimes?'

'I wanted to catch you before you disappeared off with Giles again. I want to show you my school today.'

'Though that task list of yours is still pages long?'

'I know, but I was afraid you would leave before I

had the chance to take you there, and it's what you came here for, after all.'

'Yes. Yes, I suppose it is,' Virgil said, though he had almost forgotten. It was Kate who kept him here when he should have continued on his planned journey north. The thought of Kate's kisses and Kate's touch. Passion, so long dormant, had refused to go back into hibernation. He dreamt of her, and knowing how impossible it was only served to legitimise his wanting.

Eleven years ago, he had surrendered wanting. Eleven years ago, he had ceded all rights to the comfort of affection, to the deeper dangers of love. But since he could never love Kate, he could want her. He could have her because they could never mean anything to each other. It was the kind of logic which made perfect sense when she was standing beside him. He longed to touch her and so he did. Just her hand, that was all. 'I will be leaving before your new relative arrives,' he said, to remind himself of that fact, to remind himself that they could measure the time left to them in hours, if they were so inclined.

She caught his hand between hers. His right hand. The brand was on the inside of his forearm, above the wrist, where the skin was most tender. It was covered, usually, by his sleeve. As her eyes fell on it, he tried to conceal it with his left hand, but she was too quick.

'*B. VA.* What does that mean?'

'Booth. Virginia.' Virgil tried to snatch his hand away, but Kate would not let go.

'Booth. Was that the name of the plantation?'

'And the owner.' It had been his name, too, before he was sold, though he had never claimed it.

Kate's face was ashen. 'I didn't know they branded you.'

'They didn't unless you were inclined to run away.' He hated the mark. It reminded him of his guilt and filled him with shame. The brand kept the memories of that place, that day, etched fresh. Virgil broke free of Kate's hold, turning away from her to roll down his sleeve. He didn't want her to look at it. He didn't want her to see what it told of him.

He did not want his wounds touched, nor his past discussed, he'd made that quite clear, but this time Kate could not let it be. Horrified by the brand, she took his arm again, pushed up the sleeve and touched it. The letters were indented in his skin, the skin itself puckered, a darker colour than the rest. It would have been a long time healing. She traced the shape of the letters with her fingertip.

Virgil stood stock-still. She sensed him, bunched tight, ready to spring, flee, repulse her, but he didn't. Wanting only to heal, she bent over his arm and kissed him. Her tongue traced the letters. The skin felt tight over them, stretched, as if it was struggling to contain the darkness underneath. She kissed the brand softly, then kissed it again and again, little sucking kisses, as if she could draw out the poison which was embedded in those three vicious letters.

Still Virgil did not move, but she could feel his chest rising and falling more quickly. She ached with tenderness for him. Hot tears dropped from her lashes onto his skin. She licked them away, the salt of her tears mingling with the salt of Virgil's sweat on her tongue. She kissed her way up his forearm to the crease of his elbow. Then she was caught, yanked close, and Virgil's mouth descended on hers in a kiss which stole her breath away.

Polly was right. Sweat. Muscle. Skin. There was something about that combination. Raw man, strength which could snap her but which was instead channelled into holding her, at the same time drinking from her, extracting the passion which she hadn't known was pent-up there, and fanning its flames. Virgil's arms were tight around her. She was pressed hard against his chest, bowed back in his arms, her mouth ravaged. He was kissing her as she had never been kissed before, his tongue first duelling with hers, then thrusting, claiming her mouth for his own.

He tasted feral, his touch was fierce, making her own equally so. She tore at his shirt, her hands feverish on his back, her fingers clawing the linen free from his buck-skins so that she could feel the flesh of his stomach, his chest. Skin. Heated skin. His heart beat wildly under her palm. Their kisses were wild. Long and deep, then urgent and quick, then harder, more penetrating. His manhood was hard against her thigh. His hands were like hers, feverish on her back, her bottom, cupping her into him. She rubbed herself against him and he moaned. Her nipples thrust against her chemise, hard and aching, though they were enclosed in silk and satin.

She had no idea how they came to be inside the outbuilding. She did not recall moving, and was only vaguely aware of the door closing behind her before her back slammed against it. It was gloomy inside, for the one window was thick with dust, but Kate could see enough. Virgil's hands on the buttons of her jacket. His eyes, blazing down at her. His face set, focused, concentrated, entirely on her, as if she was all there was.

When he cupped her breasts through her chemise, she thought she would faint from the sensations he aroused. There was nothing soothing or gentle about what his touch did to her. She recognised nothing of the past, none of the mildly pleasant feelings which had faded into mild disappointment with Anthony. Virgil made her wild. His kisses stripped her of everything but a craving for more. When his touch was not enough, she tugged at the ribbons of her chemise herself to give him skin, pulled his head towards her breasts, wanting him to taste her, unable to bear waiting any longer to feel his lips on her. Her corset was dark blue today, edged with black lace. He barely seemed to notice as he freed her breasts, and she forgot to care when he took her nipple in his mouth and sucked.

She cried out. Her knees would have buckled under her if he had not supported her with the weight of his body against the door. He sucked, and his hand grazed her other nipple, tugging sparks of heat, sending lightning shards of pleasure directly to her sex. Her belly clenched. He sucked again. She sank her fingers into the leather of his buckskins, clutching the hard mounds of his buttocks. A trickle of perspiration ran down her back. She felt anxious. Tense. Waiting. She knew it would be worth waiting for.

She moaned when Virgil lifted his mouth from her breast, but then he claimed her lips again, and she sank into his kiss with a hunger that made him jerk against her.

Kate ran her hands up Virgil's back, over his shirt. Bunched muscles, damp with sweat. She wanted to see him. Touch his skin. Feel his muscles. Taste his sweat. Some of the woodchips which had stuck to him were sticking to her now. Together they smelt of resin and sweat and something else tangy, musky. She tugged at his shirt, but he stepped just out of her reach.

'No. Not me. I want to see you,' Virgil muttered, tucking his shirt back into his breeches. Her jacket was hanging open. Her breasts were quite bare. Her nipples were dark. And hard. He dropped his gaze. She wore a white thing, a shift, but it was silk not cotton, and the ribbons which tied the low neckline were satin. Over it she wore stays, but they were stays about as far from ladylike as any he could imagine. Dark blue silk, bordered with black lace. It made him wonder what she wore underneath. Boots? Or stockings?

He covered her breast with his hand. She shuddered, and his shaft tightened in response. He dipped his head to kiss her. Slowly this time, lingeringly. She tasted so sweet. He wanted to taste her. All of her.

Sweet Jesus, how he wanted her. It frightened him. He wanted her too much for it to be explained away by turning points or crossroads or wanting what you could never have. He wanted her with a pureness of need which scared the hell out of him.

He would have stopped, but he did not have to, for Kate pulled herself free quite suddenly. 'I have work to do,' she said.

A few days ago he would have happily accepted this, but perversely, though he had every reason to welcome her calling a halt, though it was what he should have done, Virgil was hurt by her having done so. 'What's wrong?'

'The morning will have run away from me if I do not make haste.' She looked shocked, almost dazed, as she turned her back on him to right her clothing.

'Are you afraid someone will see us?' Virgil asked.

Kate whirled around at this. 'No, though I ought to have been. I am afraid of what you do to me, if you must have it,' she said shakily. 'It frightens me. I don't know what to do with all these feelings. I don't understand them. I've never felt—not like this…. It's too much.'

'Never?' He remembered then, she'd said something similar in the Dower House that day. 'Kate, you cannot possibly have thought that you're incapable, cold?'

'I don't *know* what I think! I don't want to talk about it. I thought it was all in the past. I thought I was over it, I thought I had dealt with it, don't you see?'

'No, I don't see. You're not making sense.'

'I *know*,' Kate exclaimed wretchedly. 'None of this makes sense. For God's sake, Virgil, you are not the only one who is scarred.'

'What do you mean?' Virgil snapped, immediately defensive.

'You think I didn't guess why you tucked your shirt back so hastily? They whipped you, did they not? Do you think I am so shallow as to find such marks repellent? The very first night we met, I guessed you could never have been anything other than a renegade slave. I did not know about the branding, but I am not so naive as to be unaware of the punishments meted out for disobedience. They whipped you and you don't wish me to see your scars.'

She thought him vain. Or ashamed. For a terrible moment, he'd thought she'd somehow guessed at the scars he bore inside him, guessed the truth of what the physical ones represented. She had not, how could she have, but his relief was short-lived. 'What did you mean, I am not the only one? Was it that man…?'

'You can unclench your fists, you are five years too late. Besides, you are well off the mark. Anthony never beat me.'

Kate forced the last button through her jacket and squared her shoulders. She had not answered his question. He could see from that defiant glare that she would not. She was going. It was what he wanted, even though it was not how he wanted it. It hurt. He should have remembered that. Desire and pain went hand in hand, how could he have forgotten?

'I appreciate the effort you've made with the garden,' Kate said in clipped tones, 'but it was not necessary. I'm sure Wright will turn up.' She turned to go, but it was not in her nature to be so ungracious. 'I do appreciate it,' she said, her voice softening. 'It was very kind of you, but there's really no need to do any more.'

'I'll finish.' Virgil summoned what most people would take as a smile. 'It will be one less thing for you to worry about.'

Kate left him to his chopping. She felt defeated and angry. Her body, so strung out with anticipation, throbbed in protest at the anticlimax. She understood now what Polly had been whispering about. She wished she didn't. She'd rather not have known what she was missing.

At least her frustration was understandable. Why was she so angry? For the rest of the morning, Kate worked frantically in an effort to regain her frayed temper, ticking off task after task from her list. The force of her feelings astonished her. It was not just their intensity, she realised as she supervised the village women in the final cleaning and disposition of furniture, it was the fact that they existed in the first place.

All these years she had thought herself cold, had accepted Anthony's judgement of her, and by implication the world's condemnation. She had come to believe herself lacking, and as such responsible, at least in part, for what had happened to her. For the past five years, she'd carried that burden of guilt unnecessarily. It was that, she thought as she discussed the ordering of supplies with the new cook, which rankled most. That, and the fact that her family, and in particular Aunt Wilhelmina, had acted as if she deserved her fate.

Five years. Five whole years! And now it turned out that she was not cold, and that realisation turned everything she thought she knew about herself on its head. She had been foolish, there was no question of that. She wished she had had the confidence to act on her instincts earlier. But that didn't alter the fact that she had also been unfairly judged, and had unfairly judged herself.

Lord, but she was *furious*! Virgil had unlocked a passionate nature she hadn't known she possessed, but he'd also unwittingly let loose a torrent of pent-up emotions. Until today, if anyone had asked her—though they never had—she'd have sworn she was over it. Over Anthony, over the guilt, over the shame. She'd have said that it all meant nothing to her now, save that she was determined not to repeat her mistakes. Virgil had seen that for the lie it was. Right from the start, when she'd told him the bare bones of her history with Anthony, he'd heard the anger in her voice. Why had not she? Why had it tumbled out this morning as it had? Was she scarred? She had thought herself healed.

For the next few hours as she worked and fumed, she

was at the same time acutely aware of Virgil out there in the garden. When the women stopped for the lunch which Kate had sent over from the Castonbury kitchens, he lit a bonfire on the lawn. She watched, calmer now, from the window of the bedroom which had been prepared for the house's new mistress, as one by one her helpers joined him. They sat, Virgil and the village women, eating game pie in the autumn sunshine warmed by the blaze of the fire. He seemed just as much at his ease as he had in the servants' hall. She could hear the women's laughter through the half-open window. She recognised in it the hint of admiration. She could see, from the way they looked at him, that they were as fascinated by Virgil as she. She felt excluded. She could not possibly be jealous! Kate turned on her heel and headed for the linen cupboard. There were sheets to count.

But sorting bed linen did not occupy her mind nearly enough. Virgil's scars were certainly real. The whipping he had received must have been vicious indeed to have raised such long-lasting welts on his back. How many years ago? How many times? He was such a confident man, such a powerfully attractive one, she was taken aback by his self-consciousness. Like the brand, she supposed his scars were symbolic of a past he wished to forget.

Kate added another pillowcase to the pile of darning.

She had thought she had forgotten her past. No, not forgotten, but come to terms with it. She thumped her fist down on a pile of table linen. She had worked so hard to deny Anthony the power of having hurt her, but it was still there, after all. She *was* scarred. The words, said in an excess of defensiveness, were true. Scarred and scared. And since she was being soul-searingly honest with only the linen for company, she was also perversely wishing she had not called a halt this morning. Virgil had proved Anthony wrong there. She was certainly not incapable of pleasure. Virgil made her body thrum. Her body's thrumming terrified her almost as much as it excited her. If she could somehow reconcile the one over the other...

The doorbell clanged in the hall, breaking into this tangle of thoughts. Kate leaned over the banister and saw that some of her new sister-in-law's staff had arrived. Alicia herself would be at Castonbury a couple of days after the dance at Buxton, and Virgil said he would go before then. She didn't want him to go, though she knew he must. He would go to Robert Owen's model village and then he would return home to America and she was very unlikely to meet him again. As she descended the stairs, Kate decided that that was probably the most melancholy fact of all.

Chapter Six

Kate returned to the house hoping for some time alone before dinner, but her plans were scuppered by a summons from her aunt. Word on Cousin Ross had finally reached Castonbury. It was therefore with her mind still in a state of turmoil that she tapped on Aunt Wilhelmina's bedchamber door.

'He is married! He has actually married that—that maidservant.' The disgust in Mrs Landes-Fraser's voice could not have been exaggerated had her cousin married one of Polly's former associates, Kate thought ruefully.

'I hoped he might,' she said. 'He and Lisette seemed to be deeply attached.'

Aunt Wilhelmina had been lying prone on her bed clutching her sal volatile, but at this she sat up. 'Surely, Katherine, you do not condone this match?'

'It is not for me to condone or condemn. Ross is of age

and, luckily for him, of independent means. If Lisette makes him happy, then I am happy for him. Do they intend to make their home in India?'

'Yes, I thank goodness.' Mrs Landes-Fraser gave a shudder. 'At least we will be spared the shame of having him set up home with a servant in England.'

'She is not a servant, Aunt. I am not quite sure why she was forced to play the part of Araminta's maid, but she was clearly gently bred. And whatever were her origins, she is now Ross's wife. If she is good enough for Ross, she should be good enough for all of us.'

'I believe I have had cause in the past to remark upon your unorthodox tendencies. I had not quite appreciated that they encapsulated your own kin.' Mrs Landes-Fraser rose from her bed to loom over her niece, who was seated by the window perusing her cousin's letter. 'I do trust, Katherine, that you have not been similarly unorthodox in your dealings with that American?'

Her aunt's gaze was sharp and Kate had never been adept at lying. 'I have barely seen Mr Jackson,' she said, keeping her eyes on Ross's strong, slanting script. 'He has spent the better part of his stay in Giles's company, as you well know.'

'I know he was not with Giles today.'

Kate said nothing. She knew her brother well enough to guess that he would not willingly have disclosed

Virgil's whereabouts to their aunt. Giles never willingly disclosed anything to anyone. It was one of his strong points, and one of his most infuriating ones.

Mrs Landes-Fraser sighed, and sat down beside her. 'You understand, Katherine, that while your acquaintance with this man is tolerated at Castonbury because Giles is here to lend you countenance and because your misguided attempts to educate the villagers make you too well-liked for malice, but were the world at large to discover you had been spending time alone with such a man it would be impossible to protect you.'

Kate bridled. 'Protect me from what, precisely? Thanks in no small part to you and my father, I have very little reputation left to protect.'

Her aunt's lips tightened. 'Had you listened to my advice, your reputation would be spotless.'

It was too much. She had not planned to give vent to her feelings, but she could not, after such a pointed remark, rein them in. 'Had I listened to your advice,' Kate said grimly, 'I would have married a man who blackmailed me into doing his will.'

'Oh, for heaven's sake, don't exaggerate.' Mrs Landes-Fraser threw herself to her feet and began to pace the room. 'You make it sound as if poor Anthony was some sort of criminal. You were to be his wife, Katherine. He had every right to expect your—your co-operation when it came to doing your matrimonial duty. If you had not been so unaccountably eager to do that same duty in the first place...'

'I may never have discovered that the man I was planning to marry was a bully,' Kate interrupted bitterly.

'It does not occur to you that it was your own actions which caused him to treat you with such a lack of respect? After all, by your own admission, you gave him freely what you should have kept for the wedding night.'

'It was not so freely given in the end, Aunt. I told you that.'

'And I told you that you must bear the consequences of your ill judgement.'

Kate clenched her fists beneath the folds of her gown. Not since the day she had announced she was putting an end to her betrothal had she felt such unbridled anger. 'Indeed,' she said through gritted teeth, 'you ensured I would suffer, you and my father.'

Her aunt froze. 'What do you mean by that?'

'Oh, for heaven's sake, you know perfectly well what I mean!' Kate jumped up from the window seat, glaring at her aunt across the room. 'You could have stood by me. You could have denied the lies Anthony was spreading. You could have tried, just for once, to see things from my side of the fence.'

'Katherine! What has got into you? Why are you

bringing this up now, after all this time? We discussed this five years ago.'

'But we did not resolve it! He all but forced me, Aunt. I know you have chosen to think that I jilted him because I did not enjoy what he did to me, but it wasn't that. I did have expectations that were not fulfilled, I did think that our—relations—should have been more...but it wasn't that. He blackmailed me. Coerced me. Call it what you will, he bent my will to his in order to have me do something I no longer wished to. If he could act in such a way before we were wed, what more would he do to me with the bonds of marriage to back him up?'

'Lord Anthony Featherstone is a gentleman,' Mrs Landes-Fraser said haughtily.

It was a shame, Kate thought, that Anthony had never treated her as a lady, but she held her tongue. Her aunt would never understand. She could not possibly be as cruel as she seemed, though she was certainly utterly misguided. 'I doubt we will ever agree upon the subject,' she said wearily.

But, as ever, Aunt Wilhelmina must have the last word. 'What about the others? There have been several less eligible but, under the circumstances, wholly acceptable offers for your hand, yet you have not even made a pretence of considering them, Katherine. You are surely not going to tell me that you thought each and every one of them a bully! Why, you were hardly acquainted with some of them.'

'I had no wish to be further acquainted with any of them.' Kate had thought her anger abated, but it flared up abruptly again. 'It *hurt*, can't you see that? You hurt me. Anthony hurt me. Even my father hurt me. It was all so unfair. How do you think I felt, all those whisperings, those turned shoulders, while Anthony was welcomed with open arms? Why was it acceptable for him to have taken me to bed, but not acceptable for me to have allowed it? I did not deserve the half of it, but that does not mean I think myself innocent. I behaved stupidly. I knew, deep down, I knew that I did not want to marry Anthony, but I allowed myself to be persuaded, and when I was still uncertain I thought to persuade myself. You say I deserved to be treated without respect— well, you will be pleased to know, Aunt, that I agree with you. Not because I anticipated my wedding vows, but because I did not trust my own judgement.'

Kate broke off, her chest heaving. Her cheeks were overheated. She could feel the burn of tears at the back of her eyes, and was determined not to let them fall. All this rage, she had not realised she had bottled it up so much. 'I do not know how we came upon this subject,' she said shortly, 'but I think we should let it go before either of us says something we may regret.'

Mrs Landes-Fraser dropped onto the edge of the bed. 'We came upon this subject, as you put it, because I wished to warn you about your acquaintance with that American.'

Aunt Wilhelmina sounded shaken. Was her complexion paler than usual? After all these years, had she actually listened? Kate tried to believe it, but the hurt went too deep for her to be generous enough to do so. More likely she was simply outraged at her niece's insubordination. 'Mr Jackson is leaving soon,' she said wearily. 'Before our new relative arrives, as you well know.'

'That is as well. You will oblige me by keeping out of his company until then. It is ridiculous, of course, for you are a duke's daughter, when all is said and done, and he is a—a...' Mrs Landes-Fraser caught Kate's eye, and obviously thought the better of however she was about to describe Virgil.

'If it is so ridiculous, I wonder why you put yourself to the bother of warning me.'

Kate's aunt smiled thinly. 'We are never likely to see eye to eye. Certainly my sense of duty and yours rarely coincide, but my promise to my sister was not made lightly. I told her I would do my best by her children, and I would not be doing my best if I did not caution you. However, I see it is unnecessary. You have made your sentiments regarding the opposite sex quite clear.

You and I are cut from the same cloth in many ways, Katherine. I myself found the physical side of my marriage most...unpleasant. Perhaps if you had been able to disguise your disgust as I did, Lord Anthony would have treated you better.'

This astounding insight would have silenced Kate, were it not for the underlying implication. Upon one thing alone she and her aunt could agree: they would never see eye to eye.

'You may leave me now, the bell has long gone to dress for dinner.' Aunt Wilhelmina got to her feet. 'I am glad we cleared the air. I trust we understand each other a little better.'

Kate studied her aunt's countenance, but she could see no trace of irony there. 'What of Ross's letter?' she asked, at a complete loss. 'Has my father seen it? What does he have to say?'

'Obviously he will have nothing more to do with his nephew. Were it not for the imminent arrival of this putative grandchild, I suspect His Grace would say a lot more, but as it is, your father is somewhat distracted.'

'You will be pleased to know that I am confident the Dower House will be ready in plenty of time for our new relative,' Kate said with satisfaction.

'Save for the gardens, of course. I am afraid Wright

cannot be spared at present, the orangery is taking up all his attention,' Mrs Landes-Fraser retorted.

'Oh, I got someone else to take care of that.' Kate headed for the door.

'How so? Wright would not have sanctioned an outsider coming to tend his garden.'

'He didn't. And it wasn't.' Kate smiled sweetly at her aunt. 'Mr Jackson saw to it.'

As a result of Ross's letter, Giles dined with his father, and Aunt Wilhelmina's presence was required in the duke's suite, too, after dinner. Though she was obviously loath to leave her nieces alone with 'the American', Mrs Landes-Fraser could not bring herself to refuse His Grace. In point of fact, it was His Grace's valet, Smithins, who communicated the request, but though the words were framed as an invitation, no one in the drawing room could be in any doubt that Mrs Landes-Fraser had been summoned.

Though she tried, before quitting the room, to persuade her nieces that a quarter before nine was more than past their retiring time, neither paid her any attention. The door had barely closed on Aunt Wilhelmina's trailing fringes when Phaedra leapt to her feet.

'Thank goodness she's gone. Now I can go down to the stables to check on Isolde. My bay mare,' she explained to Virgil. 'She was quite out of temper this morning, and though Tom Anderson says it is nothing to worry about, I just want to make sure.'

'Phaedra, it is dark outside.' But her sister had already whisked herself away. Kate shook her head. 'I swear, if she thought she could get away with it, Phaedra would sleep in the stables.'

Virgil ignored this remark, getting up from the gilded sofa to look out of the window. 'I take it you and your aunt view your cousin's marriage rather differently,' he said. 'Is that why you quarrelled?'

Kate stiffened. 'What makes you say that?'

'The atmosphere at dinner was positively frigid.'

'We did have a disagreement, but it was nothing to do with Ross.'

'It was about me, then.'

'Not directly.' Kate tried to smile, but her mouth refused to co-operate. The contretemps with Aunt Wilhelmina had left her drained, and she had not even begun to work out how she felt about this morning.

As if he read her mind, Virgil left his post at the window to sit beside her on the sofa. 'Kate, this morning—I am not accustomed to explaining myself. It's been so long since I— But if I've upset you...'

'You haven't. No, I mean you did. I was angry with

you, but it wasn't really your fault.' Kate rubbed her eyes wearily. 'It doesn't matter.'

'It obviously does, but I guess I'm not the only one who doesn't like to explain himself,' Virgil said, taking her hand.

'I guess,' Kate said with a faint smile. 'You'll be leaving soon,' she added after a moment's silence. Did this make it more or less easy to discuss how she felt? Her hand was lost in his. His clasp was warm, reassuring. 'Do you know, I think this is the first time we've ever been alone together in this house.'

'I reckon if you open the door you'll find Lumsden about two steps away. Your aunt will have asked him to make sure I don't ravish you in her absence.'

'You will be pleased to know that my aunt no longer fears any such thing.' Kate smiled abstractedly, smoothing the sash of her gown with her free hand. 'That's how it started, our quarrel before dinner, if you really want to know. She did set out to warn me against being seen too much in your company, but by the end of our conversation she had decided that it was quite unnecessary, for not only are we worlds apart, you and I, there is the fact of my being frigid to be taken into account.'

'Frigid!' Virgil looked at her searchingly. 'Is this your English idea of a joke?'

'No, I was perfectly serious and so, it seems, was my aunt.'

'So it's a pretty safe bet that we weren't spotted this morning,' Virgil said.

'Is that *your* idea of a joke? Was that what was worrying you? Was that why you stopped?'

'It was you who stopped.'

Kate had been studying their clasped hands, but now she met his look squarely. 'If I had not, you would have. How long has it been, Virgil?'

He released her hand and moved a little further away from her on the sofa. 'It doesn't matter.'

'Ah, but it obviously does,' Kate said, quoting his own words back at him. She began to smooth her sash again, frowning down at her feet as she did so. The urge to confide was strong, for she desperately wanted to make sense of her jumbled feelings. It did not come naturally to her, trusting anyone with her innermost thoughts, but of everyone she knew, Virgil was the least likely to judge her, the most likely to understand her. She wanted to be understood. She wanted to understand herself. She wanted *him* to understand.

Kate abandoned her sash and resettled herself on the sofa, shuffling round to face Virgil. 'I was frightened this morning, that was why I stopped. Not of you, but of myself. There were things I thought buried and forgotten which our— When we kissed, it brought it all to the surface, somehow. I had no idea what I meant when I told you I was scarred, it just came out. Then later— and talking to my aunt—I was so angry. You were the cause indirectly, I suppose, but it was not your fault.'

She had his attention now. His expression had lost that remote look which he used to intimidate. His eyes were fixed on her. She could almost feel him listening, so intently was he concentrating.

'What frightened you, Kate?'

'It sounds silly now, but I was frightened of what I was feeling. I'm not—I haven't ever felt like that before, you see, and I thought…with Anthony— Oh, heavens, I am making such a mull of this. I'm sorry, but I can't even make sense of it myself, let alone explain it. Forget I spoke. It is too— Let us just forget it.'

She made to get up, but Virgil was too quick for her, pulling her back down onto the sofa. 'Do you want to make sense of it?' he asked gently. She nodded. 'Then tell me,' he said, 'from the beginning.'

Kate stared across the room. She could see their re-flections in the window. They were sitting far too close. Tall as she was, she looked so slight compared to Virgil. He was such a very definite shape. Such a very distinc-tively masculine one. She turned back to him resolutely. 'I've already told you the beginning. I told you I was ruined. I told you I was a social pariah. What I didn't tell you was the full story.'

It was impossible to speak with him so close, so she crossed the room to stare out into the night as he had done earlier. It was easier, not seeing his face. 'The truth is, that we—that Anthony and I—we were lovers.'

There! She had said it. Kate forced herself to turn from the window, but Virgil's expression was quite unreadable. 'I've shocked you,' she said, seeking a reaction, but Virgil was not to be drawn.

'Are you saying that this became public knowledge? That's it?'

'Yes.'

'But how? You would surely not have—do you mean *he* made it public knowledge?'

She could have no doubt of his feelings now. Virgil looked utterly astounded. 'He denied it, but it could only have come from him. When I broke off the betrothal he was furious, you see. Anthony has almost as high an opinion of himself as my father.'

'But what of your father? He is the Duke of Rothermere. Surely if he denied— You're his daughter, for God's sake. Didn't he stand by you?'

Kate laughed, a bitter little sound, and threw herself down on an adjacent sofa. 'My father wanted me to marry Anthony. When the whispers started he could easily have quashed them, but he chose not to, thinking that I would choose marriage over infamy.'

'And your aunt?'

It had taken until today for her to realise just how much hurt her aunt's failure to take her side had inflicted. Kate swallowed hard, and dashed a hand across her eyes. 'Sorry,' she said, lacing her fingers tightly together in an effort to regain control. She hated to cry.

'She took your father's view,' Virgil said flatly.

'Yes.' Her voice was tear-filled, but when Virgil looked as if he would comfort her, she shook her head. If he touched her— She could not risk tears. They had been so long pent-up, she was afraid she would not be able to stop them, and besides the fact that she did not wish Virgil to see her as a watering pot, she was horribly conscious of the fact that they could be interrupted at any moment.

'Kate, why did you break it off? You said you discovered you did not suit, but if things between you had become so intimate—you must at one point have believed you were in love?'

'Not in love, I told you it was an alliance. Compatible, I suppose is what I thought. I don't know what I thought, really. I was nineteen. I was curious. With hindsight, I think I was never sure that Anthony and I would suit, but at the time...' Kate sighed and rubbed her eyes. 'At the time, I believed that anticipating our vows would bring us closer together. I wanted affection from my husband, Virgil. I wanted him to care for me. He said he did. He said that it would be proof that he did, if I allowed him. But he didn't force me, not at first. I was stupid. Misguided. And I *wanted* to please. Anthony. My father. My aunt. I know you will think me weak-willed, I think it so myself now, but at the time...'

'At the time you were nineteen years old! What does anyone know of caution at that age?' Virgil exclaimed.

His angry tone grabbed her attention. 'You sound as if you speak from experience,' Kate said.

'I was nineteen when I spearheaded the rebellion which led to my being sold. I remember what it was like to be so sure of yourself that you can't see past your certainties. If someone had cautioned me...'

His eyes glazed as his voice faded. He was obviously lost in the past. Kate waited nervously. It was the first time he had confided in her without prompting, the first hint he had given her of the darkness which was his past. His expression hardened, then he blinked, and she could almost see him packing up whatever images he had conjured back into the boxes where he stored them. 'You said he did not force you at first,' he said, and she knew the moment was lost. 'What did you mean, Kate?'

She cleared her throat. Better to get it over with. 'He

never forced me, not physically, but I did not enjoy our encounters as he seemed to, and when I tried to refuse him he told me I had surrendered the right to do so by consenting and that if I didn't want him to stray before we had even said our vows that I must...'

She resumed the pleating of her sash and spoke hurriedly, determined to get her confession out of the way, though with every word she felt herself diminishing, not just in Virgil's eyes but her own. 'It was that, you see. His threats. I realised then what being married to him would mean. If he could coerce me into this, what else would he wish from me? It is such a one-sided bargain, marriage. I would not have the right to gainsay him and I could not trust him.'

'He blackmailed you.'

The anger in Virgil's voice gave Kate courage. His anger made his skin seem stretched too tight across his face, emphasising the beauty of his bone structure, the strong jaw, the slanting lines of his cheeks. His eyes were dark, fierce. He looked like a warrior, a predator, frighteningly powerful, terrifyingly, fatally attractive. And he understood. At last, someone did understand. 'Yes,' Kate said gratefully.

'And your aunt—did you tell her the truth?' Virgil said grimly.

She dug her nails into her palms. 'I did.' Her voice

was reduced to a whisper. 'Aunt Wilhelmina said that duty was not always pleasant.'

'She advised you to marry a man who was forcing himself on you?' Virgil swore viciously under his breath. 'It must have taken a hell of a lot of guts to break it off.'

'All the guts I had,' Kate said with a shaky laugh. 'But I did it, and—well, you know the consequences. Anthony put it about that I was unwomanly. He implied that the decision to call off the wedding was his, but that he had allowed it to appear to be mine because he was a gentleman. Until I met you I believed him. That's what frightened me this morning, and that's what made me angry, Virgil. And somehow, when I got angry it was like a release. I realised I was furious with my aunt, and so when the subject turned back on the whole affair this afternoon, I lost my temper and—and that's what we quarrelled about.'

She slumped back against the embroidered blue silk of the settee. She felt no sense of relief, only as if all the air had been let out of her. Deflated, that was the word. And tired. 'I thought I was done with it, and today made me realise that all I've been doing is burying it. I've been pretending it didn't matter when it does. My aunt is the nearest thing I have to a mother. Knowing I was right doesn't stop it hurting. And I behaved so stupidly. It is all very well to say I was just nineteen, but I can't run away from the fact that I was responsible. I wish I had not—but there is no point in wishing. No matter how hard I try, I can never be the person my family think I ought to be.' She paused. 'I wish you would say something, Virgil.'

He smiled at that. 'I like the person you are, though I doubt that's any consolation,' he said, getting up from his sofa and sitting beside her, putting his arm around her and pulling her against the comforting shelter of his shoulder. 'Before you say it, I don't give a damn if Lumsden walks in.'

His fingers stroked the exposed flesh between the puffed sleeve of her evening gown and the top of her kid gloves. The superfine of his coat was rough against her cheek. Kate let herself relax against him, closing her eyes, relishing his strength, his solidness, the smell of wool and linen and soap and deliciously musky man.

'It's been eleven years.'

He spoke so quietly that she thought at first she had misheard. 'What has?'

'You asked how long it's been since I made love. Eleven years, that's how long.'

Kate sat up. Virgil's eyes were dark, bleak. Her heart contracted. 'What happened?'

'I lost someone.'

'Oh, Virgil, I'm so sorry.'

'No. I don't want your pity. I just wanted you to know. This morning, you weren't the only one to worry about it being too much. I don't mean it was the same. It could never be the same. But I guess we both underestimated the strength of our attraction. I guess that was it.'

It could never be the same. That hurt, but did it also make sense of how she felt? 'Do you mean—is it possible to be so attracted without it meaning anything?'

Virgil's brow cleared. He smiled down at her, his mouth curling sensuously in a way that made her belly clench. He touched the skin below her ear, and she felt the pulse flutter under his fingers. Her breathing quickened. 'I think we've already proved that, don't you?'

'I thought it was different for women. One of the things which has always seemed to me most unfair is the way the world takes it for granted that men indulge their appetites. I assumed it was so because women are different.'

'It's not different. Didn't you ever—with that man?'

'Never.'

As Kate felt the flush creeping over her cheeks, Virgil's smile became positively devilish. 'It would be different with me. You can trust me.'

She was tempted, but it was too much. Kate jerked herself free and got to her feet. 'Can I? I don't think I'm the trusting type. And besides, you're leaving soon. I shan't see you again.'

'Isn't that the point?'

'I don't know what the point is. This morning you were as happy to call a halt as I. Tonight you seem to have changed your mind. I don't know whether I am on my head or heels.'

She made for the door, but Virgil grabbed her before she could open it. 'You're not the only one who's confused. You're not the only one with scars. Remember that.'

He flung open the drawing room door and strode out into the marble hall, startling Lumsden, who had been dozing in a chair. As the butler stumbled to his feet, Virgil made for the staircase which led downstairs, obviously intent on escape. Exhaustion hit Kate. She wanted nothing more than the comfort of her bed.

Despite having walked for over an hour round the grounds, Virgil was wide awake. He paced his room, then tossed restlessly in bed, going over the day's events. He had to admire Kate for her courage in confronting all that had happened head-on. It went against the grain with her to confide, he could see that, but that hadn't stopped her dealing with some very painful facts. She had real guts. And she was loaded down with guilt. That, too, he recognised.

How he'd like to get his hands on Lord Anthony Featherstone. The bastard deserved a hiding for what he'd done to Kate. And as to her family. That father of hers, who spent all his time these days hiding in his room and nursing his wounds instead of facing up to reality. And her aunt—she was the worst. She at least should have understood. The more he thought about it, the more he realised how much strength of will it must have taken for Kate to stick to her guns in the face of such opposition.

He hadn't asked what her brothers had thought of the matter. But five years ago both Giles and the dead heir, James, would have been abroad fighting. And the other one, Ned, the one whose name Kate could not say without crying. Most likely he'd been away, or too young to help. They were a patriotic lot, the Montagues. Shame they did not think to look closer to home for their battles. Though they had a hell of a fight on their hands now. Virgil had not given much thought to the implications of the dowager marchioness's claim to the dukedom on her son's behalf, but he suspended his anger long enough to wish the woman well. It would serve the Montagues right to have an heir foisted upon them.

It was dawn. Virgil sat on the window seat watching

the early-morning mist swirl over the lakes. They were both confused, both scarred, he and Kate. Neither of them trusted their feelings. Neither of them wanted to feel, yet together there was such passion between them. What he felt for Kate was nothing like what he'd felt for Millie. Not love, but a desire so strong it had overwhelmed him yesterday. Too exhausted to pretend, he had to admit that he was tempted. He knew she was, too, though she would not trust him enough to admit it. And why should she, when he had given her no cause?

Worse. She had shown him her scars, and he had given her almost nothing in return. He'd met her courage with a blank wall. His fingers traced the brand on his arm, shadowing how Kate had touched him. He reached behind him, feeling the welts of the whip marks beneath his linen nightshirt. He thought more of her, not less, for what she had revealed. But the mere thought of telling her all made him sick.

Outside, the mist had lifted. A slight figure dressed in white slipped like a wraith from the fishing pavilion and stood on the edge of the upper lake. Virgil opened the casement window, straining his eyes. The figure was poised, slim and female. His body knew, before his brain assimilated it, that he was watching Kate. She stretched her arms to the grey sky, then to his utter astonishment sprang into the air and dived into the water.

He was still fastening his buckskin breeches over his nightshirt as he ran barefoot down the curved corridor, where Kate's ancestors eyed him askance from their gilded frames. Down to the gloomy entrance hall, where the marble pillars were like a regulated forest in the shadowy light. Without caring who heard him, Virgil yanked open the locks and bolts on the heavy front door and sprinted towards the lake.

He couldn't see her. For one heart-stopping moment, he thought that she must have gone under, but then he remembered that graceful dive. She could obviously swim, but where was she? His feet sank into the mud, which oozed between his toes. The water was icy. There was an island about four hundred yards out, but it was a wild tangle of trees and bushes, impenetrable to the naked eye from here. A faint splash caught his attention. He would get a better view from the bridge, but if she needed help, then he'd be further away. He was being irrational; she could swim, she would be perfectly safe, Virgil told himself as he waded through the reeds until he was thigh-deep and dived in after her.

The cold took his breath away. His feet had stirred up mud and leaves, making the water cloudy. He came up for air spluttering, heading half blind towards the island. He had learned to swim in the creek at the plantation, where the water had been a delightfully refreshing

relief from the summer humidity. The Castonbury lake
was fed from water which originated in the Peaks. The
cold gripped him like a vice, making his breathing painfully sharp. The water soaked the leather of his breeches,
dragging his body downwards to the murky depths.

Virgil struck out with renewed determination. He was
panting heavily as he reached the sandy banks of the little island. Chest heaving, water streaming from the tails
of his nightshirt and the cuffs of his breeches, he forced
his way through the bushes to the other side, just in time
to see her at the far end of the lake, next to the bridge,
heading back round. Unlike him, she seemed perfectly
at home in the water. She swam with effortless grace,
arm over arm, her head under the water, then up for air,
sleek as an otter, cleaving through the lake with barely
a ripple, clearly in no need of rescue. He watched her,
thinking that he would be content to watch her for ever,
while at the same time feeling excluded, shut out from
whatever place it was her mind had gone to, for she
seemed to make her way by some other sense than sight.

As she rounded the corner out of sight again, Virgil
made his way back into the centre of the island in two
minds. He wanted to call to her, but he didn't want to
disturb what was obviously a customary swim and a
private moment. He would wait until she circled back
again, then he would make his own way back to shore

without her seeing him. He felt foolish now at having come rushing out half naked to rescue someone in absolutely no need of help. There was a clearing in the middle of the shrubs and trees, a little hollow of ground quite hidden from view. A circle of blackened stones had obviously been used for a fire. Around it the ground was bare, packed dirt and sand, where the undergrowth had been worn away from use.

Chapter Seven

'We used to come here as children.' Virgil started. Kate was standing in the clearing behind him. He hadn't heard her approach. 'It's one of the few places at Castonbury out of Aunt Wilhelmina's reach,' she said. 'There's a box down by the beach with wood and kindling—will you help me fetch it?'

Virgil dragged the heavy chest through the undergrowth, and Kate opened the lid. She took out a quilt and handed another to him. 'You look as if you need this. I'm used to it, but I expect you found the water cold. What are you doing here?'

'I saw you dive in from the window of my bedchamber.'

'Did you think I needed rescuing?'

'Not once I saw you swimming. You're very…lovely.'

He'd meant to say *good* or *strong* or even *graceful*, but the truth slipped out before he could stop it. The quilt was draped over her shoulders. She wore what looked like underwear, a short, sleeveless cotton chemise and a pair of knee-length drawers. The sodden material clung to her figure, revealing tantalising glimpses of the pink flesh beneath, hugging every contour, from the swell of her breasts, the flare of her hips, to the dark cluster of curls between her long legs. Her nipples were hard peaks, clearly visible. Long damp tendrils of her hair had escaped the bun on top of her head and stuck to her throat, her neck, her cheeks. Water dripped from her lashes. It dripped from the ends of the ribbons which tied her drawers at her knees and at her neckline. 'Charybdis,' Virgil said with a smile, 'daughter of Poseidon.'

He still held the quilt folded in his hands. If he would wrap it around himself, then she wouldn't have to look at him, Kate thought. Dripping wet. His skin dark, glistening through his shirt. Was it a shirt? It looked more like a nightshirt. She should be cold, but under her skin she felt unaccountably hot. She laughed nervously. 'That's not very flattering. Charybdis makes whirlpools to drown men at sea.'

'I know, but she was once a nymph.'

'So it's a compliment?' It was the swimming which made her sound so breathless. It must be the swimming which was making her shaky too. She'd overdone it. Was it the swimming which was making her mouth dry? It was definitely the cold which was making her nipples ache. Virgil looked—oh, heavens, there was no getting away from it—he looked magnificent.

'I'll light a fire.' Kate hunkered down over the chest, fumbling for the kindling. 'You'll catch cold, else.' It didn't occur to her to suggest that Virgil would be better getting back to a warm bath and dry clothes.

'Let me.'

He tended to the fire efficiently and quickly. Of long habit, Kate sank onto the sandy hollow and pulled her quilt around her as the flames took life. Virgil had abandoned his quilt. The ridges of his whip marks could clearly be seen through his shirt. They were vicious, long welts, some overlapping. More than one whipping or one particularly fierce event? He looked as if he'd been flayed. She swallowed the lump in her throat, determined not to show him she'd noticed.

Virgil dropped down beside her. Through the cold lake water, his body was already starting to emanate heat. 'Last night, it must have taken a great deal to say what you did,' he said.

Kate turned round to face him, dislodging the quilt from her shoulders. 'You don't despise me?'

'On the contrary. You are very hard on yourself, Kate.' Virgil wiped a drop of lake water from her cheek with his thumb. Her skin was softened by the water, chilly to touch, whereas he felt as if he were burning up. 'Yesterday, it wasn't that I was afraid of your reaction to my scars, I was afraid of my own.' He still was, but he could manage it. He could. He owed her this much. No, it was more than that, he wanted to show her. Virgil lifted up the hem of his nightshirt and pulled it over his head. 'These are not just from one whipping. I don't know how many. I lost count,' he said, swivelling round to show her his back.

Kate gasped. He wasn't surprised; he knew it was a horrific sight. He'd seen it reflected in the mirror, though it was a long, long time since he'd seen it reflected in anyone's face. 'At the slave market, it's what saved me.' The words came out stiff, cold, but at least they came out. 'It shows I lack discipline, you see. My scars, they mark me out as a rebel. A clean back would have brought a much higher price for Master Booth. This back, it's what made Malcolm Jackson buy me.'

'Why?' Kate asked.

Her voice was ragged with horror. She hadn't touched him. Virgil managed a shrug. 'He said it was because he saw a free spirit. A man with dreams, he said I was. A stubborn man. A man who would fight for his cause. He took a chance on me, and I made sure it paid off.'

Another debt. In Glasgow at least he would have the opportunity to pay that one in full.

Kate touched him. Virgil flinched at the unexpectedness of it. 'Did I hurt you?' she whispered.

'No.' These scars no longer ached, though what they stood for would hurt him always.

Kate's fingers traced the fretwork of lines, some threads, some thick like ropes, where his flesh had been opened and healed, opened and healed. The skin was tight in the bigger scars. It still pulled sometimes, tugged at him, wanting him to remember, making sure he could not forget. *You are not healed. You will never heal.* His scars spoke to him.

'Did you run away?' Kate asked.

Her hands smoothed over his back now, as if she would erase the mess, as if she would make him new. As if she could. He wished she could. Virgil nodded. 'Once. Mostly I refused to do as I was bid. Spoke when I wasn't supposed to. Looked them in the eye when they spoke. Once, they wanted me to fight and I wouldn't.'

'You mean box? Young Charlie was right?'

'No! I wouldn't fight. I saw Molineaux once. Prizefighting is how he earned his freedom in the end, but I wouldn't let myself be treated like that, like an animal. I never fought that way, but I fought them every other way. Working too slow. Not working. Working too fast. I learned to read and write and they didn't like that.'

'They whipped you because you could read?'

He would have laughed at the utter shock in her voice, only it hit him like a punch in the stomach that she was right. It *was* beyond belief. He'd survived because he hadn't let himself think about what was happening to him. He was afraid the horror of it would sap his strength. He had no energy to waste on railing against what he could not change. 'They whipped us for any reason, and for none at all, but the last time I guess I gave them cause. I led a rebellion.'

Talking of his plans to force concessions by striking, to add weight to their strike by spreading it through neighbouring plantations, Virgil remembered what he had forgotten all these years, that despite all the evidence to the contrary, he'd believed that reason would triumph. 'I thought if they could just be forced to see our point of view, they'd realise how wrong it all was.' He laughed bitterly. 'I thought that if we could show them we had some power, if they could see that we were strong enough to stand together, they'd realise they would have to change. I was so wrong.'

'What happened?' He could see she already knew. Could tell from the way she gripped her hands together in her lap that she wanted to be wrong.

'Just exactly what you think,' Virgil said with a twisted smile. 'It's one thing to make promises, another to keep them when you know what the consequences are likely to be. Some didn't strike. Some caved early.'

'But not you?'

If only he had. Virgil shook his head. 'Not me.' He told her of that final whipping. He told her about the hellhole. And then he stopped.

Kate swore long and viciously in response, words even Virgil would not have spoken. Then she wrapped her arms around him, and leaned her body against the breadth of his back. 'I would kill them.'

She took it for the end and he was too relieved to do anything but follow her lead. Her voice contained real menace. 'I believe you,' Virgil said. If it came to it, he doubted she would, but he believed she would want to, as he had, and it was a sweet revenge in its way, knowing that a duke's daughter wanted to do what he had chosen not to. His vengeance had been slow in coming, but it was worth every second of hard slog it had taken. He had proved himself better. Now he would make sure others like him could do the same.

He could feel Kate's breasts flattened against him. Her breath was warm on his neck. Her hands were wrapped around his body, her palms resting on his chest. 'We should get back,' he said, telling himself that he meant it.

Her arms tightened around him. 'No.'

She nestled closer. Despite the cold, Virgil's manhood stirred to life. 'Kate...'

'Did you tell me all that to show me I can trust you?'

'And because I wanted to.'

'Do you want *me*, Virgil?'

The evidence of just how much he wanted her was taking solid shape in the chafing leather of his buckskins. 'You know I do.' He twisted around in her embrace. Her mouth was soft, trembling, pink. Her eyes were grey rather than blue. 'Kate, I don't want to hurt you. I would never use you or force you or any of the things you're afraid of, but if you're not sure...'

'I am. I think I am.'

Was he? He was sure he wanted her. He was sure it was different. The power of it came from passion heightened by abstinence, not love. But his abstinence had been one of the sources of his strength. Still, he wanted her and there were ways for both of them to have what they wanted without risk. Without compromise. Without hurt. He did want her. He was so tired of fighting it.

Virgil wrapped his arms around her and pulled her down onto the quilt which had fallen from her shoulders, and kissed her.

Was she sure? Kate locked her arms around Virgil's neck and kissed him back. She was sure of him. Sure she wanted him. Sure she wanted what she had never had, what Anthony had taken from her.

He tasted of lake water. His lips were warm against hers. He rolled her onto her back and covered her body with his own. So large. Kissing, she stroked the breadth of his shoulders, then let her fingers flutter over the tortuous mess of his back. And so powerful. His kisses heated her. His hands on her face, her shoulders, her breasts, made her shiver in anticipation.

He kissed her deeply, his tongue thrusting into her mouth, then tangling with hers, teasing, tasting, then taking again. He kissed her neck, her throat, the valley between her breasts. The damp cotton of her chemise clung stubbornly to her body, but he was patient, untying the ribbons and buttons, feasting on each inch of skin as he opened it. Hot mouth on cold nipples. She arched up in delight, for his actions connected straight to her throbbing sex.

He kissed her lips again, as if he couldn't get enough of her mouth, and that, too, delighted her. She watched him avidly as he kissed his way back down between her breasts, cupping them, his thumbs stroking, as his mouth nipped and licked at her ribs, her belly. Skin. The delicious abrasion of his skin on hers. Was there anything more delightful?

There was. The ribbons on her drawers were knotted. When she would have torn them, he untied them with care, easing them down her legs. His face was taut, his eyes glittering, fierce and focused. The way he looked at her filled her with the most glorious sensation. She knew herself powerful. She knew herself wanted. Truly wanted. She let him look, made shameless with his need, her own need making her wanton. She kept her eyes open, fixed on him, his hands, his face, his mouth, his body.

She fumbled with the fastenings of his buckskins, but the leather was so wet her fingers could make no sense of them. She could have cried out in frustration but Virgil saved her, sitting up, quickly dispensing with buttons and falls, pulling them down his long, muscled legs.

He was utterly naked. Kate looked. She had seen a naked man before. She knew what an erect member looked like. She had been curious enough to look, and Anthony had been determined that she touch, but this was different. She'd thought the male body strange. Ugly, almost. Now, fascinated by the differences between them, she thought Virgil simply beautiful.

He sat down on the quilt opposite her and pulled her to him so that they were facing, her legs over his thighs. They studied each other, touching, tracing their shapes with their fingertips, exploring. They kissed. Virgil cupped her breasts, kissed her nipples. Kate arched back, her heels digging into the sandy floor of the hollow behind his back. He touched her belly. He kissed her again. He stroked her flanks, and then the soft flesh inside her thighs.

But when he began to stroke into the folds of her sex, she tensed, and Virgil stopped. 'What's wrong?' he asked.

'I'm afraid I'll fail you,' Kate whispered.

'Did *he* say that?' Virgil swore. 'Kate, *he* failed *you*.'

He tilted her chin up, forcing her to meet his eyes. 'What do you mean?' she asked.

'Just trust me.' He kissed her. He kissed her breasts. Then he kissed her mouth again. When her breath came shallow against his, he eased her back and stroked her thighs. Then stroked again, and slid easily past the folds of her sex and inside her. She gasped. Her muscles tensed around his finger. He eased into her a little more.

'Do you like this?' he asked. When she nodded, he took her hand and wrapped it around his shaft. They both stared, fascinated by the contrast of her skin on his.

The muscles in Virgil's belly tightened. His erection thickened. He eased his finger higher inside her, seeing from the way her eyes widened that she liked it. 'Stroke me, like this,' he said, showing her, for he had no faith in her previous experience, and was glad, if he was honest, that she seemed so unsure.

She did as he asked; he had to close his eyes to hold

himself back. 'Again,' he said, thrusting into her as she stroked, watching her as she touched him and he touched her. He could see his desire reflected in her eyes. It was intoxicating. He could see that she found it so too. He kissed her. Her lips were hard on his now, her tongue thrusting into his mouth.

Kissing. Stroking. Thrusting. 'This,' Virgil said, pushing harder and higher with his fingers, stroking over the smooth moist nub of her with his thumb, 'this is what you're doing to me.' He could feel her swelling. He could feel himself thickening, pulsing. Her face was a mixture of confusion and delight. The knowledge that in this way he would be her first gave him immense satisfaction. He thrust and stroked and stroked and thrust, and then he kissed her, claiming her mouth with his tongue as she tightened around him and cried out, the pulsing heat of her, and the taste of her, and the feel of her hand, her fingers, on the length of him sending him over the edge seconds later, dragging a deep moan from his depths as he spilled his seed onto her hand and she slumped against him.

Solid. Virgil was so solid. Kate clung to him as if she were drowning. She felt as if she had been broken apart. Her body throbbed, wave after wave of sensation rippling out from the heat between her legs up, down, making her lightheaded, dizzy. She had been so furled tight and now she was—she didn't know what she was. Unsprung? Was that a word? Like a clock which had been overwound. What she felt was red and sparkling and bright, bright, bright. Like a shower of sparks. A cascade. Her heart was pounding against Virgil's chest. Or it was his heart. His hands on her back, his arms circling her so easily. When she wrapped her arms around him like this, her hands struggled to meet. His skin was like velvet, not soft, not rough, just velvet. Except his back. She traced his scars. She smoothed his scars. She nestled her face into the crook of his neck and kissed him. He smelled of lake and sweat and what they had just done. She didn't know a name for it. No, Polly had given her several names, all of them far too vulgar-sounding for what she'd just experienced. It most certainly didn't feel the least like a tickle.

Virgil hadn't shaved; his chin was rough with stubble, though she could barely see it. She didn't want to spoil the moment, but she had to ask the question which had been bothering her most of the night. 'The girl you lost, did you love her?'

He tensed. 'Yes.'

It was terrible of her, horrible, but Kate's first emotion was jealousy. Virgil had loved someone. It was like picking at a scar, but she had to know. 'How did you lose her?'

He put her from him, and got up, pulling his breeches on. His face was hard, his eyes hooded. 'We should get dressed.'

'I thought you trusted me.' It was unfair of her. She could tell from the set of his shoulders, from the way he held himself, tight, the muscles on his abdomen clenched so hard she could count them. Kate scrabbled to her feet and began to drag her sopping swimming attire on. 'Don't answer that. I didn't mean it. I shouldn't have said it.'

'No, you shouldn't.'

She had as well cut the connection between them with a knife, but what had she expected? It was just physical, what they had shared. Pleasure, nothing more. It was not life-changing or any other sort of changing. They were still the same two people, scarred and confused both of them. She had acquired no extra rights over him.

Virgil folded the quilts and tamped down the fire as she struggled with her buttons and ribbons. He picked up the heavy chest and disappeared down to the beach to return it to its hiding place.

'I can fetch the rowing boat, if you don't wish to take another wetting,' she said when he returned.

'Don't be ridiculous.' Virgil ran his hand through his

cropped hair. 'She died. Her name was Millie, and she died. It's not a question of trust, Kate. It's none of your business.'

She was shivering as she followed Virgil down to the water's edge and began to wade in to the lake. Virgil dived in and began to swim in a powerful if rather splashy style for the shore. Kate took her time. Swimming always helped her think. Virgil was right, Millie was long dead and none of her business, but she wished all the same that she could ask more. What happened to her? Were they separated when Virgil was sold, or had she died before? Eleven years ago he'd only been nineteen. The same age as she had been when she'd broken her betrothal. Just a boy. No. Nineteen years on a plantation would have made a man of him many years before then.

Whatever had happened had scarred him more deeply than the savage marks on his back, that much was certain. Perhaps that was why his lovemaking had taken the form it had. They had not been truly joined. She was not Millie. Virgil, thank goodness, was not Anthony. Though those first few times with her betrothed, she hadn't been completely indifferent. She'd forgotten that. Funny, but what she remembered until now had been boredom, indifference morphing into pain and humiliation, but in the early days she'd been interested enough to feel let down afterwards, disappointed. Now she knew what she'd been missing, she could quite see that what she'd experienced back then was a shadow of what it could have been.

Virgil was wading onto the grass at the side of the lake. As she walked towards him, she could almost touch the barricade he seemed to have erected around himself. He wanted to be alone. 'Go back to the house,' she said. 'I have dry things in the changing room below the fishing pavilion—there is no need for you to wait for me.'

He hesitated, then turned away. Kate watched him go. On the horizon, in direct contradiction of her own mood, the sun began to break through.

A few days later, despite the cold which hinted at the winter to come, Kate and Virgil walked through the woods to the village. Finally, the visit to the school had been arranged. Conversation between them was stilted at first, but their shared enthusiasm for Robert Owen's educational experiment soon broke down any awkwardness.

The Castonbury school was a single-storey purpose-built building with an enclosed garden to the rear. The local vicar, the adopted father of Lily, Giles's betrothed, awaited them with Miss Thomson, the schoolmistress, in the bright entranceway. 'Mr Jackson, it is an honour.' Reverend Seagrove was a portly man whose benevolence was writ large on his beaming countenance, and his handshake was as warm as his smile was genuine. 'Lady Kate, always a pleasure. And this is Miss Thomson.'

The schoolmistress dropped a shy curtsey. Allowing the vicar to do the honours, for he was every bit as proud of the school as she was, Kate watched Virgil's reaction on tenterhooks.

The school room itself was spacious, with two rows of desks separated by a central aisle. The children were ranked, with the littlest ones at the front and the eldest at the back. The entire wall at the rear of the room was covered with a depiction of the two central hemispheres, and a large globe stood beside them. Light streamed through the long windows, and every other bit of wall space was taken up with bright pictures of animals and wildlife, both familiar and exotic. The atmosphere was happy and relaxed. The children were smiling, clean and alert. As he followed the vicar and the schoolmistress around the room, watching as Miss Thomson led a spirited history lesson which included a battle re-enactment, Virgil was extremely impressed.

'Mr Owen believes that a happy child will be more receptive to learning,' Reverend Seagrove said, beaming at him, as the children gathered round a table for morning milk. 'We try to mix some play with our lessons. It is not good for the children to be seated at their desks for hours on end.'

'You have quite an age range here,' Virgil said to Miss Thomson, 'how do you manage?'

'We have the older children help the littlest ones with their reading and numbers, and I have a young woman who helps me three days a week,' the schoolteacher replied, blushing.

'Lady Kate is eager to recruit another full-time teacher,' Reverend Seagrove said, 'but we must first persuade the villagers of the benefits of keeping their children in school past working age. Unfortunately, Mr Jackson, many families depend upon their children's income, and do not have the foresight to understand that the income could be significantly increased in the future were they permitted to learn more.'

'What about educating the parents?' Virgil asked.

Miss Thomson looked shocked, but Reverend Seagrove was much struck with this idea. 'Lady Kate has been telling me all about Mr Owen of New Lanark. I believe he has established some form of institute which purports to offer an education to the adult members of his community.'

'It is that aspect of New Lanark I'm most interested in,' Virgil replied. 'Without learning, you can never be free to choose.'

'Most profound, if I may say so,' the vicar said, nodding vehemently. 'I will use that for a sermon, if I may.' He smiled at Kate. 'Perhaps we shall persuade the good people of Castonbury that there is a place for grown men in the schoolroom, after all.'

'And grown women, too, I hope,' Kate replied drily.

Reverend Seagrove chuckled. 'Quite right, my dear. What do you think, then, of our little school, Mr Jackson?'

'I think it's a lot more than a *little* school. Your ideas are revolutionary.'

'Lady Kate's ideas, for the most part,' Reverend Seagrove said. 'It was she who insisted on our modern heating system. Most of our patrons felt it quite unnecessary to heat a school room. And the lessons, too, the participative elements you have seen...'

'Come, Reverend Seagrove, you are making me blush. I merely followed Mr Owen's tenets. I could never have raised the funds without your help, and while I am happy to take some credit for the principles upon which we teach, it is Miss Thomson here who has put them into practice.'

'Then you are a remarkable team,' Virgil said seriously. 'You should all be proud of Castonbury school. You've given me much food for thought.'

Kate's family were by degrees mildly interested, dismissive and scathing of the hard work she had invested in this enterprise. Many of the children's parents had taken a great deal of persuading to allow their offspring to attend. While Reverend Seagrove and Miss Thomson had been unfailingly supportive and the school's board of governors were slowly coming round to the ethos upon which it had been established, she was quite unused to praise. She had never doubted the worth of what she was doing, but having someone else perceive it and credit her with some of its success almost overset her. She had tried to pretend it didn't matter what anyone thought. She had mostly succeeded. But it did matter, and Virgil's opinion, whether she wanted to admit it or not, meant more than anyone's.

'Lady Kate does not know what to do with compliments,' Virgil said to Reverend Seagrove, seeing her blush, 'but nonetheless, I must tell you all, I think this is a remarkable place.'

Replete and revived by their morning victuals, the first awe which had overwhelmed them upon meeting their American visitor dissipated, the children gathered around Virgil, clamouring for stories, besieging him with questions, not all of which had any grounding in reality, having arisen from the various stories they had heard at home. Receiving Miss Thomson's assent, he sat down on the floor with them in a circle around him and told them stories of the New World.

It was as if he wove a spell, Kate thought, watching. He held them captive, enthralled and yet totally at ease, just exactly as he had done with the servants at Castonbury. His tales of Anansi the spider were not what the school's board of governors would call nice. They were subtly subversive, exactly the kind of story to make the children laugh gleefully, at the triumph not of good over bad, but of small over large.

'I meant it, Kate,' Virgil said as they made their way back through the woods at Castonbury afterwards. 'You should be proud of what you have achieved there. I gather from the reverend that it was no easy task to persuade some of the villagers to send their children to school rather than into employment.'

'There is so much more I'd like to do.'

'There is always more. You cannot do it all.'

'Yet that is exactly what you aim to do, judging by the plans you were discussing with Reverend Seagrove. I hadn't realised they were so far-reaching. It sounds as if you wish to take on the burden of educating every freed slave in America.'

'It's the least I can do.'

She was startled by the sudden weariness in his tone.

'You sound as if you carry the burden of slavery upon your own shoulders. *You*, of all people, have nothing to feel guilty about.'

'Kate, you don't know what you're talking about.'

The atmosphere which had come between them since the morning at the lake returned. 'Virgil, I...'

'Kate, we need to talk.'

She almost panicked. The past two nights had been spent assuring herself that what had happened between them had been purely physical. It had been intensely pleasurable, but it meant nothing more. By day, she could maintain a calm front, assuring herself that nothing had changed save she knew herself capable of pleasure. By day, she had the strength of her conviction. By night, she was as weak as a kitten. And it frightened her.

She had not loved Anthony, but she had cared for him and hoped to learn to love him. What she had discovered was that her feelings could be easily abused, she herself easily manipulated as a result. It had taken her five years to regain control of that life. She was *damn* sure she wasn't going to do an about-turn and hand her heart over to a man who not only swore he could never care for her, but in a few weeks hence would be on the other side of the world. She almost panicked, because for a terrible moment she thought Virgil was about to declare himself, and for an even more terrible moment she thought herself about to accept him. Then she saw his face. Tight. Controlled. Fierce. And she knew she'd got it quite wrong.

'You are leaving?' she said with a sinking heart, because it was the only other thing she could think of.

'You know I am, sometime before that claimant to the Castonbury throne arrives, but that's not what I wanted to discuss.'

'What, then?'

'Is there somewhere we can be private near here?'

'There is the orangery, but I think Wright is still working there. Or the fishing pavilion.'

They walked quickly and in silence. The pavilion sat over the lake with a view out to the island, a small square building which smelled of damp wood. Not the most romantic of places, Kate thought, then told herself that was exactly as it should be. An odd assortment of chairs and stools were huddled together by the window.

She sat in a wooden ladderback chair, but Virgil remained standing. He paced the room like a restless tiger, abstractedly inspecting fishing tackle, picking up a piece of rope and working a knot in it free. Casting it aside, he pulled a three-legged stool over to sit opposite her. 'Millie,' he said resolutely, 'I need to tell you about Millie. You need to understand, Kate, how impossible it is that there could ever be anything between us.'

'Virgil, I already understand that.'

Did she? The problem was, the difficulty was that he wasn't sure *he* did, not after—no, don't think about that. Virgil felt like a knight who had voluntarily laid down his armour thinking the battle won, only to discover that another was starting and his armour no longer fit. He could not allow Kate to penetrate his defences. What he needed to do was to remind himself of that. And if that meant the brutal truth, peeling back his scars to the raw flesh to remind himself, then that is what he would do.

He loosened his neck cloth. This was the only way. He had to close it down, this thing between them. He had to find a way to stop himself thinking of her, dreaming of her, *wanting* her. He had to get her out of his mind. This was for his sake, but even to say so would give her the wrong idea.

'Kate.' Virgil caught himself. Don't say her name, not like that! He tried again. 'Kate.' Better. She looked… anxious. Couldn't be helped. He could do it. The pain would cauterise whatever it was he was feeling, stop it in its tracks. *Damn it*, he had to do it. Virgil breathed deep, as if to dredge it all up from his guts. He felt sick. Good. That was good.

He closed his eyes. Another deep breath and he was back in the South. Harvest time. He opened his eyes and forced himself to look at Kate. Her face had that fierce look, her brows drawn together, her fine features pinched with concentration. Good. Good.

'There's a heaviness to the air in Virginia in the summer that saps your energy,' he began. 'Everything smells ripe, rotten. There's an art to getting the tobacco leaves in at just the right time, to having them dried in the sheds and packed in the hogsheads ready for the ships arriving so you can get the best price. If you leave them on the plants too long, you lose them.'

'That was why you chose to strike then. I remember you saying so.'

'Yes. As the time passed, the end was inevitable. I saw the men's resolve crumbling, Kate. I could almost taste their fear, but I hung on.'

'And you were punished.' She reached for his hand, but he brushed her away. He couldn't touch her. He would not have her comfort; he did not deserve her admiration. He would put an end to that. 'I was so damned certain I was right. They stuck by me, the men at the Booth place. God forgive me for that. They stuck by me long past the time when I thought we'd have been sure to win, but I hadn't counted on Master Booth's sheer determination, and I hadn't counted on his being smart enough to know that if he conceded just one thing it would be the end. I thought we had the most to lose, but I was wrong. When they sent men from the neighbouring plantations to do our jobs, I knew we'd lost. Yes, they whipped us. They flayed me so badly I thought I would die, but you'd be amazed just how much punishment a body can take.'

There was a sheen of tears in Kate's eyes. He could see her struggling valiantly not to let them fall. How she hated to cry. 'You mustn't feel guilty,' she said. 'Those other men, I'm sure they didn't blame you.'

'That's not it.' Tension enhanced the drawl in his voice, brought out the distinctive accent of the South. He held himself rigid on the stool.

'What else?' Kate asked.

There was doubt in her voice. She didn't want to hear. That was good. He didn't want to tell, but it was too late now to call a halt. 'Millie,' Virgil said. 'We weren't married. Some of the plantation owners encouraged it—they figured a family man was less likely to run away and they could always sell the children for profit, though it didn't stop them splitting those same families up if it suited them—but Master Booth wasn't one who went along with that view. He thought family ties made us more rebellious. We weren't married, but we planned to be.'

Kate flinched. Her eyes were dark, her skin not so much creamy as pale. She hadn't expected that, obviously. She didn't like it. Because she cared? He couldn't let himself think that way. Hell, that was the whole point.

Virgil tugged at his neck cloth and it came away in his hand. He began to wrap the length of linen round his knuckles, pulling it tight. 'Millie, she was mightily against our uprising. She begged me not to do it, but I was so sure I knew best. It was for our future, I told her.' He cleared his throat. 'What I did, it made sure we didn't have a future.'

He told her, and in the telling it was like it was happening again, fresh and stark, every detail etched on his memory, waiting all these years to be released for the first time. The sting of the sun blinding him as he emerged from the hellhole. The way fear tasted, sharp like sweat. Apprehension morphing into disbelief, then horror, as he saw his fellow slaves lined up. The look on Master Booth's face. On Harlow, the overseer's. And Millie. Millie's face. Millie calling his name. Millie, suffering for his crimes. Millie paying for his insubordination. 'They knocked me out. I heard her screaming, I tried to get to her, but they knocked me out. I couldn't get to her. I tried, but I couldn't get to her. I couldn't save her.'

His voice cracked, be he made himself finish. 'When I came back to consciousness, I thought it was over. I knew I would be sold. I thought most likely they'd send me north, because my reputation was too bad to make me anything but worthless in the South. I planned to come back for her. I wanted to tell her but they wouldn't let me see her. I never got to tell her. I thought she would know, but by the next morning—by the morning—it was too late. She killed herself.'

The agony of it all, which he had locked away, which he had kept so firmly tamped down, weighting it with the sheer slog which had been his determination to succeed, binding it tight with the penance which was at the root of his philanthropy, overwhelmed him. Virgil dropped his head in his hands.

Chapter Eight

Dry, hacking sobs echoed around the small room. Virgil's shoulders heaved. Kate had never before seen a man in such agony. That it was this man, so powerful, so seemingly invincible, made it all the more unbearable to watch. She ached for him, but she knew better than to offer him comfort. She wiped her own tears away frantically. What he had told her was beyond anything she had imagined. *Why* he had put himself through the trauma of reliving it, she could not quite understand.

Her own feelings strained at the leash she had put around them, like hunting dogs fresh on a scent. It was an enormous effort to control them, but she knew she could not afford to fail. That Virgil may be struggling, too, she had not for a moment imagined. Was he afraid, as she was?

Looking at his hunched, distraught figure, the horror

of his story fresh in her mind, Kate could not believe that. Such a trauma would surely sever all emotions for ever. No wonder he had chosen celibacy. No wonder he had been so reserved since the island. He obviously felt he had been unfaithful to Millie's memory. *It could never be the same*, he'd said. She understood that fully now. It hurt. It was good that it hurt. He'd put himself through this for her sake, Kate realised. He knew she was not indifferent. He'd seen what she would not admit to herself. His seeing made her realise how far from indifferent she had allowed herself to become. But it was not too late.

Virgil got to his feet and stared out of the window. Kate joined him, close but not touching. There was a heron on the lake shore, its wings spread to dry. When he began to speak again, his voice was flat, drained, exhausted. 'So now you know it all. I killed her. My stubbornness, my ambition, my certainty, killed the woman I loved. If I had listened to her, if I'd thought for one moment about the consequences of what I was doing, I wouldn't have done it. Surely to God, I wouldn't have done it.'

Kate stared at him, stunned. He couldn't possibly blame himself, but he quite obviously did. 'You can't have guessed what they would do to her!'

'I should have. It wasn't the first time I'd been whipped for insurrection, and this was one hell of an insurrection. We must have scared them. A whipping was never going to be enough, and I knew when they put me in the hellhole that they weren't going to hang me. I should have known.'

'No!' Kate exclaimed, the single word rebounding violently round the wooden walls of the pavilion. 'How can you say that? Virgil, for goodness' sake, if anyone is to blame it is that man, Booth.'

'I put myself first. I didn't think about her. The woman I wanted to marry, and I didn't think about her. It's not a lesson I ever want to repeat. When they told me she was dead—then I felt flayed. I don't ever want to go through that again, Kate. Do you understand that?'

There could be no mistaking the warning note in his voice. Though it hurt her, Kate told herself the pain was welcome. It was a warning she would be a fool to ignore. 'You could not be clearer, Virgil. I assure you, I understand completely. How could I not? What you have suffered...'

'I don't want your pity,' he exclaimed sharply. 'What I've suffered is nothing. I wanted to kill them at first, when I was in the hellhole, before it—before Millie—but I knew there was a better way. When Malcolm Jackson brought me to Boston, I felt like providence had finally given me a card I could play. I would show them I was

better than them, and I have. Better. Stronger. More powerful. And I did it on my terms.'

'That's what's driven you all these years?'

'That's part of it. I've had my revenge. Now I can
make good for what I did to Millie.'

There was so much, too much, for her to assimilate.
Kate smiled weakly. 'With schools?'

'And homes. And work. A library. I don't know what
else.'

Emotional isolation, Kate thought. Physical depriva-
tion. 'So I was right,' she said instead. 'You do want to
take on the burden of providing a future for every freed
slave in America. How will you know when you've done
enough, Virgil? When will you have paid?'

'I took a life. How can I ever repay that?'

'Millie took her own life,' Kate said gently.

'Because of me.'

She would not have given up, Kate thought, but bit
her tongue. How could she possibly tell what she would
have done? She could not even begin to put herself in
Millie's position. 'You were nineteen, Virgil. "What does
anyone know of caution at that age?" That's what you
said to me, remember? Don't you think it's time to forgive yourself?'

Virgil had been leaning against the wooden wall. Now

he stood up, rolling his shoulders. 'Don't you think you should be asking yourself that question?'

He sounded utterly drained. Kate, too, felt quite empty save for a gnawing sense of loss. She caught his hand and rubbed it against her cheek. 'I can't begin to tell you—to imagine…' She blinked furiously. No tears. 'It wasn't your fault, Virgil. I wish you could see that, but I can see there is no point in my trying to persuade you. What I'm trying to say is, I understand. Why you told me, I mean. You have no cause to worry, I understand completely.'

They agreed that it would be for the best that he leave Castonbury and continue north with his planned visit to New Lanark sooner rather than later. Paradoxically, the certainty that he was leaving and the knowledge that his truly shocking history made the very notion that he could care for her impossible allowed Kate to admit to herself that she *had* begun to care for him. Virgil's tortured confession had torn at her heart, but the warning behind it had been entirely effective. She had no option now but to pull herself back from the precarious brink upon which she had, quite obliviously, been teetering.

'Yes,' she agreed as they walked back to the great house from the fishing pavilion, 'it is for the best that you leave.' But saying what she ought and accepting its consequences were two different things. She had never been inclined to melancholy, but she could sense its grey mantle hovering over her as she pictured a Virgil-less Castonbury. 'Though now we are in accord, perhaps there is no need for you to go straight away,' she said cautiously.

Beside her, she sensed Virgil hesitating. 'I do have some business I haven't had the chance to tie up for Giles. And there is the Buxton assembly the day after tomorrow, if you still wish to go?'

They could dance together. Since no one else was like to ask her, they would be obliged to dance together, Kate thought. 'There can be no harm in us dancing, surely.'

'Surely,' Virgil agreed with a semblance of a smile. 'I shall make arrangements to leave the following morning. In fact, I think I'll walk back to the village and book a place on the mail right now.'

It was not that he was eager to be rid of her, Kate told herself as she watched him striding off. Were he so, he would not have agreed to stay a moment longer at Castonbury than necessary. This business with Giles could be quickly concluded. And as to the dance...

She had mentioned it to no one. Not even Aunt Wilhelmina knew she was considering attending with only Virgil as a chaperon. She had assumed that Virgil would invite Giles and Lily, but he had not. Under other circumstances, of course, she would have suggested it herself, but with Virgil leaving Castonbury so soon, this would be their last chance to be alone together. Alone together in a crowded ballroom, that is, but at least they would be free of the oppressive atmosphere which prevailed whenever Aunt Wilhelmina and Virgil were in the same room.

Kate's mood lightened a fraction. She would not ask permission. She was four-and-twenty; there was no need for her to ask permission of anyone. She would order the carriage for after dinner, and she would wear her best dress, and she would hold her head high in front of all who snubbed her, and she would dance with Virgil for the first and last time.

'What will you wear tonight, my lady?' Polly's head poked over the screen behind which Kate was bathing in a large copper tub in front of the fire. 'The claret velvet? Or what about the green silk with the French trim? Only I heard His Grace was joining you, so you'll want something a bit grander than usual.'

Kate dropped the lavender-scented soap into the water. 'My father is coming to dinner?'

'So I heard downstairs. Didn't Mrs Landes-Fraser tell you?'

Kate made a wry face. 'I've been avoiding my aunt

today. The truth is, Polly, that I'm going to the assembly at Buxton tonight, and I haven't told her.'

'You're going dancing?' Polly edged around the screen, her eyes narrowed. 'You never go to public assemblies. *Why* haven't you told that aunt of yours? Who is escorting you?'

Kate picked up a large sponge and set about soaping it industriously. 'Mr Jackson.'

Polly swore colourfully. 'You've got some brass. They'll never let you go, especially not now that His Grace will be at dinner.'

'I don't see how it makes the slightest bit of difference. Virgil—Mr Jackson—has been a guest in this house for some time, and my father has shown absolutely no inclination to meet him. Yet on the eve of his departure...'

'So that's it,' Polly exclaimed.

'What do you mean?'

'Come on, my lady, you don't fool me. He's leaving tomorrow. It's a last fling, isn't it?'

'I don't know what you mean by *fling*...'

Polly pursed her lips. 'I think you do—leastways, I think you know more about it now than you did before your Mr Jackson came to visit.'

'He is not my Mr Jackson.'

'No, nor likely ever to be. His Grace would have you banished.'

'It has nothing to do with my father, Polly. Mr Jackson is not—we are not— There is no question of such a thing. We are friends, merely. And he's leaving tomorrow.'

'And you want one last night with him, and I don't blame you. If he was mine—'

'He is *not* mine,' Kate interrupted, trying not to notice the wistful note in her own voice.

Polly ignored her. 'Right, then. The blue crepe, I think—you've never worn it. Have you ordered the carriage? Good. Now, let's get your hair washed. We need to make sure you look your best.'

Two hours later, Kate stood in front of the looking glass. Her gown of celestial blue crepe was worn over a white satin slip and trimmed with a deep border of tulle embroidered with silks and chenille in a variety of contrasting shades. The sleeves were puffed, the décolleté low, trimmed with net lace and tulle, which frothed seductively over her tightly laced bosom. Polly had dressed her hair high on her head, teasing several wispy curls out from the severe chignon, which suited her far better than the fashionable Grecian styles. She wore only pearls—a tight choker with a diamond clasp around her throat, several bracelets over her French kid gloves and a pair of pearl and diamond drops in her ears. Her silk slippers were the same celestial blue as her gown. Her chemise was white silk, as were her stockings, though they were white tied with dark blue garters, the same colour as her corset.

Kate smiled with satisfaction. 'I look very well. Thank you, Polly.'

'You look lovely.' Polly handed Kate her reticule. 'Don't you dare lose courage, my lady. No matter what His Grace says.'

'No,' Kate said with far more conviction than she felt. She took a last look in the mirror. Her heart was fluttering with excitement. Anyone would think she was a girl making her debut, not a grown woman, for goodness' sake. 'Wish me luck, Polly.'

'Knock 'em dead, my lady. And if you don't,' Polly said grimly, 'I will.'

Though she knew that Virgil's valet would have been as well-informed as Polly regarding the duke's presence, Kate made sure to be the first in the drawing room. They saw so little of her father since Jamie and Ned had died, that at times she quite forgot all about him. Smithins, His Grace's proprietorial valet, kept him abreast of household matters, but as her father's health deteriorated so, too, had his interest in these affairs. Giles, she knew, kept the duke in ignorance of a great deal of his worries for fear of the effect it would have on him. She suspected that Smithins, too, filtered out much of the household gossip. Though the impending arrival of the child he already claimed for his grandson had revived the duke somewhat, Kate was rather astonished at his decision to take dinner *en famille* tonight. Virgil's last night. Could it be that her father actually felt guilty at not having met the man who had been his guest? No, she thought with a curl of her lip, more likely her father wished to flaunt his heritage at an American who, she had no doubt Aunt Wilhelmina would have informed him, had not a drop of aristocratic blood in his body.

'Have you heard?' Giles stormed into the room, looking harassed. 'Our father has deigned to join us for dinner tonight. I tried to stop him, but he was insistent. Said he wanted to meet the American, something about showing him how the Old World did things.'

'Oh, Lord, are we to dine in state, then?'

'Heaven knows how many courses. At least it will give that Frenchman who rules the kitchens something to do. Didn't you know? I thought you must, when I saw you in your finery.'

Kate took the glass of Madeira gratefully. 'This, brother dear, is a ball gown,' she said. 'I thought you were a connoisseur of women's clothing too.'

Giles grinned. 'Those days are well in the past now. I'm a happily— What do you mean, a ball gown?'

'I'm going to the Buxton assembly. It was all arranged before I discovered our revered sire was joining us.'

'*I* never heard anything. Who is escorting you?'

'Virgil.'

It was not often that her brother was at a loss for words. Kate raised an eyebrow at him, and sipped her Madeira.

'You can't!'

'Why ever not?'

'Kate, I know you have no time for the proprieties…'

'Why should I? I am a ruined woman, as my aunt never fails to point out. For heaven's sake, Giles, it is a public ball. No one would bat an eye were you to go unescorted.'

'You wouldn't catch me dead there, unless I was dragged kicking and screaming.'

'Which is quite beside the point. You cannot have it both ways, you know. Either I am ruined and it matters not what I do, or what I did with Anthony Featherstone did not ruin me and therefore does not matter.'

'Sophistry, sister dear!' Giles drummed his fingers on the high mantel, where he had taken up his accustomed position, standing with his back to the fire. 'You are set on this?'

Kate nodded.

'May I ask why?'

'I am tired of allowing the opinions of others to decide my actions. Anthony is happily married and, as ever, the darling of society. I did nothing more than he did. Less, for I did not talk. Why should I continue to pay when he does not? It's not fair.'

'Kate, it's how things are,' Giles said with a sigh. 'If you wish to return to society, why did you not discuss it with me? With my sponsorship—'

'Had Papa and Aunt Wilhelmina *sponsored* me five years ago, you would not have to offer now.'

'You feel they let you down?' Giles nodded slowly. 'Yes, I can see that you do, and I admit you have cause. Had I been here—'

'But you were not, and I doubt you'd have persuaded Papa to listen back then, in any case.'

'You do see, Kate, that turning up without any female to lend you countenance, in the company of an unmarried man, and one who moreover is not even related to you—'

'And an *American* into the bargain,' Kate interjected sarcastically.

'It has nothing to do with his heritage,' Giles said. 'Virgil Jackson is the kind of man who will be treated with respect wherever he goes. What do you think we've been doing while you've been setting the Dower House to rights? There's barely a house in the county Virgil hasn't visited with me, and in every single one he's been well received, not to say downright toad-eaten. I'll wager he's plagued with invitations, though he's chosen to accept none of them. You'd best make sure he marks your dance card before you go, or you'll find yourself without a partner.'

'He has said nothing of all this to me.'

'Why would he, save to rub your nose in it? Most of these people won't open their doors to you. Virgil's not so insensitive.'

'No.' Kate finished her Madeira. 'Does this mean you won't object to my going to the ball, then?'

Giles gave a bark of laughter. 'Was there ever any chance I could stop you?'

The drawing room door opened and Virgil entered. 'What is the joke?'

'You and my sister,' Giles said. 'Lord, I'm looking forward to seeing the old man's face when you tell him you're taking her to the Buxton assembly.'

'Yes, I heard His Grace was joining us at dinner. Do you wish to change your mind about the dance, my lady?' Virgil turned towards Kate as he spoke. She rose from the gilded settee, and had the satisfaction of seeing her appearance reflected in his expression. 'That is a very beautiful ball gown,' he said. 'And you look quite breathtaking,' he added softly, taking her hand between his.

She blushed. 'You look very smart too,' which was an understatement. In silk knee breeches and a tightly fitting black coat, with a white shirt, white waistcoat and white stockings, Virgil looked starkly magnificent. She could not quite believe that after tomorrow morning she would never see him again. Though she knew this for a fact, it was one thing, she was discovering, for her to know, and another for her to accept. She didn't want him to go, though she knew there was no reason at all for him to stay, nor ever could be.

He really was magnificent. She watched him, standing beside Giles. The two men were of very similar build. Funny, she'd never thought her brother either attractive or handsome, but he was both. She wondered now if Lily felt, when she looked at Giles, as Kate felt when she looked at Virgil.

Not that the cases were the same, for Giles and Lily were in love, whereas she and Virgil were…in lust? No, it wasn't that. Though her heart was beating quite erratically. And her corsets felt too tight. And she couldn't help thinking of the skin and muscle under those tight-fitting breeches. The curve of his buttocks. The span of his chest. The seductive potency of his manhood.

'Katherine?'

Kate jumped. 'Aunt Wilhelmina.'

'Why are you wearing a ball gown?'

'His Grace, the Duke of Rothermere,' Lumsden intoned, as if he were announcing war.

Giles rolled his eyes as the door was flung open. Phaedra stopped short, a comical look of dismay on her face. Kate smothered a smile. Obviously her sister had not benefited from any sort of warning.

'Your Grace.' Mrs Landes-Fraser, more than usually draped and bedecked in shawls and turbans and feathers, abandoned her interrogation of her niece to drop into a curtsey so low Kate feared she may require help in recovering. It was an absurd gesture, in her opinion, but her father seemed to appreciate it, for he held out his hand and allowed it to be kissed, for all the world as if he were a prince.

He was looking much frailer than when she had last seen him. He had been a tall man, but he was stooped now, bent over like a question mark, his evening clothes loose on his wasted frame, the last remnants of his white hair wispy on his mottled pate. His once hawk-like features were blunted by saggy skin and watery eyes. Crispin Torquil Fitzmerrion Montague had the appearance of a man headed shortly for the grave.

'Father.' Giles made a curt bow. 'May I present our guest, Mr Virgil Jackson.'

'Your Grace.'

Kate was pleased to note that Virgil's bow was neither deferential nor particularly low. His tone was not cold, but nor did it contain any warmth. He did not say it was an honour. Her father, too, noted all this. His brows snapped together. His expression, which had been benignly supercilious, now hardened, giving his audience a fleeting glimpse of the ruthless despot he had once been. 'I believe my daughter invited you, Mr Jackson,' he said. 'Under the mistaken belief that she will warm me to this abolition nonsense, no doubt. Katherine's propensity for supporting lost causes knows no bounds.'

'Papa! How—'

'Mr Jackson is as much my guest as Kate's,' Giles intervened hastily, 'as you are perfectly well aware, Your Grace, for I have informed you myself. Mr Jackson is an extremely astute businessman and has, amongst other things, been so kind as to give me some very sound advice regarding your investments.'

'Giles!' Mrs Landes-Fraser exclaimed. 'There are ladies present. I am shocked that you should raise such matters in mixed company. Girls, where are your manners? You have not yet greeted His Grace.'

'Papa.'

'Phaedra. You smell of horse.'

'I am just back from the stables, Papa. There was no time to bathe. No one told me you were joining us,' Phaedra muttered, glaring at her aunt.

'And, Katherine.'

'Papa.' Kate made a very small curtsey.

'I believe I have you to blame for oversetting my arrangements for my grandson. The boy is my heir. It is not at all fitting that he stay in the Dower House.'

Giles sighed heavily. 'We have been over that, Father. We agreed—'

'I did nothing of the sort. I may be sick in body, but I am quite in control of my own mind. I want that boy here, under my roof in the Castonbury nursery. This will all be his one day.'

'*If* he proves to be Jamie's child,' Giles said.

'Of course he is Jamie's child,' the duke snapped. 'He must be.'

Giles, abandoning any pretence of keeping the peace, opened his mouth to argue, but was interrupted by the clash of the dinner gong and Lumsden's stately announcement that His Grace was served. When Mrs Landes-Fraser would have taken the duke's arm to support him in the short journey across the marble hall to the dining room, Smithins appeared like a ghost, leaving her to be escorted by a most reluctant Giles.

'I'm sorry,' Kate whispered as Virgil took her arm, motioning to Phaedra to take the other, 'my father is unforgivably rude.'

Virgil shrugged, and squeezed her fingers. 'You think I care about him looking down his patrician nose at me? What's unforgivable is the way he treats you.'

'Oh, that was nothing,' Phaedra said chirpily. 'Before Jamie and Ned died, Papa and Kate used to argue hammer and tongs. Why are you wearing a ball gown, Kate?'

'Because she's going to a ball,' Virgil replied. 'With me.'

'Just you?' Phaedra eyed Kate with respect as they entered the dining room. 'Goodness, dinner is going to be interesting.'

Interesting, Kate thought grimly as course followed course, was one way of putting it. Tedious, fraught, embarrassing and interminable were others. His Grace had Virgil sit on his left-hand side in what should have been a position of honour. It was, however, patently obvious that the duke wished merely to have the convenience of alternately interrogating his guest and snubbing him without the inconvenience of having to turn his head too far or raise his voice. Several times Giles tried to intervene, but when it became obvious that Virgil was neither intimidated nor insulted, merely blandly indifferent, Giles grinned at Kate and devoted himself to his dinner.

It was a most magnificent repast. Monsieur André, Castonbury's haughty French chef, had obviously relished the challenge of putting a meal worthy of the duke on the table. It groaned under the weight of carp Chambord studded with truffles and braised in red wine; lobster Parisienne; cold scallops glazed in aspic and decorated with artichokes; veal Périgourdine, cooked in butter and stuffed with fois gras; noisettes of lamb; pigeons *bonne-femme*; a whole pickled tongue; soup julienne à la Russe; stuffed cucumbers; eggs Polonaise; and any number of vegetable dishes in aspic jelly moulded into extraordinary shapes.

The duke ate sparingly. 'I believe you visited that school my daughter has established,' he said, graciously allowing Lumsden to help him to a sliver of lobster.

'I was impressed,' Virgil replied. 'Castonbury now has as fine a place to educate its young as any other in the country. I think even Robert Owen would be pleased.'

'That man is a subversive!' the duke exclaimed. 'Servants and farmers and mill workers have no use for reading and writing.'

'Perhaps not, if they are to remain mere servants and farmers and mill workers,' Virgil said mildly. 'But what if they wish something more?'

'More?' His Grace looked incredulous. 'What more could they possibly want?'

'Lady Kate wishes to offer the villagers the chance to attend classes at night.'

'It is time that my daughter learned that her wishes are of absolutely no consequence. Her place is with her family. When my grandson arrives, Katherine will have no time for these misguided attempts at charity. Since she has signally failed to do her duty by marrying, the least she can do is devote herself to the service of her nephew. I fear my ill health has of late allowed her too much latitude. *That*,' the duke said with an air of finality, 'will come to an end now that I am a little recovered.'

For a moment, it looked as if Virgil would rise to the bait. Instead he pushed his chair back abruptly. 'You will excuse us, Your Grace, but I am afraid we have a prior engagement.'

An expectant hush made Kate's heart bump hard against her chest. She put her napkin on her plate of untouched food, acutely aware of the eyes of every one of her relatives, fixed fascinated, astounded and disbelieving, upon her. Not since she had jilted Anthony had she openly defied her father. This time, she was no frightened child but a grown woman. She smiled up at Virgil as he pulled her chair back, and then smiled benignly over at the duke. Their confrontations, as Phaedra had so inelegantly put it, had always been hammer and tongs. Tonight, watching him become increasingly querulous as his barbs failed to wound and his most pointed insults were greeted by Virgil with bland indifference, she saw that her tactics had been quite wrong. It had been a struggle not to rise to the baited remarks about her future, but she had gritted her teeth and held her peace, and it had paid off.

'How dare you, sir!' The duke, turning an alarming shade of puce, broke the silence. 'Katherine! Where the devil do you think you're going?'

Aunt Wilhelmina cast her a furious look. 'Katherine! We have not finished dinner.'

'*I* have. Mr Jackson and I, as he has already informed you, have a prior engagement. We are going to the Assembly Rooms at Buxton.'

The duke gasped. Phaedra muffled her nervous laugh with her napkin. Mrs Landes-Fraser looked as if she would swoon. 'Katherine Mary Cecily Montague,' she hissed, 'you cannot be serious. Have you any idea what people will say?'

Kate laced her fingers tightly together behind her back. 'How can I not, Aunt Wilhelmina, when you remind me on a daily basis.'

'Sit down at once!'

'Get her out of my sight,' the duke cried, clutching his chest. 'That any daughter of mine should— You will go to your room, Katherine, and you will remain there until you see the error of your ways.'

'Oh, for heaven's sake, she's not a child. This is turning into a farce.' Giles pushed back his chair so violently it fell over. 'Get out, Kate, go to Buxton before he has an apoplexy. Lumsden, call Smithins. Phaedra, stop smirking.'

As Polly, waiting in the marble hall, helped Kate into her evening cloak, and the dining room door burst open again, her sister came bounding out with Giles in her wake. 'That was marvellous. I haven't enjoyed dinner so much in an age. Have a lovely time,' she said, surprising Kate with a hug before disappearing down the back stairs, obviously headed for the stables.

'I hope you know what you're doing,' Giles said to Kate. With a curt nod at Virgil, he, too, disappeared.

Virgil took Kate's arm. 'Well, I think you've certainly made your point. Are you sure you want to go?'

She smiled up at him. Tomorrow she would face the consequences of her insubordination, but tonight she did not give a fig. 'Just try and stop me,' she said.

Chapter Nine

The Buxton Assembly Rooms were brightly lit, with a crowd of carriages jostling for position in the cobbled street outside. Flambeaux lit the way as Kate and Virgil mounted the shallow flight of steps to the main entranceway, where they discarded their outerwear before ascending to the ballroom on the second floor. Two rows of marble columns supported the high ceiling of the long room, which was lit by three glittering chandeliers. A card room and withdrawing room served those who wished to play and those who sought relief from heat and the crush of dancers.

As Kate entered on Virgil's arm, a country dance was under way. She recognised the young woman at the head of the set in a gown of primrose jaconet as the daughter of a neighbour, and her partner as one of Giles's boyhood friends. Around the rooms, seated on gilded chairs, were the cream of the county, almost every one an acquaintance of her father, her aunt and formerly of herself. With a sinking heart, she realised that the eyes and lorgnettes of most of them were turned upon her and Virgil. She stiffened.

'Don't show them you care,' Virgil said softly. 'You have no reason at all to be intimidated by them. I doubt very much if any of them could lay claim to the kind of spotless reputation they pretend to. Think of it as a game, Kate. Don't be the first to back down.'

She tried to do as he bid her, meeting disapproving gazes with a bland smile, and holding her head high. To her surprise, several women nodded—not the friendliest of nods, but they did not shun her. Virgil led her determinedly from one group of people to another, and she recalled the reaction he had generated the first time they'd met, several weeks ago now, though it felt like months, at Maer Hall. All eyes turned towards him. Whispers turned into murmurs of appreciation. Ladies vied surreptitiously to greet him. Gentlemen edged closer, as if he exerted some sort of invisible attraction. It was just as Giles had predicted. Virgil was received with effusion and bombarded with suggestions that he partner this daughter, this niece, this granddaughter, in the next country dance or cotillion or quadrille.

He agreed to some, but only those for which Kate was

also solicited, and he insisted that the first dance and the waltz—which the master of ceremonies had daringly introduced some months before—were saved for her. 'You see,' he said to her as they joined their cotillion set, 'if you lead, they will follow.'

Kate laughed. 'It's true, only a very few people actually snubbed me, but I think it was rather the case that if *you* lead they will follow.'

'Stop undermining yourself. You are the one who looked them all in the eye and held your nerve. And while we are on the subject, I must congratulate you for the way you handled that tyrannical old goat who is your father tonight. He couldn't believe it when there was not a rise to be got from you.'

'I took my lead from you.'

'Well, now you know what to do, you can take the lead from yourself. You don't need me, Kate. Have a little faith in your own ability.'

Their set was now formed, with six other couples. For the first time since they had arrived, Virgil looked doubtful. 'I have not danced the cotillion very often.'

'I have not danced one in years.' Kate looked towards the orchestra, where the master of ceremonies was consulting a card. 'It looks like he will call the changes, at least. I shan't mention it if you stand on my toes provided you return the favour,' she said with a teasing smile.

'Kate.'

It was the way he said her name that made her heart flutter. No one ever said her name like that. And the way he looked at her, really looked at her, his tawny eyes focused only on her, that made the muscles in her belly clench. She forgot about the disastrous dinner and the strain of facing the world and even the six other couples in their cotillion set. She forgot all about the need to restrain her feelings, to keep a leash on her thoughts, and gave herself up to the raw strength of the attraction between them. It was still there, fiercer than ever. He felt it too. She saw it reflected in his eyes.

The orchestra struck up and the dance began. Each touch of their hands ran like a shock up her arm, making her skin tingle. When they separated, their eyes retained the contact. Glove on glove felt like skin on skin. Every glance was a caress. She was barely aware of the other dancers, barely aware of the changes, tuned in not to the orchestra, but to some internal rhythm known only to the two of them.

When it was over, the polite applause startled them both. They blinked as if waking from a reverie. For the next two hours they danced with other partners, but the connection between them grew as they exchanged glances across the throng, as Virgil's hand sought hers under cover of the folds of her gown when he stood beside her talking at tea, as his arm brushed against hers, or hers against his thigh. By the time the last dance, their first and only waltz, was called, Kate felt strung tight as a bow.

'I see you are not so unaccustomed to the waltz as the cotillion,' she said, striving to retain a little control of herself as they made their first circuit of the floor. Having his hand on her waist was conjuring up all sorts of memories. Of his skin against hers. Of his lips on hers. Of the way he felt against her, hard and muscled and yet velvet-smooth. Her voice sounded breathless. He would think it was the dance.

'I've danced it several times back home. If a man is to be a success, he cannot be completely antisocial.'

'So you charm the ladies of Boston with your dancing and your polite conversation so that they will persuade their husbands to do business with you?'

Virgil's smile faded. 'I succeed on my own terms, Kate. I don't need anyone to oil the wheels for me, and I never cross the line of what is proper. I mean that I'm part of that society, so I can't live outside it.'

'I know what you meant, I was only teasing.'

His hand tightened on her waist. 'I'm sorry. I guess I've had enough of socialising for tonight. I was beginning to think it would never end. No, don't look like

that. I didn't mean I was bored. I meant—damn it, I just
meant I wanted to dance with *you*.'

'Oh.'

'Just "oh"? You're supposed to say that you only
wanted to dance with me.'

'I would, if I could be certain you wouldn't remind
me of how impossible it is.'

'Do I have to?'

'No,' she said sadly. 'You're leaving tomorrow and I
shan't see you again. I know that.'

Virgil pulled her closer as they turned. 'Let's not talk
about tomorrow,' he said harshly. 'Let's just enjoy what
is left of tonight.'

She was happy to do so. As the dance progressed, she
began to see why it was deemed so shocking. Above
the waist they held themselves rigid, but below, their
legs, thighs, knees brushed and touched, a constant teasing, tantalising contact. They did not talk, but their eyes
spoke. Yearning and loss. A flare of passion quickly repressed. Desire flickered, was tamped down, then flickered back to life. By the time the waltz ended it had
taken hold. They did not wait to bid anyone goodnight,
but made their way quickly down the central staircase,
among the first to collect their coats.

John Coachman was waiting with the landau. The
hood was up. They sat together, facing forward in the

dim of the interior as the coach rumbled over the cobblestones of Buxton.

'Kate.' Even in the dark, he could find the pulse below her ear. He had taken off his gloves as soon as they had left the ballroom. His lips were warm on her skin. His fingers stroked the nape of her neck. His thigh was solid against hers. 'You are so beautiful,' he whispered.

'In the way that a greyhound is,' she said, remembering that first night.

'In the way only you can be. You are Kate. Perfectly Kate. Don't let them change you. Don't ever change.'

She swallowed hard. She would not have his last memories of her be marred by tears. 'I shall try not to.'

'What he said, your father, about the future. You will not allow him to force you into the role of an old aunt?'

Had he any idea what he was asking of her, to live at Castonbury and to defy its lord and master? To be herself, as he asked, would mean she could never please. 'I shall try,' Kate said hesitantly, for she would not lie to him.

Virgil sighed. 'There is no alternative, but to remain there?'

'If I made an effort to become truly eccentric, I suppose there is a chance they would exile me to the Dower House. Always assuming that Jamie's wife chooses not to live there. Always assuming that she *is* Jamie's wife.'

'Your father seems to have decided.'

'The lawyers will require more concrete proof than a ring and a child,' Kate said.

'Giles cannot accept that his brother would have married without informing him, I know.'

'Giles has confided in you?'

Virgil shook his head. 'He had no need. It's obvious.'

'To you, perhaps. You are very perceptive.'

The crump of the landau's wheels on the gravel of Castonbury's driveway took them both by surprise. The journey had been too short. As they proceeded towards the house, Kate began to panic. She was not ready to say goodbye.

'Virgil, I...'

'Come for a walk with me. It's cold, but it's a clear night. Let's go look at the stars by the lake,' he said, handing her out.

Kate looked towards the door, where Lumsden stood waiting. 'I can't. My aunt—'

'Wait here.'

She had no idea what he said to the butler, but as John Coachman headed for the stables, the front door closed and Virgil rejoined her. 'He won't wait up, and he won't tell.'

They walked in silence towards the lake. Above them the stars glittered in the midnight blue of an unusually clear night. It was cold. Winter was not long away. At the head of the north lake they stood looking out at the island. The water lapped gently on the pebbles and Virgil pulled her into his arms, crushing her to his chest so tightly she could hardly breathe. 'I won't forget you, Kate.'

She swallowed hard. She clenched her fists, digging her nails into her palms in an effort to control the sudden spasm of tears which threatened to overwhelm her. She hadn't thought about this moment, she wasn't ready for it, but she would not spoil it. 'I won't forget you either.'

He tilted her chin up. His face was set, fierce, but she knew him better now. He was not angry. 'Will you kiss me goodbye?'

He did not wait for her answer. His lips were gentle, but she was having none of that. Kate pressed herself against him, twining her arms around his neck, and kissed him hard, pouring all her regrets and all the passion they could not share into that one moment. When he would have pulled away, she pulled him back.

With a groan which seemed to come from the depths of his being, Virgil surrendered to the kiss and the moment. This wasn't what he'd planned, but then since he'd met Kate nothing had gone as he'd planned. He couldn't pretend he didn't want her. It didn't change a damn thing, but he couldn't lie to himself. Not tonight.

He kissed her. Then he told himself to stop, and kissed her again. When he kissed her again, he was still sure it was not too late. But then he kissed her again, and she made that little growling noise deep in her throat, and he knew that it was. 'Kate,' he said, meaning *stop*, but it came out sounding the opposite. How could he not want her, with her breath on his cheek, the scent of her perfume and her skin and her Kate-ness going straight to his head and his groin, her body pressed, melting, pliant into his?

He wanted her. He couldn't imagine a time when he would not want her, though he knew this would be the only time he could ever have her. 'Kate, we can't.'

'Don't you want to?'

'You know I do.'

'Then show me,' she whispered, 'but not here.'

She led him to the Dower House, retrieving the key from its hiding place in the portico, lighting the lamp which sat on the marble hall table. Of one accord they climbed the stairs to the room with the fantastically carved mythological bed. Kate placed the lamp on the chest of drawers and turned to him, suddenly nervous.

'Are you sure?' Virgil asked her.

'Are you?'

'Right now, I am.'

Kate smiled. 'That's all that matters.'

They both knew differently. In the morning he would be gone. In the morning they would face their different futures alone. But right now, at this moment, his imminent departure was an urge to completion.

Virgil's kiss was deeply sensual. It seemed to reach right down inside her and extract the sweetest, most delicious ache. Kate twined her arms around his neck and kissed him back fervently, spilling all the pent-up emotion of the night into him. She felt drugged, heavy, weighted, weightless, by what he was doing to her. His tongue stroked and licked, his mouth shaped hers and heated hers. His lips were like velvet.

He dropped his greatcoat onto the floor, then undid the clasp of her cloak. The velvet pooled at her feet. The tiny buttons on her gloves were next. He undid them slowly, licking the exposed skin of her wrist before pulling them down over her arms, trailing kisses in the wake of the soft French kid, on the crook of her elbow, her forearm, her wrist again, each one of her fingers. And then the other hand. She shivered violently.

He shrugged out of his coat. Her fingers plucked at his clothing but he slowed her, muttering her name like an incantation, smoothing his hands over her, taking his time, as if they had all the time in the world.

He ran his fingers through her hair, casting pearl-tipped pins onto the floor. His hands were like magic. Could hair feel? It was tingling at the roots. He kissed her mouth, her eyes, her throat.

His hands traced the shape of her body through her evening gown, skimming over her breasts, her belly, her hips. Heating her from the inside. His mouth drove her wild. His kisses grew more focused. He turned her around and kissed her neck. His fingers on the laces and hooks of her robe were less certain, but still he wouldn't hurry, slipping it down, kissing the crook of her elbow as he freed her from each sleeve, cupping the flesh of her bottom, her thighs, as he helped her step out of it.

Moonlight slanted through the windows, casting a ghostly light over the carved bed. Nymphs, goddesses and fantastical sea creatures peered out at them, watching. Virgil said her name again as he looked at her. She could melt from the way he said it. He undid her stays slowly, his smile taking on a new sensuality as he enjoyed the look of her in dark blue satin and pristine white lace. She had always thought the purpose of wearing such exotic undergarments was for her pleasure alone. Until now. The way he looked at her made her bones liquid.

She tugged at his waistcoat. He quickly unbuttoned it, casting it off with his neck cloth and shirt. Her breath caught in her throat at the sight of him. Smooth skin, barely a mark on his chest in contrast to his back. Muscles that strained at his skin. Gleaming ebony. She ran her fingers over him, marvelling at the way he shivered under her touch, counting down his ribs.

He sat her on the edge of the bed and pulled off her slippers. They were damp with dew, quite ruined. He rolled down her stockings and kissed her knees, her feet, each one of her toes. He kicked off his own shoes, his silk knee breeches, his hose. She had forgotten how beautiful he was. Her imagination had failed her. His body was hard-packed, the muscles rounded, the whole infinitely male. She reached for him, and his touch became more urgent, tearing at the last of her undergarments, oblivious of the silk and lace and ribbons, interested only in that most intimate of covering, her skin.

Finally, he lay her down on the bed. She relished the weight of him on top of her, the breadth of him, the solidness of him as he held her, breast to breast, thigh to thigh, the hard length of his erection nestling between her legs. Kate moaned, low and guttural.

He kissed her mouth again. Then he kissed her breasts. Hands and mouth on her nipples, on her flank, kissing, teasing, tugging, much more urgent. She was not prepared for how fast it built, her climax. She was sky-high, taut, unbearably tense as he cupped her sex, just cupped her, the heel of his hand pressing against her, nothing more, and she thought she might explode.

Kate clenched tight. Not yet. She bucked under him. Not yet. She mimicked the way he cupped her, and felt him tighten in her palm. Not yet. Virgil moaned. His fingers slipped inside her and she gasped with pleasure. He slid in so easily, she was so wet. Not yet. Not yet, please, not yet. She was tight, tight, tight. His fingers slid over her, over the tightest, hottest bit of her, and she felt herself unravelling.

She slid her hand up the length of his shaft. Thick. Hard. Silky. She wanted him inside her. 'Please,' she breathed desperately. He kissed her. He thrust his tongue into her mouth. He stroked inside the folds of her sex, over the hot, tight, hard part of her. She couldn't hold back. She felt herself toppling, shattering, crying out, and then he thrust, one long hard thrust deep inside her and she shattered.

She came, pulsing, throbbing, crying out, but he didn't let up. He tilted her up, he wrapped his arm around her back to brace her, and thrust again. She hadn't ever felt anything like it. Virgil inside her, thick and hard and pushing higher, her own muscles pulsing around her, her climax ebbing and then building, like an echo, as he pushed into her. She held him tight there, clinging to him, watching the effect of what she did to him dancing across his face as he withdrew and she clung and then opened for his next thrust. And his next. It was like a race now. He was pushing her hard and though she wanted to give in to him she didn't want him to stop, not yet. Higher and harder, she clung and she gasped and then it happened so suddenly, not an echo but something more, as he touched a spot she hadn't known existed high up and she let go, truly let go, had no choice but to let herself fall, and with a harsh cry Virgil pulled himself free, spilling onto her belly.

He wiped her clean with his kerchief. Such a little thing, but it brought a lump to her throat, for Anthony had never shown such care. Grabbing her cloak from the floor, Virgil threw it over them, and then pulled her back into his arms, spooning her against him, nestling her bottom into his thighs, one hand over each breast, nuzzling the back of her neck. It brought a whole new meaning to the word *bliss*. Kate closed her eyes and floated.

Later, not much later, Virgil stirred. He kissed her mouth again. Then her breasts. Then lower. Her thighs. And then her sex. He didn't just taste her, he savoured her, licking into her, around her, thrusting his tongue inside her. Kate was too aroused to be shocked. His tongue teased and stroked and circled. He seemed to know exactly how to bring her close to the edge, and then to leave her there teetering, hovering, wanting to fall, wanting to cling on. She arched shamelessly against his mouth. It felt different this time. More intense. A brighter colour. A wrenching of her guts. When she came he stayed with her, and when she thought she was done, he licked her into another of those rippling echoes.

Afterwards, she rolled over on top of him, taking him by surprise, wanting to taste him and to taste what he did to her. She could feel him, hard and hot between her legs. She wriggled down his body, enjoying the way his skin rubbed on her breasts, relishing the contrast of her skin on his. She slid down, until she had the tip of his shaft against her lips. His eyes were glittering when she looked up. She licked him and felt him jerk under her. She licked him again. He moaned. She liked making him moan. She flicked her tongue down the length of his shaft. She licked back up. She drew him into her mouth. A tiny bit. A bit more. She could feel him swelling. That's how he knew to tease, she thought with satisfaction, to bring her to the brink. So she stopped.

She looked at his face, and saw exactly what she'd felt when he'd done it to her. She took him in her mouth again. Stopped again. But when she went to do it again, he caught her by surprise, his arms on her waist, pulling her up his body, positioning her, and instead of her mouth, the pulsing tip of him was inside her and she forgot all about teasing and slid down on him and set about riding them both hard to a climax that felt as if it turned her inside out.

She forgot to be careful but he did not. He lifted her clear of him as he came. Wrapping her hand around him to capture the last pulsing of his seed, Kate felt a deep sense of loss.

Time marched relentlessly on. They touched but did not speak. Words were pointless. They had said everything. Kate resented every moment that passed, hated every minute which brought them closer to the hour of his departure.

They made their way, still silent, back to the big house. One last kiss at the door. Bittersweet. More bitter than sweet. She would not cry in front of him. In the morning she must say a composed goodbye. Covering her mouth with her hand, Kate fled up the stairs to her bedchamber.

She did not sleep. Heavy-eyed but determined to say farewell with the dignity Virgil expected of her, Kate was dressed and downstairs for breakfast by seven the next morning, but he was already gone.

'The mail leaves the Rothermere Arms at seven,' Giles told her.

'He told me nine. Did he leave a message?'

'Said all that was proper.' Her brother drew her one of his sharp looks. 'Was there something in particular you were expecting him to say?'

'No.' Kate poured herself a cup of coffee. Her hands shook. She sat down at the table and began to pick at a bread roll.

'I liked him, Kate. He's a sensible man. An impressive one. But...' Giles broke off frowning, and took a long draught from his tankard. 'I hate to agree with our aunt, but in this she was right. It would never do.'

'I know that.' Giles pressed her hand. It was this small token of affection, so very unlike him, which was Kate's undoing. 'I know!' she said, dashing her hand over her eyes, for to cry in front of him would be to admit that there was something to cry about and how could there be?

Kate pushed her cup aside. Coffee splattered over the polished surface of the table. 'I must get on. I have a hundred things to do today,' she said, and fled from the room.

There was no sanctuary in her bedchamber, where Daisy was making up the bed. 'Mrs Landes-Fraser was looking for you, my lady,' the chambermaid told her. 'Said to tell you that she was going over to inspect the Dower House to make sure all is well for the lady's arrival tomorrow, and that she'd expect you there at your convenience. I told her I was sure you'd got everything under control, but you know what she's like, Lady Kate. Thinks no one can do anything properly but herself.'

Kate liked Daisy, and encouraged the girl, who was in her opinion far too bright to earn her living as a servant, to work at her lessons with a view to helping Miss Thomson out at the school. This morning, however, she managed only a perfunctory smile. She couldn't face her aunt yet. She couldn't face anyone at the moment. Alone in her bed last night, she'd worked so hard at persuading herself that Virgil's leaving was not the momentous event it felt. Finding him gone had made her face up to the fact that she'd retained a tiny sliver of hope that he would stay. With that hope extinguished, she was forced to admit that she had wished for more. A lot more.

'If my aunt asks, you haven't seen me,' she told Daisy. 'I'm going for a swim.'

It didn't do much good. Her thoughts circled as she made her laps of the lake, but the usual calm which the physical effort of swimming invariably gave her failed to descend. She understood that he had left without seeing her again to spare them both pain, but she couldn't help wondering if he was running away.

As she abraded her icy skin with a towel in the little changing room under the fishing pavilion, shivering, her numbed fingers struggling with the ties of her garters, she told herself she was being irrational. She pulled her gown over her head and began to wrestle with the fastenings.

'To be sure,' she muttered to herself, 'Virgil Jackson is a fascinating person but there are surely lots of equally fascinating people in the world.' Though not another who had understood her the way he had. 'That is simply because I've never confided in anyone else,' she told her shoes firmly, slipping her cold feet into them. 'Virgil is gone and will not be coming back. I should be grateful to have met him, and I won't forget him, and absolutely will never forget last night, but I must put all these other silly thoughts out of my head else I will end up a weeping willow with absolutely no cause.' She nodded decisively. 'It is a mistake to waste energy on things one cannot control. Far better that I focus on what I can. Like making sure that this poor woman is given the welcome she deserves. Always assuming she deserves it. Which I must do, until it is proved otherwise. So that is what I shall do,' she told the changing room door staunchly.

Closing it behind her, quite convinced, for the moment, that she meant every word she said, Kate strode off towards the Dower House to see what havoc her aunt had wreaked in her absence.

* * *

It would have been some consolation to Kate to know that Virgil was having a similarly difficult time in rationalising his feelings. Thinking him by now well on the way to Manchester, she would have been extremely surprised to learn that he had in fact been forced to delay his departure by at least one and likely two days. Snow had come suddenly and unseasonably early in the north and the mail coach had fallen victim the day before, breaking an axle, delaying its journey south and thus its return journey north, so the landlord of the Rothermere Arms explained to him.

It had been a wrench to leave Castonbury without saying goodbye to Kate, though he had no doubt it was for the best. It would be a mistake to return, no matter how much he longed to do so. For Kate's sake, he told himself. He would like to reassure himself that she was coping. But that putative relative of hers arrived tomorrow, and they had, after all, said their goodbyes.

Sitting in the private parlour he had bespoken at the inn, Virgil tried to distract himself with business, but images of Kate smiling, laughing, frowning, Kate kissing and Kate swimming and Kate lying in his arms, and Kate crying out as she climaxed, crowded his head. He put aside his notes on the new venture with Josiah

Wedgwood and turned to a collection of recent essays by Robert Owen on the formation of the human character.

It was not easy, but Virgil was a very determined man, and by the time dinner was served, he was quite caught up on Owen's *New View of Society*.

The Dowager Marchioness of Hatherton arrived in the ducal landau the next morning, having been collected by John Coachman from the Rothermere Arms, where the London mail had deposited her. It being another pleasant day, the hood of the carriage was down. As John Coachman brought the horses to a halt, and Joe Coyle opened the door with a flourish, Kate thought for a moment that the woman inside looked terrified. But when she looked again, her countenance was smooth and shyly smiling.

Giles was making a stiff bow. 'Welcome to Castonbury.'

Ross had not underplayed the lady's charms, was Kate's first thought. Jamie's wife was very pretty indeed. Petite, slender and angelically fair, she had a pair of blue eyes which Kate had no difficulty at all in believing Jamie had fallen victim to. Her travelling dress was neat but shabby, several seasons out of date, but she carried herself with dignity, and her smile was just the correct mix of confidence and deference.

'This is Lady Katherine, my sister, who has been making all the arrangements for you and your boy, ma'am.'

Giles's introduction was cool. Despite the fact that her brother was dead set against inheriting the title, he seemed also dead set on proving this woman a sham. It made Kate all the more determined to welcome her. She beamed, and instead of dropping a curtsey, enfolded her new relative in a warm hug. 'You must call me Kate, since we are to be sisters,' she said, unable to resist casting a defiant look at Giles over her shoulder.

'Then you must call me Alicia, if you please. I don't feel entitled to call myself a dowager marchioness, for Jamie and I were married such a brief time.'

'Long enough,' Giles said shortly. 'Is this the boy?'

The child, whom John Coachman had lifted down, shrank against his mother's skirts. 'Yes, this is Crispin James. He is a little tired from the journey, my lord.'

Giles eyed the child with obvious scepticism. Fair-haired like his mother, he had also inherited her blue eyes, but his features had still too much of a chubby infant about them to be definitive in any way. 'They all look the same to me at that age, he could be anyone's.'

'Giles! For heaven's sake...'

'Please, my lady—I mean, Kate—it's perfectly natural that your brother should question.... I am sure this has been a shock to you, as indeed Jamie's death was a shock to me. I did not expect to be coming here to Castonbury under such circumstances. It is such a—a— I find it difficult to believe that one day all this will belong to my son.'

'*If* he is proved also to be my brother's son,' Giles said, unmoved by the flutter of a lace handkerchief over a pair of big blue eyes drowned in tears.

'You must forgive my brother, he is a little overwrought,' Kate said, putting a protective arm around the widow. 'Now, come into the house and meet the rest of the family.' She held out her hand to the little boy, giving him a warm smile. 'Monsieur André, our chef, has made a special treat just for you. A sugar castle, what do you think of that?'

The child's eyes widened in astonishment. Waiting only for a nod from his mama, he took Kate's hand and tripped happily up the sweep of stairs into the magnificence of the marble hall, which had been opened up in preference to the usual entranceway downstairs for the occasion.

The Duke of Rothermere himself it was who had insisted on the formal line-up of Castonbury servants to greet the new heir. Kate stopped short in the doorway at the sight of the military line of menservants on one side, women on the other, and her father seated in state at the top with Aunt Wilhelmina in regal purple, not one but three nodding ostrich feathers in her turban, standing behind him like a queen consort. No wonder Giles was in a mood. Papa was making it very clear where his alliances were. Poor Giles, Kate thought. And come to that, poor Alicia, who was like to lose her precious child if her father had anything to do with it.

Chapter Ten

With Alicia settled in the Dower House and her most pressing duties over, Kate wanted to escape, and decided to go for a drive. It was John Coachman who told her. 'Snow in the north,' he said as he got the gig ready for her. 'That Mr Jackson's been kicking his heels at the inn for two days now.'

'Mr Jackson?'

'Aye, my lady. Though it looks like he'll be off tomorrow right enough. Weather's turned again. You know what it's like at this time of year.'

'Mr Jackson is still here?'

'Didn't you know, my lady?'

'No,' Kate replied, 'I did not. I wonder why he—oh, Alicia, of course.'

'My lady?'

'John, I'm sorry, I was talking to myself. I shan't need the gig, I've changed my mind.'

She hurried off in the direction of the village. Virgil was still here at Castonbury. It was because of Alicia. He knew Alicia was arriving today, that was why he had not been in touch.

As she made her way along the path through the woods, it occurred to her that perhaps he had stayed away for another reason. He had not said goodbye for fear of upsetting her. He would be worried that another goodbye would be more upsetting, no doubt, but truly, he was quite wrong. Since he had left, she had been perfectly fine.

Apart from the lack of sleep, but that was nothing, completely irrelevant. Everyone had sleepless nights. Besides, Virgil would be wondering how Alicia had been received. She could reassure him and bring him up to date and say goodbye in a civilised manner all in one visit. It would be wrong of her to forego the opportunity to do so. Very wrong indeed.

Albert Moffat, the landlord of the Rothermere Arms, raked a hand through his wiry thatch of salt-and-pepper hair. 'Mr Jackson, yes, he's here all right. He's in the best parlour, my lady. If you'll wait here, I'll go and fetch him.'

Now that she had arrived, Kate's confidence was beginning to falter. Virgil had made his feelings quite clear, and he was not a man who liked to have his hand forced.

But it was too late, she was here now, and he was so tantalisingly close she could not go away without one last chance to see him.

'I shall announce myself,' she told Albert, 'I know the way.' Without giving herself the chance to change her mind—or indeed Virgil the opportunity to refuse her—Kate ran quickly up the stairs, tapped lightly on the door and pushed it open.

'Kate! What are you doing here?'

'Good afternoon, Virgil. I heard you were delayed. The snow. And I thought you would wish for news of how Alicia's arrival went. And I thought that— You did not say goodbye.'

Virgil had been trying to work. He had been only partially successful. He had never before found it difficult to concentrate; his utter focus had been one of the keys to his success. He blamed the noise of the inn. He blamed the inconvenience of the delay. It was frustrating, to be frittering his time away here. He blamed himself for having taken so much time away from business while staying at Castonbury. He was out of the habit of work, but it would come back to him if he persisted. So he had persisted. He just needed to persist a bit more. What he didn't need was Kate, her skin flushed from the cold, looking at him with her chin tilted in that defiant way of hers, looking at him as if she was half afraid he might show her straight out the door, half wishing he would kiss her.

She was dressed more elegantly than usual. Not her customary riding habit but a dress of dark claret trimmed with black beadwork. Instead of her usual jacket she wore a full-length fitted pelisse with very tight sleeves. The simple lines suited her svelte figure. He wished he didn't remember every lean line of her. The elegant curve of her neck. The long, supple length of her legs. Virgil got to his feet slowly. 'You shouldn't have come.' Which was true, but he couldn't find it in him to regret that she had. 'But you're here now. Come in and tell me the news.'

She remained leaning against the door. 'You need not worry. I'm perfectly fine. I have not come here to—to cause a scene.'

He had to laugh at that. 'I can think of nothing more unlikely.'

Still she did not move. 'I am quite resigned to your going, Virgil. In fact, that is one of the reasons I'm here. To—to reassure you.'

He held out his hand. 'I'd be more reassured if you came over here to the fire. It's freezing out.'

Kate took a couple of steps into the room. 'I went for a swim the other morning.'

'And you didn't turn into an icicle?' She was nervous, Virgil realised. The last time they'd been together—best not to think about that. He smiled at her, more warmly this time. 'Come over to the fire, Kate. You should have stayed away, but there's no harm done. We're in a public inn, we're hardly likely to— I mean, I won't—we won't…' What he had to do was stop thinking about it. 'Tell me about Alicia. And your aunt. Is she still talking to you?'

Kate finally left the door, unbuttoned her pelisse and cast it carelessly over a chair, before sitting opposite Virgil at the fire. 'No. She addresses everything through whoever else happens to be in the room. "Lumsden, you will inform Lady Katherine," she says, or "Giles, you will instruct your sister not to," and once, when there was no one else, it was, "Margaret, you will let Lady Katherine know,"' she said with a chuckle.

'Who is Margaret?'

'Daisy, but my aunt will not lower herself to remembering the names of the housemaids, so she calls them all Margaret. She always has. Oh, Virgil, the day after the ball she gave me such a lecture—it was so absurd, I wish you could have heard it. According to her I am ungrateful, immoral and undutiful. I'm not exactly sure where it is I can expect to end my days in exile, but according to Aunt Wilhelmina, it is some sort of frozen wasteland full of old maids with only cats for company and gruel to eat.'

'The Dower House, does she mean?'

'Oh, no, that is far too close.'

Virgil cursed under his breath as an awkward silence fell. Why had he mentioned the Dower House? Now they were both thinking of that night. That bed. 'And your father?' he asked, grasping at the subject most likely to quench any thoughts of passion. 'How did he receive his grandson?'

Kate rolled her eyes. 'With all the pomp and ceremony you'd expect. He had the entire household lined up to welcome them, though he did not, incidentally, deign to speak to me. Unless I apologise on bended knee, I doubt he ever will, which is absolutely fine by me.'

'And what do you think of her, your brother's wife-apparent?'

Kate pursed her lips. 'I'm not sure. She is very pretty, but she is no mere cipher. I would say she is holding her own. She was quite happy to have little Crispin—that is the child, named for my father, which needless to say has confirmed him in his belief that the boy cannot be anything other than his legitimate flesh and blood, though she could have easily picked the name by looking up the title in *Debrett's Peerage*. Anyway, she allowed the boy to be dandled on my father's knee, and tomorrow, I believe, the pair of them are to be given a tour of the house, but she was quite adamant that she have sole care of the child in the Dower House. The ducal cradle in the Castonbury nursery remains empty. Not but what the child is far too old for a cradle.'

Virgil began to relax. He had missed Kate's acerbic tongue and caustic wit. He had missed her conversation, and the way she told a story. She always viewed things from a different angle, usually a wholly unexpected one. There could be no harm in talking, after all. They were only talking. He sat back in his chair and stretched his legs out towards the fire. Kate had on short boots today of black leather. He could see them peeping out from under her skirts. Her feet were narrow, high-arched. Her stockings would be black, too, he reckoned. She'd told him once they were her favourite. He caught himself just in time as he began to speculate about what colour her corsets were. 'And was your father right? Does the child look anything like your brother?'

'Lord, what do I know? I think one blond-haired mop- pet looks very much like another at that age, though nat- urally my aunt disagrees, and as you know, my father had already made up his mind before they arrived any- way. Alicia is having her lawyer review the trust deed, incidentally, and the guardianship too.'

Virgil raised his eyebrows. 'Another female in the

Castonbury household who will not fall into line. Your father will not be amused. Either the widow has an astute business head on her shoulders, or she doesn't trust your family.'

'Would you? If my father had his way—but Giles will make sure he does not. He believes that the child needs his mother, which I have to confess rather surprised me.'

'Do *you* think she's a fraud?' Virgil asked.

Kate shrugged. 'Like Giles, I find it very difficult to believe that Jamie would have married without telling us. He is—he was—the heir to a dukedom, and no matter how pretty and astute she may be, Alicia is, in my father's terms, a nobody.'

'Perhaps your brother was in love?'

'And knowing that my father would forbid the match, he simply decided not to ask for permission? It's possible, I suppose, only from what I gather they had not known each other very long.' Kate pursed her lips. 'Alicia does not talk like a woman in love—at least, she most certainly does not go starry-eyed when she mentions Jamie, and she does not actually mention him very often. *Can* you fall in love upon such short acquaintance?'

The question hung in the air between them for a few seconds, before Kate rushed on. 'It is different in wartime, I expect. Under normal circumstances—but there is no point in speculating about it for it is quite beside the point and— Oh, the funniest thing, when I was discussing the matter with Giles and I asked him if he had sought Papa's permission to marry Lily, he said, "Of course not! Who I marry is my own business" in that snappy way of his.'

'Why *has* Giles not married Lily yet? I had the impression he was very eager to tie the knot. What is he waiting for?'

'The resolution of Jamie's affairs. At present Giles is still nominally the heir, and so tied to Castonbury. Neither he nor Lily wish to make their home there, and so until matters become clearer they have chosen to wait. It is one of the many things which makes my brother ill-tempered, but I cannot blame him. He must feel as if his life is suspended, and not his own.'

Her voice trailed away. She was nervous again, looking not at him, but into the fire. Her hands smoothed her gown. She always did that when she was thinking. What *was* she thinking? Virgil wondered. 'So, Giles is still determined not to allow this child to step into your brother's shoes, then? Even though the last thing he wishes is to inherit himself?'

'He certainly doesn't want to live there after he is married. Jamie loved the place, he was raised knowing it would all be his one day. It's different for Giles,' Kate said, still staring into the flames.

'He told me once that Castonbury stifles him.'

'Did he?' Kate looked up. Her smile was crooked. 'I can certainly understand that. I know it's fanciful, but there are times when I feel that every one of our ancestors in those portraits which line the guest corridor are looking at me disapprovingly.'

'I don't think you fanciful at all—they do the same to me. Kate, you won't let them turn you into...'

'Aunt Wilhelmina? Can you see me in a turban?'

'Don't joke, you know what I mean.'

She nodded slowly. 'You asked me before, remember? That night at the Dower House, you asked me, and I said I would try. And I will, Virgil, but I cannot pretend it will be anything other than a battle. I think—I can see now, mostly thanks to you, that there are different ways of fighting. I can never be what they want me to be, but I don't have to be so confrontational about it, and I certainly don't have to feel guilty about it. You were right about that—despite what I thought, I do still wish to please my father, and it's an impossible task.'

'What of your aunt?'

'*That* is not so clear-cut. She is neither malicious nor a despot. I do believe that she means well, but she will never really understand me. Perhaps we can reach a détente, I don't know.'

'You will be happy, Kate?' It was only as he said it

that Virgil realised how much it mattered to him. If he could know she was happy, it would make it easier to go. He had no doubt he was doing the right thing—it had not crossed his mind that there was any other way—but if he could be sure that Kate felt it too...

'Kate?'

'You ask a lot of me. I have never been one to lament what I cannot change. I mean my situation,' she added hurriedly, 'not you. I shall keep on with my own projects, but I cannot ignore the fact that I owe my father my bread and butter and, while Castonbury is my home, I still have a duty to perform at least some *auntly* tasks. I shall be content enough. What about you, Virgil?'

Now she did look at him directly. Her eyes were more blue than grey today. When she looked at him like that, he always felt she saw too much. 'I shall be content enough,' he said, choosing to echo her own words. 'When I return to Boston, I'm planning to make a fresh start on my plans. Once I've seen New Lanark for myself, I'll have a better idea of what I want to do. And there is the new business with Josiah too. I will have plenty to keep me occupied.'

He sounded bleak. Why did he sound so bleak? He needed to get on, that's what it was. All his plans, he was anxious to put them into motion. He didn't like the way Kate was looking at him. As if she didn't believe him. As if she felt sorry for him. Why should she feel sorry for him? Perhaps if he told her about his business in Glasgow, then she'd understand that he really was making a new beginning. Then she would see, as he did, that he was putting the past behind him and building a whole new future. She needed to be reassured, that was all. He could do that quite easily.

'I haven't explained,' Virgil said, getting to his feet, 'what it is that takes me to Glasgow.'

'You said it was business.'

'There is always business,' he said with a grin, 'but it's more than that. Wait here.' He returned a moment later with the locket from his portmanteau, and handed it to her.

It was a simple piece of jewellery. A hinged oval of chased gold decorated with sapphires. Kate had gone quite pale as she held it in her hand. 'Is it Millie's?'

'No!' It hadn't even occurred to him that she would think that. The denial came out far too harshly. Kate flinched. 'Of course it's not Millie's,' Virgil said in a quieter voice. 'What would a slave have been doing with something so valuable?'

'I'm sorry, I just assumed…'

'It belonged to Malcolm Jackson. To be completely accurate, it belonged to Malcolm Jackson's betrothed. That's her inside. Here, let me show you.' He took the locket from her and opened it, then returned it to her. On one side was a miniature executed in watercolours, somewhat faded. On the other side was a lock of hair. 'Louisa Gordon, that was her name,' Virgil said, squatting down beside Kate's chair. 'She wanted to marry him before he left Scotland for America, but he was set upon making a home for her first, and left her behind. She was killed in a carriage accident about a year later. The letter telling him of her death crossed his asking her to come to him, he told me.'

'That's tragic.' Kate touched the lock of hair. It was brown, slightly lighter than her own. Louisa's eyes were brown too. 'And your Mr Jackson, he never married. He must have loved her very much.'

'I guess,' Virgil said uncomfortably. 'The point is, he asked me to bring this back, to bury it beside her.'

'So that he could feel he was with her, you mean? Your Mr Jackson sounds as if he was quite the romantic. How he must have repented leaving her behind. I feel sure she would have preferred to be with him in the New World, no matter how difficult or dangerous. I feel sure he underestimated her. Look at her, she has a very determined set to her mouth.'

'Kate, you can't know that. It's just a picture, and poorly executed at that. She died almost forty years ago.'

'And he never forgot her.'

'More likely he discovered that he was perfectly content without her. He could easily have married if he wanted to.'

Kate shut the locket with a snap. 'Why did you show me this?'

Virgil took it from her and slipped it into his coat pocket as he got to his feet. She was angry. What had he said to make her angry? He tugged at his neck cloth. He'd sent Watson back to London, but somehow he'd got into the valet's habit of tying it too tight. 'I thought you'd understand. When he asked me to bury the locket, I didn't plan to come all this way across the Atlantic just for that obviously, but the opportunity to do business with Josiah came up, and I read about New Lanark, and it was as though—I felt it was the chance to make a fresh start.'

'To bury the past, you mean?'

'Yes.'

'But it's not your past, it's Malcolm Jackson's,' Kate said with a frown. 'When you talked about your future a few moments ago, it was all about schools and libraries and houses. How many must you build before you forgive yourself, Virgil?'

'You asked me that before, and I told you. I can never forgive myself.'

'Then burying a locket won't make you free,' Kate said sadly as she got to her feet and picked up her pelisse.

'What about you, Kate?' Virgil grabbed her by the arm and spun her towards him. 'You wouldn't have to worry about dwindling into an aunt if you married. You could leave Castonbury, have your own home, your own family, but you won't, will you? Because you can't forgive yourself either, can you? Admit it, there's a bit of you that thinks you deserve your fate, isn't there? And there's a bit of you that thinks every man you meet is like Lord Anthony Featherstone. And there's another bit of you that's afraid, is there not? Between that cold-blooded family of yours and that ambitious bastard you were betrothed to, they've got you thinking that no one could love you. Well, isn't there?'

'Why are you shouting at me? Why are you so angry? You have no right to tell me what I should or shouldn't do with my life.'

'Any more than you have to tell me, but that didn't stop you.'

'You have it all wrong. I'm not at all afraid of—of love,' Kate said furiously. 'I could marry if I chose to, I have not lacked offers. I simply don't choose to, that is all. You sound as if you want me to throw myself at the first man who comes my way.'

'I don't.' He didn't want to think of her with any other

man, but he knew that was wrong. 'Kate, don't cry. I didn't mean to make you cry.'

'I'm not crying,' she said, scrubbing at her eyes with the backs of her hands.

Virgil pulled out his kerchief and dabbed at her cheeks. 'I just want you to be happy.'

'I don't need a man to make me happy, any more than you need a woman.' Kate sniffed. 'You are right, I should not have come here today.'

'Don't say that. Kate, I just— I want— Oh, hell, Kate don't cry. Don't go. Not like this.' He didn't mean to but he couldn't not. His arms went around her. He dragged her hard, tight up against him, and he kissed her.

If she had not kissed him back. If she had not been so upset. If she had not thrown all those things at him that he didn't want to hear, he wouldn't have had to block them out. If she hadn't looked so tragic and so brave at the same time. If he hadn't been thinking of her day and night since he left her. Then…then he would have been able to stop.

But she did kiss him back. And she made that little noise that sent the blood rushing to his groin. And her kisses were so angry and so hungry, just exactly like his own. She savaged him with her mouth and he thrust his tongue into hers. She arched against him; he pushed her up against the door, the better to mould her to him.

She said his name, the way no one else said his name, and he said hers, the name which could only be hers. Passion consumed them. He hadn't thought it was possible to burn so hot and so high so quickly. There was no gentle build, no slow burn, but a white-hot searing which made him achingly hard and had her panting, her fingers clutching at him, tugging at his clothes without any sort of finesse.

'We can't, not here,' he said, at the same time as he pulled her clear of the door only to ram a wooden chair under the handle.

'Albert could walk in at any time,' Kate agreed, as she unbuttoned his waistcoat and yanked it with his coat down over his arms.

They staggered, entwined and kissing frantically, towards the table. Virgil lifted her onto it. Her dress buttoned up the front. Tiny buttons. He tried to undo them, but they defeated him and so he pulled at the fabric, scattering jet buttons across the floor. Her corsets underneath were black silk. 'Sweet heaven, Kate. If anyone knew how you look underneath. Have you any idea what it does to me?' He breathed in the sweet scent of her, kissing her throat, and down, to the mound of her breasts. Her skin was flushed. He could feel her heart hammering. Same as his own.

Kate moaned. She yanked at Virgil's shirt. 'Take this off. I want to see you. Take it *off.*'

He pulled it quickly over his head and tossed it over his shoulder. The action drew in his abdomen, making his chest expand. She could count the muscles. He was like velvet. Every time she saw his skin that's what she thought of. Dark, luscious velvet that cried out to be touched. His muscles weren't sinewy but round and hard. She hadn't ever seen muscles like that. She was so tense she thought she might break. Hot and shivery. Throbbing and fluttering.

He pulled her back to him, to the edge of the table, and kissed her again. Her hands stroked and plucked at his skin, his shoulders, his chest, his nipples, the shadow of his rib cage. She didn't have enough hands. His lips were hot on hers, and hard. He rucked up her dress. 'Black,' he said, looking at her stockings with satisfaction. 'I knew they would be black.'

His hands stroked up to the flesh at the top of her stockings, then hovered over her sex. 'I don't want you, Virgil,' Kate said, digging her nails into his shoulders. Still he hovered. 'I don't need you,' she said.

With his other hand, he pushed her skirts higher. 'You don't need any man,' he agreed, stroking her.

'No.' It was a struggle to keep her eyes open, but she managed it, holding his gaze, tawny rimmed with gold.

He had hardly touched her, but she was struggling to contain her release. 'I don't.'

'You don't,' Virgil agreed.

He kissed her mouth hard. Then he tipped her, suddenly, back onto the table, and dropped down to his knees before her, and licked into her. She cried out as his tongue flicked over her sensitive flesh. She could have sworn he made sparks shoot out. It felt like all her blood rushed to that single spot as he licked and sucked, and she tumbled, headlong and out of control, shoving her fist into her mouth to stop herself from screaming.

Virgil pulled her towards him, sliding his finger inside her, feeling the clenching of her climax around him. She pulled at his wrist, put his finger in her mouth, then kissed him, mingling the taste of them, the essence of her. He thought he would explode, the way she did it. Deliberate. Challenging.

'I don't need you,' she said, her voice husky with sex.

He needed to be inside her. Urgently. 'No more than I need you,' Virgil said, unfastening his buckskins, pulling her to the very edge of the table, wrapping her legs around his thighs, and entering her, pushing right into her, into the sleek, slick heat of her, in one thrust.

Her eyes darkened. She said his name. Urgent, just as he felt. She wrapped her arms around his neck. She tightened her ankles around his waist and tilted so that he pushed higher inside her.

Her eyes were fixed on his. She clenched around him, holding him completely still. He let her, for a moment. Then he moved and her eyes widened. He slipped his hands under her bottom to lift her, and thrust. Her hands were icy on his neck. He thrust again, and felt the delicious eddy of her climax. Another thrust, and she gave a muffled groan, and it was like being caught in a maelstrom inside her. He was whipped up, tossed high, pounded, helpless. He lost control, thrusting into her again and again until it took him, too, and at that moment he would have given anything to be able to spill himself into her. But he pulled himself free just in time, and afterwards, as he held her, clutched tight around him, he had never felt emptier.

Kate sat on the edge of the table, stunned by what had happened. Virgil was pulling on his clothes. She tried to fasten her gown, but half the buttons seemed to be missing. It didn't matter, she could button her pelisse over it. She couldn't believe what they'd just done, in Albert Moffat's best parlour. If she was a different kind of woman she would be ashamed of herself. If Virgil was a different kind of man…

If he was a different man, he wouldn't be Virgil. She retied one of her garters and made a vague attempt to pat her hair into order. She most likely looked as if she'd been dragged through a hedge backwards, but she couldn't bring herself to care. She dragged her pelisse over her dress and fastened it.

This time, she had no doubt it was goodbye. At the Dower House, she realised, she'd still had some hope. She had none now, but still she felt a sadistic urge just to make sure. 'It is impossible, isn't it?'

Virgil had been looking out of the window while she dressed, but he turned now, and came to stand beside her, taking her hands. He held them against his chest, bracing her. She didn't want him to brace her; it meant he thought she was going to be hurt. 'Don't answer that,' Kate said hurriedly. 'I know the answer.'

'You will take care of yourself, won't you, Kate?'

She nodded. 'And you.' She pinned a smile to her face. 'I will see myself out. Don't watch me go. I won't look back.'

She thought he would kiss her again. She thought it was something akin to pain she saw in his eyes, but it was gone before she could be sure. 'Goodbye, Kate.'

'Goodbye, Virgil.'

He pulled the chair away from the door and opened it

for her. Kate made her way down the stairs of the inn, feeling as though she were descending into Hades. She didn't look back.

She did not remember the walk back to Castonbury. In her bedchamber, she rang the bell for Polly and a bath, then sank down on the window seat as the tub was filled. She was aware of Polly casting her anxious looks, and thankful that she said nothing until the bath was ready, the screens draped with towels set up by the fire.

For once, she allowed Polly to help her undress. 'What happened to your gown? You look as if you've been in a fight.'

Kate shook her head, biting her lip. Tears again. What was the point in tears? She had nothing at all to cry about. 'Nothing. I don't want to talk about it.' She sank gratefully into the depths of the lavender-scented water.

'I heard Mr Jackson was still at the inn. Snow, I heard, though it's to clear by the morning.'

Kate said nothing.

'John Coachman said you didn't take the gig. He said you went walking instead. Did you see him? Mr Jackson, I mean.'

'Yes,' Kate said with a sigh. 'I did. I wanted to say goodbye.'

'You didn't— I hope you were careful, my lady.

There's ways and means if you weren't, but they're not pleasant and they don't always work.'

She considered pretending ignorance, but Polly was too perceptive and Kate was a terrible liar. 'There's no need to worry. Virgil was—was careful.'

Polly nodded. 'He's a good man, but it wouldn't have done, my lady. They would never have tolerated it.'

'There was never any question of that, Polly. It was just—we were just— I am not in love with him, and he's certainly not in love with me. It was just—what did you call it? A fling. And now it's over, and I'm fine. I'm absolutely fine.'

'Of course you are, my lady. You don't need him. You don't need any man.'

'No, I don't,' Kate said. Her lip quivered. It was ironic that the only person in the world—in her world—who knew her well enough to see beyond her words was a woman who had spent the better part of her life selling her body on the streets of London. She burst into tears.

Kate spent the following days keeping extremely busy, ensuring that Alicia was comfortable in the Dower House, taking her and the child on short drives around the countryside when the weather permitted, keeping out of Aunt Wilhelmina's way and reviewing her plans for extending the Castonbury school. She did not think, would not let herself think, about Virgil, in the daylight hours. She was bright and cheerful and useful, and that was enough, she told herself. At night it was a different matter. She did not cry, but she ached. Under cover of darkness she could admit that she missed him, but that was as far as she would go. She would not hope or even dream. There was no point and no need. She was lonely here at Castonbury, but she had always been lonely. It was just she hadn't noticed before.

In Scotland, Virgil emerged from the noise of the mill house at New Lanark in much the same frame of mind. Three waterwheels and thousands of spindles worked by over five hundred people made it a noisy place, no matter how light and clean it was in comparison to other mills. Walking down the main thoroughfare of the model village, he passed the other two mill buildings and headed towards the school which formed the kernel of Owen's Institute for the Formation of Character. There were aspects of his host's philosophy with which Virgil disagreed, but he was awed by the man's vision and utterly convinced by his arguments that education was fundamental to social reform. This visit had given him ideas enough to last him decades.

Through the windows of the school, he could see the little ones at their desks, their faces rapt with attention as James Buchanan, weaver turned teacher, told them a story. He had intended going in to take more notes, but a restlessness kept him going down the cobbled road towards the majestic Falls of Clyde, thinking for the thousandth time how much Kate would have enjoyed this visit. It wasn't that he missed her so much as that he regretted the missed opportunity. He would have liked to have seen her reaction to it all, heard her opinions of it—which would be bound *not* to be anything like he imagined. Without her, the experience was somehow less than he expected.

Autumn was almost over this far north. The trees which bordered the falls were bereft of leaves. There was a decided nip to the air. The cascade which frothed and thundered over the river on its way down to propel the water wheels which powered the mills was mesmerising. The spray was icy. It made him think of the lake at Castonbury. The lake made him think of Kate, though not even she would consider swimming in water this cold. Kate, nymph-like and naked, her wet skin gleaming. Kate kissing him. Kate, hot and damp for him. Kate's climax, the look of shocked delight on her face. The jolting pleasure of his own release.

Virgil swore, and began the by now tried and tested process of forgetting about Kate by thinking of other things. He had plans now, thanks to Robert Owen, not for just one village but for a whole string of institutes and schools.

How much would ever be enough? Kate's question haunted him. This was what he'd worked for so tirelessly these past eleven years. This was what would start to make good some of his guilt for what he had done to Millie. So why was he feeling so down? Not just down, but tired, worn out, his energy sapped. The future he had worked so hard for, the castle he had built in the air which was now within his reach, they had lost their appeal. It wasn't that he didn't want it all, the schools and all the rest of it, but he did keep wondering, damn it, if he could ever do enough.

He was tired of carrying the burden of guilt around with him, but he couldn't see it ever easing. Why was he so tired? Was he being punished for having broken faith with his celibacy? Until he met Kate, it was a pact he had never thought of breaking. Well, Kate was in the past now, and so he would have no trouble keeping to it again. He wouldn't ever hold her again. Or kiss her. Or hear her laugh. Or…

Virgil jumped to his feet with an exclamation of disgust. What he had to do was get on with his life. He would go to Glasgow tomorrow. He would put his past to rest. And today, he would write to Kate and tell her all about New Lanark. He owed her that much.

Chapter Eleven

The grey December sky reflected Kate's mood. It was not raining but the air was damp and it was cold. It looked like it might rain, it looked as if it might clear up, it couldn't make up its mind. Ambivalent. Could weather be ambivalent? More like confused, she thought, that's what she was. She was sitting in the dining room drinking a cup of cold coffee when Lumsden informed her that Giles wished to see her as soon as conveniently possible.

Thinking that her aunt must have lodged another complaint, Kate made her way to her brother's private study with a heavy heart.

'You look tired,' Giles said.

'Can't sleep,' Kate replied, in quite his own terse style.

Giles grinned. 'Mind my own business, you mean. Well, I will, since I've a hundred other things to think about, provided you can assure me you've done nothing new to set our aunt off.'

'She seems quite taken up with little Crispin,' Kate said, dodging the question.

Her brother gave her one of his searching looks, but Kate returned it blandly, and he shrugged. 'We've had a letter from Harry,' he said. 'He sent it from Madrid. It's—well, interesting. Here, read it for yourself.'

Kate unfolded the missive. Harry's scrawl, unusually for a man who most often considered three or four lines sufficient, covered the entire sheet of paper, leaving barely enough room for his signature. The contents were, as Giles had said, interesting. 'So there's hope, then, that he might get the evidence he needs to prove Jamie's death?'

'Looks like it. If he does, at least it means we'll be able to access the funds.'

'And you may be a step closer to marrying Lily.'

'I wish it were more than a step. This waiting is the very devil,' Giles said grimly. 'Let us not talk about my affairs, it is frankly too painful. I haven't told Father about the letter. His health is still so frail. If Harry can't track down this chap in Seville, if it proves another false lead, then we're back to where we started. I haven't said anything to our aunt either.'

'Quite right. Aunt Wilhelmina wouldn't be able to resist telling Papa. It's best to keep this to ourselves until we have more certain news.'

'Good. I'm glad you agree with me, I was pretty sure you would.' Giles folded the letter up and tucked it into a drawer in his desk under a pile of other papers. 'What about the widow though? I don't feel right keeping it from her. Apart from anything else, if Harry can talk to this chap, the one who was with Jamie at the end, it may well be that it helps her cause. He'd have been bound to mention his marriage, wouldn't he?'

'I don't know. What do you think, are you still sceptical of her claim?'

'Honestly?' Giles locked the drawer. 'She seems genuine. She's not a money-grabber, though she's protective of the boy's rights, and that's natural enough. I could wish she did not allow him so often in the company of our father, but I can't deny it gives him pleasure. But honestly, Kate? I just can't get rid of the feeling that there's something—I don't know, something not right about Jamie's death. If we could just get the full story—but I won't count on it, not until we hear from Harry again.'

'Nor I.' Kate touched his hand briefly in sympathy. They were not a demonstrative family; this was the nearest she could imagine to hugging Giles. She hadn't noticed, not until she met Virgil, how little physical contact she had with anyone. 'We'll just have to bide our time and hope that Harry comes through, one way or another. In the meantime, do you wish me to tell Alicia the news?'

'If you would. It will be better coming from a woman.'

'Which means it will save you the bother of coping with her tears,' Kate said, laughing. 'Tell me, Giles, do you run the other way when Lily cries?'

'No, I try to make damn sure she has no cause to,' her brother retorted.

She almost ran into Aunt Wilhelmina on the staircase. 'I am going to Buxton with your sister-in-law,' Mrs Landes-Fraser, who had thawed enough since Alicia's arrival to address Kate directly once more, informed her. 'His Grace has commented several times now on the dowdiness of her wardrobe, and whether she proves to be an imposter or not, we cannot have it said that we dressed the woman in rags. I shall stop at Ripley and Hall in the village to select some silks, then we shall go on to Buxton to have them made up. We shall take the landau and shall be gone the better part of the day. I would ask you to accompany us, but she won't go without the boy, and you would be quite cramped. If you are in need of occupation I suggest that you turn your hand to the pile of sheets which you removed from the Dower House. Such common work should not be beyond your rather meagre skills. Your sister-in-law sets a surprisingly beautiful stitch.'

Suppressing the urge to set a beautiful stitch to hold her aunt's mouth shut, Kate continued up the stairs to her chamber. Was this what she was to be reduced to—darning sheets! Alicia did not even trust her to play nursemaid. Giles, who was off to inspect a horse somewhere, had asked Phaedra to accompany him. Giles had always favoured Phaedra. In a family of six siblings—eight if you counted Ross and Araminta—there were bound to be alliances and differences, but while she was undoubtedly well down the chain of popularity, Kate couldn't count herself as the favourite of a single one. Even dearest Ned had preferred Giles.

She threw herself onto the window seat and drew a frowning moon face in the condensation caused by her breath on the window pane. Drawing was another accomplishment she had not mastered. Her attempt at a horse had reduced Phaedra to tears of laughter once. She wiped the face away with her hand. It wasn't like her to be moody. She wondered how Virgil was getting on at New Lanark. She envied Virgil this trip. She envied Robert Owen Virgil's company.

Heavens, but she missed Virgil. There, she could admit that. No one could see inside her head the way he did. No one seemed particularly interested in her, the way he was. No one had ever made her feel the way he did.

Goodness, but she wanted him too. His body. His touch. His kisses. Their passion. Remembering what it had been like to have Virgil inside her made her muscles clench into a shiver. Alone in bed, she touched herself as Virgil had done, but it wasn't the same. She wanted *his* fingers. *His* mouth. His body.

Giles hadn't asked after Virgil once since he had gone, despite the fact that he'd been more than happy to monopolise him when he was here. It could be tact, of course, but Kate wasn't in the frame of mind conducive to giving anyone any credit. A man of ideas, Giles had called Virgil, but he had never considered him as anything other than a mild distraction from the burdens of trying to pull the estate out of the financial crisis in which their father's unfortunate investments had left them. Aunt Wilhelmina had practically danced in the wake of Virgil's departure. And Phaedra was so caught up in her horses that she barely noticed anything or anyone else. Whereas Kate…

Outside in the driveway, her aunt was being helped into the landau by John Coachman. She and Aunt Wilhelmina would never be close, but the stand-off they had reached, if not outright peace, was at least better than open warfare. Though her aunt remained almost

as sceptical as Giles about Alicia's claims, contradicto-
rily, she seemed to accept without question the child's
parentage. She remarked pointedly and repeatedly that
Crispin's arrival gave Kate the perfect opportunity to
practice her role as aunt.

But the fact was, Kate thought, watching Alicia lifting
the boy into the carriage, now that the hiatus of Alicia's
arrival was over, and Alicia herself was patently able to
take care of her own interests and equally wary of the
friendship Kate offered, there was very little for Kate
to do. Alicia's lawyer was negotiating a settlement for
her. He was insisting on joint guardianship. His Grace
would be obliged to consult her on all matters pertinent
to Crispin's well-being. She would take care, too, she
told Kate, that His Grace understood that nothing short
of death would separate her from her child. She would
see that Crispin had what was entitled to him.

Alicia was evidently not so fragile as her appearance
gave everyone to believe. Kate was relieved. She looked
forward to the day, which must surely come, when Alicia
did pitched battle with the duke. She would not lay odds
against her.

'Devil take it, I will not spend the day mending
sheets!' Kate threw herself from the window seat, then
stopped short. There were plenty of things she could be

doing. Much more important things. If only she could think of them.

'Lady Kate, I'm so sorry, but this letter was overlooked in the mailbag this morning.'

Daisy's head poked round the bedchamber door. Kate's mouth went quite dry as she took the epistle. She had never seen the neat script before. There was no cause at all to imagine that it would be from him, and even if it was, it did not necessarily mean anything. 'Thank you.'

Kate locked the door behind Daisy and with trembling hands sat down again on the window seat to break the wafer.

It was from Virgil, and it was everything and nothing. Scanning it quickly, aware that her heart was beating fast, that she was shaking, Kate lurched from anticipation to extreme disappointment in the space of a few seconds. She read it again, forcing herself to go more slowly now, but there was nothing personal in it at all. Virgil had written her an account of New Lanark *'in order that you may better understand Owen's methods as well as his theory*,' he wrote. There was no return address. Only a postscript, informing her that he would not be returning to Stoke to see Josiah, but would conclude their business in London. She would never see him again.

She had thought she had understood that. She had thought she had accepted it. She had not. Staring at the letter, reading it for a third time, and for a third time failing to find anything remotely personal, the dreadful truth which she had hidden away, ignored, denied, buried deep down inside her, peeped out.

'Oh, no, not that.' Oh, heavens, let her contrariness not have led her to that. Surely she couldn't possibly have been so stupid as to fall in love with him?

But it was too late, and it had nothing to do with contrariness, her love for Virgil. 'Well done, Kate,' she said bitterly. 'Trust you to give your heart to the one man in the world determined not to have it.'

She loved him. She had thought herself incapable of love, but it seemed she was wrong. When had she stopped being afraid? She didn't know, but sometime between the day at the Rothermere Arms and now, she seemed to have crossed the border and left the past behind. She had paid for her mistakes with Anthony in full. What's more, she had, she realised with surprise, accepted that trying to become the person her aunt and her father wished her to be was wrong. Worse than wrong, it would make her unhappy. Virgil said she had to forgive herself. She hadn't really understood what he'd meant, but it seemed she'd done it all the same.

If only Virgil could forgive himself too—but that, Kate knew, looking down at her letter, really was asking the impossible. She loved him, but he would never, ever love her back. No one understood her as Virgil did. No one would ever touch her, mind or body, as he did. She could not imagine that anyone ever would.

Tears clogged her throat, but she would not let them fall. She had promised him that she would try to be happy. In this letter he had written, there was no love, but there was much which could help her to follow some of her dreams. Sniffing resolutely, Kate took it over to her desk and began to read it again.

Robert Owen, Virgil told her, employed one of his former mill workers and a young village girl to teach the infants without books. Mr Owen boasted that his mill workers were the happiest, healthiest and most productive of any in the country, though Virgil was not convinced they were all equally so. In the evenings, they attended classes and dancing lessons. There followed a host of facts and figures which Virgil hoped would give Kate the real evidence, practical proof, to make her patrons pay attention.

Kate smiled as she read Virgil's views on some of Mr Owen's more controversial methods, then she drew a clean sheet of paper onto the blotter, dipped her pen in the inkwell and began to make notes.

Virgil reached Glasgow in the early afternoon. The crowd of ships on the river Clyde marked his progress towards the bustling city, long lines of them anchored in the channel with their heavy sails furled; the exposed rigging looked like complex trails of cobwebs slung between the masts. There was a constant to-ing and fro-ing of small boats ploughing the waters from the ships to the wharfs like worker ants.

As the Edinburgh mail approached the town itself along roads thick with mud it slowed, weaving through the clutter and throng of carts and drays, of carriages and sedan chairs, avoiding stray dogs and clucking hens and a herd of lowing cattle being brought back from the common grazing grounds in the west to their byres in the east.

The mighty cathedral rose high on the hill above the city. In amongst the cluster of smallholdings and cottages which dotted the land nearest the river, merchants made rich by tobacco, sugar and slaves had built huge mansions. The foundations of a large house stood oddly in the midst of a field planted with cabbages. Further east, just before the Trongate, inns and taverns of the lower sort contested the traditional space of houses and food markets.

Virgil stopped at the posting house only to eat the half crown ordinary of mutton and barley stew. Ramshorn Kirk, where Louisa Gordon was buried, was known locally as the Merchant's Graveyard. Armed with directions, the gold locket tucked safe in an inside pocket of his coat, he set out on foot. Glasgow owed much of its wealth to the crop he had spent a large part of his life growing and harvesting and he was eager to see what his servitude had created. Though the trade was no longer what it had been, there was a time when almost every hogshead of tobacco grown in Virginia had come through this city.

He walked up to the cathedral past the cheese and meat markets, whose business was done for the day. Descending the hill via the university and skirting the large expanse of the green where lines of washing flapped in the breeze, he came to the tower of the tollbooth prison. In the paved square outside, he stopped to watch the merchants hold court while those wishing to do business with them vied for attention.

By the warehouses and offices which lined the docks, the air was thick with the scent of spices, sugar and, above all, tobacco. That sweet, almost rotten smell made Virgil stop in his tracks, oblivious of the bustle around him, of clerks with their tied documents, of ships' crews in search of their next voyage, of the warehousemen who lurked in the alleyways taking a sly break, and through it all the merchants who strutted and preened. Eleven years ago, the tobacco which had been packed by the strike breakers would have come here. Twelve years ago, thirteen, fourteen, more, the hogsheads he had packed himself would have been sold on at this exchange, too, more than likely. Now he was probably richer than any of these merchants. If he wanted to, he could outbid them all for tobacco, sugar, molasses, silks. The knowledge gave him no pleasure. *How many schools and libraries and houses would be enough?* Kate's question haunted him. It would never be enough. Never. Because his crime was so great? Or because he was looking at it all the wrong way?

He stopped abruptly in front of the Trade's House. It looked uncannily familiar. He could not imagine why at first, and then he saw it. The carved pediment above the pillared entrance, the pleasing symmetry of the building. It reminded him of Castonbury.

Kate.

Kate had said he had to forgive himself. Kate had said that this locket he carried was someone else's past. Kate had said he would never be free. He missed her. God, he missed her. That last day, when he'd told her to be happy, he hadn't meant it. He *did* want her to be happy, but not with another man. Not with any man. Except him.

But that was impossible.

Wasn't it?

The graveyard was north of the river, just a few hundred yards from the Trade's House. It was raining as he entered it, a long narrow space enclosed by warehouses on three sides. Gloomy. Ominous. It did not feel particularly peaceful. He would not like this to be his last resting place.

Reading the stones, he could see how the place got its name. Tobacco, sugar, cloth—the remains of any number of merchants lay here with their families, touting their wealth in the huge slabs of stone which covered their crypts. Several of the tombs were large enough to be enclosed by wrought iron fencing. The Gordon tomb was one such. Virgil turned the heavy latch, relieved to find it was not locked.

Tragic, Kate had called Malcolm Jackson's story. If Louisa Gordon had married her lover and gone to the New World, she would not now be lying beneath this cold, damp sod. A month's happiness, a year's, or many more, she would have had with her husband. Had Kate been Louisa, she would not have stayed behind alone. If Kate had been Millie, she would not have killed herself.

Virgil sank down onto the gravestone and opened the locket. Kate would not have given up as Millie had. Kate would have known without him having to tell her that he would come back for her, because Kate understood him. No one had ever understood him as Kate had. Could he forgive himself?

If he did not, one thing was for sure; he would never

be free of his chains. The past kept him bound and manacled. He could not undo it, he could repent it and he could try and make good, but how much good was enough? He could build schools and libraries and model villages even. He could give others the opportunity to free themselves, but still deny himself that chance. Kate was right. He was still in shackles.

Millie would not have wanted that. Would Millie have forgiven him? Freedom was about having choices. He'd made some poor choices, and he'd paid for them, but Millie had chosen too. She'd chosen death over hope. Kate said that Millie would have forgiven him. That hadn't ever sat right with Virgil. Millie had made it impossible for Virgil to be forgiven. Wasn't the point that *he* had to forgive *her*?

He tried to remember what it felt like to be with Millie—to laugh with her, to walk with her, to make love to her—but it was like someone else's memories. Even the images from that fateful last day which had been so painfully fresh when he'd painted them for Kate seemed to be fading. Perhaps his confession had been cathartic, after all.

He'd been a boy when he'd fallen in love with Millie. Their passion had been joyful, but nowhere near as intense as what he'd felt making love to Kate. When Kate climaxed she looked right at him. When he was inside her, inside the intoxicating heat of her, he felt as if she was inside his head, as if she was communing with him. He hadn't ever felt that with Millie.

Could he really forgive himself? And even if he could, and come to terms with what Millie had done, too, where did that leave him?

It left him without Kate.

Virgil took out his pocket knife and began to dig a hole. He dropped the locket into it, and said a last prayer for Malcolm Jackson and Louisa Gordon. Maybe in the next world he and his Louisa were together.

Virgil was in this world, and he had no desire to quit it yet. If he could forgive himself, he had a future, and he was damn sure he didn't want to live it alone. Closing the gate of the crypt behind him, he made his way quickly back to the posting house. Eleven years of celibacy. It seemed so obvious now that it had been easy because he hadn't met Kate. He did love her. He had no idea what she felt for him, but he did love her. He had done everything possible to kill any feelings for him she may have had, but that last day at the inn…

Could he hope? Dare he hope? He had been afraid to love her because he was terrified of losing her, but if he didn't ask her, if he didn't try, then he'd have lost her anyway. He missed her so much. Now that he had allowed himself to consider the possibility, he couldn't bear to think of how empty his future would be without her. It was all very well to insulate yourself against hurt by denying yourself affection, but it was too late for that now. He had to see her. He could not wait to see her.

He ran the last half-mile to the posting house. 'Change of plan,' he said to the landlord. 'I need to hire a post chaise and six. Now.'

Kate rose each morning with a list of tasks constructed overnight and went about them methodically, focusing on achieving something new every day. She made the days long. She worked hard. She did not cry, or lament, or allow herself to dwell on her hopeless love. Virgil was gone. There was nothing she could do about it, and all she could do to keep her heart intact was to be true to what she had promised him. It was not her way to try to change what she could not. She was a survivor, one who coped and continued regardless, and this was how she found the reserves to face each day. She loved him and would always love him, but there was nowhere for her love to live, and so she kept it hidden, tucked up inside her like a wingless bird. Helping others had always been her consolation. She would simply have to help them a lot more now.

This morning, the first task on her list was to see

Alicia, and finally bring her up to date with the contents of Harry's letter.

'I have some news.'

They were sitting in the drawing room of the Dower House. The child, Crispin, played contentedly in the corner with a set of wooden blocks. Jamie's wife looked well, dressed in a morning gown the same colour of blue as her eyes. Her fair hair was prettily dressed, tied in a top knot which fell in a cluster of curls around her neck. She did not wear a widow's cap. Aunt Wilhelmina had been vocal upon this subject at dinner. Alicia looked much too young to be a widow. She was much too beautiful to hide her charms under a cap. Not that there was anyone in Castonbury to appreciate Alicia's charms that Kate could think of.

Had Alicia loved Jamie? Loving Virgil as she did made Kate look at everyone differently. Now she knew the signs, it was obvious to her that Giles was deeply in love with Lily. Of Alicia's feelings she was not at all certain. There were times when she seemed quite cold, indifferent almost, in the way she said Jamie's name, as if he was not her husband but a stranger. Of course, she had Crispin to remind her of Jamie and so no real need to talk about him, Kate supposed. Polly said she'd never been in love and thank the Lord for having been spared. Despite everything, Kate was glad *she* had not been spared.

'What news, Lady Kate?'

Alicia was looking at her expectantly, and Kate realised she had been daydreaming again. A new habit. 'We have had a letter from my brother Harry. As you know, he's in Spain.'

'Trying to discover what happened to my husband.'

'Jamie. Yes. Harry writes from Madrid, but he is on his way to Seville. There is a man there, Pablo Garrido, who was apparently in command of the unit to which Jamie was assigned. Harry's letter says—Harry believes that this man Garrido may be able to put him in touch with the man who was actually with Jamie when he died.'

Alicia's hands fluttered to her breast. 'You mean Xavier Sanchez?'

'I believe that was the name. You know this man?'

'No, no. Only—I have heard his name. I— Jamie must have talked of him.'

'Jamie discussed his mission with you?'

'No, that's not what I meant.' Alicia leapt to her feet and picked her child up, folding him in a tight embrace, ignoring his protests. 'I meant—I merely meant that when Jamie died, it was no secret that man Sanchez was with him.'

'Of course, it's only a slim chance, but if Harry can speak with Sanchez, perhaps then we can find out the details of how Jamie lost his life. And then there will be the proof of death that we need in order to sort out the estate.' Kate smiled encouragingly. 'It could even be that Jamie talked to Sanchez about you.'

'About me?' Alicia repeated, the colour draining from her face. 'Why should he?'

'Mama, Mama, you're hurting.'

The child set up a wail. Alicia got to her feet, kissing the boy's golden head. 'It is time for his nap,' she said to Kate.

There was no mistaking the dismissal in her voice. 'I'm sorry to throw this at you so suddenly, only Giles and I felt that you should know. We have not told anyone else. You understand, Alicia, my father knows nothing of it.'

'You need not worry, I won't say anything to the duke. Jamie is dead. What do the details matter?' Alicia said flatly. 'Excuse me, Lady Kate. I must see to my son.'

Walking back to the big house, Kate felt rebuffed. Recounting the meeting to Giles, who had been waiting for her by the bridge, her natural sense of justice restored her. 'It was a shock,' she told her brother, 'that much was obvious. She must have cared a great deal for him. It's just too painful for her to hear the details.'

'Well, you told her. She can't accuse us of not keeping her informed,' Giles said. 'Kate...'

'What is it?'

'Kate, Virgil Jackson is here.'

'What?'

'He arrived half an hour ago.'

'Is there something wrong? Has he been hurt? Why didn't you tell me? Where is he?'

'Why the devil should you think he was hurt? He looked perfectly healthy to me. He's in my study. I thought it best—no one knows save Lumsden that he's here. Kate...'

'What is it, Giles?' Kate was almost dancing in exasperation. Virgil was here. *'What?'*

'Devil take you, Kate, you know damn well what! I can't stop you. If you love him—Lily says you do, and she's—well, God help you.'

Under any other circumstances, Kate would have found this disjointed speech utterly fascinating. She didn't think she'd ever seen her brother beyond words, but right now she didn't give a damn. Picking up her skirts, she ran across the lawn at full tilt and did not stop until she burst into Giles's study, when the sight of Virgil standing there made her heart flip.

'Kate!'

'Virgil!'

'You look tired.'

'It's been a long journey.'

Kate closed the door and leaned against it. She was out of breath. Her hair was falling down. She was shaking. 'How did you get here?'

'Post chaise. I hired a carriage. Four horses. I asked for six but they said not even royalty could harness six horses to a hired chaise.'

He looked quite dishevelled. His neck cloth looked as if it had been tied without the aid of a mirror. His boots were splashed with mud. He looked anxious. Nervous. Worried. She had missed him so much. Giles seemed to think—but she would not let herself hope. 'What are you doing here?'

'I had a speech,' Virgil said. Kate hadn't moved from the door. She looked wary. He didn't like that look. 'I had a speech,' he said again. He couldn't remember a word of it. He crossed the room to stand beside her. There was only one bit of what he wanted to say that mattered right now. 'I love you, Kate.'

'How do you know?'

That made him laugh. He should have known her reaction wouldn't be what he expected. 'What you said, about never being free. When I was burying the locket, I realised you were right. Millie had a choice too. I made it difficult for her to live, but I didn't make it impossible. Once I saw that, I saw lots of other things too.'

'Such as?'

'I was afraid to care. I thought that love and loss went hand in hand. I didn't want to love you because I couldn't bear the idea of losing you, but then I realised that never having tried, regretting not trying, would be so much worse.'

'Like Louisa Gordon and Malcolm Jackson,' Kate said.

Virgil took her hands in his. 'Exactly. And more. I couldn't understand why you were so impossible to resist. I see now that it was you. It could only ever have been you. I love you, Kate. I don't know what you feel, but I'm asking you to give me a chance. It won't be easy. Your father will disown you. Even in Boston, a marriage like ours would be—there will be many people who will never accept us into their world. But if you love me, we could make our own world, Kate.'

A single tear escaped her and rolled down her cheek. He still hadn't touched her. He was afraid to touch her. He was terrified he had left it too late. 'Don't cry, Kate.'

She sniffed. 'I'm not.' She rubbed her eyes with the heel of her hand. 'If that was your speech, it was the most beautiful one I've ever heard.'

It took a moment for her words to sink in. 'I'm not too late?'

Kate shook her head.

'You love me?'

'How could you doubt it?'

'And you'll marry me?'

'Oh, Virgil, I thought you'd never ask!'

He kissed her so hard then that if she had not been leaning against the door she would have fallen. He kissed her desperately, clinging to her, murmuring her name, his hands feverish on her. He really had thought he'd lost her.

'You would never have been too late,' she whispered, kissing him back, pressing herself as close as she could against the delightfully hard, solid bulk of his body. 'Never, never, never. I love you more.'

'No, me more.'

'No, me. More.'

They were laughing and kissing at the same time. A wild euphoria ripped through them, turning their laughter into passion. Kate reached behind her to turn the key in the lock, saying a quick apology to her brother for the use they were about to make of his private room.

'We can't,' Virgil said as she rubbed herself quite blatantly against the length of his erection. 'It would be wrong.'

'All the more reason,' Kate said, stroking him through the leather of his buckskins. 'Think how outraged my aunt would be,' she said, slipping down onto her knees before him and undoing the buttons of his falls.

'We should wait. Until we are married. That's what I planned. Oh, Kate…'

With a sigh of satisfaction, she freed him and wrapped her fingers around him. Silky and potent and hers. She tasted the tip of him, relishing the way it made him shudder, drawing a groan from deep inside him. She was hot. Wet. 'I don't want to wait,' she said, slanting a mischievous look up at him before tasting him again. 'I don't think you *can* wait, my love. Doesn't it add a certain something, knowing what my family would think? This isn't wrong. It couldn't be more right, could it?'

Virgil dropped down onto his knees beside her. 'Nothing could be more right,' he said, cupping her face. His kiss left her utterly certain. 'Nothing could be more right than this,' he said, tilting her back onto the floor and kissing her again.

'And this.' He pushed her skirts high, parting the legs of her lacy drawers. 'Do you know, there is something about the curve of your knee which fascinates me. And here, the crease right here, where your bottom curves into your thigh. And here.' He cupped her sex, gazing deep into her eyes as the pressure of his palm on the swollen core of her brought her to a frenzy.

'And this.' The tip of his shaft stroked over her, throwing her over the edge as he entered her. She pulsed around him, panting and clutching at him, urging him on, harder.

'I love you, Kate,' Virgil said, and he exploded, staying inside her, holding her, shuddering against her.

Kate wrapped her arms tight around him. Her hair streamed out across the ancient rug. The leg of a chair was sticking into her shoulder. There was a large cobweb suspended from the cornicing above her. 'I love you, Virgil.' She had never been happier.

Epilogue

His Grace the Duke of Rothermere was predictably out-raged by his eldest daughter's choice of husband. Having met Virgil just once, His Grace was completely unprepared for the astounding news that his wayward daughter had fallen in love and accepted a proposal from a man who, as far as he was concerned, barely existed. That the man was an American, albeit one of that country's richest inhabitants, was bad enough. That he was a commoner, and ex-slave with a lineage which could be traced back precisely one generation and only on one side, made the marriage, as far as the duke was concerned, simply impossible.

He was incandescent. When it became clear that Virgil was not actually *asking* him for his daughter's hand but telling him that he had already been accepted, consent was refused. When it was pointed out to His

Grace by his outspoken daughter that his consent was not required, the duke informed her that she would be cut off without a penny.

'My dowry was settled on me by my mother. You cannot actually deprive me of it,' Kate said with satisfaction, having made a point of checking the matter with Giles.

'As a matter of fact, we have no need of Kate's dowry,' her future husband said.

'But it's mine. I'm entitled to it. I can't come to you with nothing.'

'You are all I need.'

At this point, the duke's daughter committed the ultimate sin of expressing her emotions in public by throwing her arms around her betrothed and kissing him. His Grace, realising nothing could be done to prevent the match, decided that nothing could make him accept it. Informing his daughter that he never wanted to lay eyes on her again, he sank onto his couch, closed his eyes and opened them only when his valet presented him with a glass of cognac and informed him that Lady Katherine and the American had gone.

Thus relieved of the duty of trying what she had always known would be a vain attempt to bring her father round, Kate set about happily making plans. Virgil, who had at first been inclined to consider using monetary measures to bring the duke on to their side, was persuaded by her complete and utter happiness not to do so. That her brother, sister and even her aunt seemed, respectively, reconciled, happy and inured to Kate's choice was more than Virgil had bargained for.

Though he missed her desperately, he was persuaded that he could leave her to make arrangements for their wedding while he made his arrangements for their departure to America and finished his business in London with Josiah Wedgwood. The potter was so delighted with the news that such a unique couple had been introduced at his own dinner party that he promised to design them their very own dinner service.

Lady Katherine Mary Cecily Montague became Mrs Virgil Jackson on Christmas Eve. It was a private ceremony in the family chapel at Castonbury. The Reverend Seagrove officiated. The groom was represented, most irregularly as Aunt Wilhelmina pointed out, by the bride's brother. This left the bride herself with no one to walk her up the aisle until she hit upon the idea of asking her aunt to give her away.

Mrs Landes-Fraser was torn. Never before had she heard of such a thing. But since it was a private ceremony, her niece pointed out, no one would ever know. And if they did, Aunt Wilhelmina should remember that this was the wedding of the Duke of Rothermere's daughter. Where a Montague led, others would follow.

Would not Aunt Wilhelmina wish to set a precedent all by herself?

Mrs Landes-Fraser was flattered.

Kate, existing in a bubble of happiness, pressed home her advantage. It was what her mother would have wanted, she said, disregarding without a qualm the fact that she barely knew her mother, and was fairly certain that she would have spent her eldest daughter's wedding day in protest alongside her husband rather than in the church. But Aunt Wilhelmina was swayed. In honour of the occasion, she purchased a new turban in a particularly regal shade of puce and proudly walked her niece the short journey up the aisle, thus finally proving to Kate that her affection, though well-buried, was sincere.

All the more sincere, Phaedra, the only other person present, whispered later to her sister, since Aunt Wilhelmina had chosen to support Kate against the express wishes of their father, who was notable by his absence.

The church, which had been built and rebuilt by the Montague family on the same site since the thirteenth century, provided any number of Kate's ancestors in the form of effigies and tombs, to make up for the absent duke. Kate, dressed in a vermillion gown cut quite inappropriately low across the bosom, didn't care. There was only one person whose attendance was vital, and he was right there at her side, placing a gold wedding band on her finger. Reverend Seagrove said later that he had never heard a couple make their responses so firmly. Aunt Wilhelmina declared that the church must be in need of airing, for the dust had made her eyes positively stream.

Though the bridal couple wanted no formal party to celebrate their nuptials, Giles insisted that there was one tradition which could not be dispensed with. The Yule log had been hauled in that day, and sat in the fireplace in the huge marble hall. Monsieur André, the French chef, had produced a sugar cake which was an exact replica of Castonbury Park itself, in honour of the occasion. The entire Castonbury staff save His Grace's faithful valet were there to greet Lady Kate and her husband. Most of them were very happy for her. Polly, who was joining her mistress in the New World, was nothing short of ecstatic.

To Kate fell the honour of lighting the fire with kindling formed from last year's Yule log. To Virgil fell the task of proposing a toast to his new bride. Looking around at the sea of faces standing under the gilded domed ceiling in the cavernous and astoundingly beautiful hall, he caught her hand. 'Are you sure you really want to leave all this behind?'

'This is the old world, Virgil. I will miss it, but I can live without it. I can't live without you.'

Every time he looked at her, he thought it wasn't possible to love her more, and every time he looked at her again he realised it was. Virgil kissed his wife's hand and raised his glass. 'To Kate,' he said, 'who is all the world to me.'

* * * * *

Read on to find out more about
Marguerite Kaye
and the

CASTONBURY
PARK
A Regency Upstairs Downstairs

series...

Born and educated in Scotland, **Marguerite Kaye** originally qualified as a lawyer but chose not to practise. Instead, she carved out a career in IT and studied history part-time, gaining a first-class honours and a Master's degree. A few decades after winning a children's national poetry competition, she decided to pursue her lifelong ambition to write and submitted her first historical romance to Mills & Boon. They accepted it and she's been writing ever since. You can contact Marguerite through her website at: www.margueritekaye.com

Previous novels by the same author:

THE WICKED LORD RASENBY
THE RAKE AND THE HEIRESS
^ INNOCENT IN THE SHEIKH'S HAREM
^ THE GOVERNESS AND THE SHEIKH
*THE HIGHLANDER'S REDEMPTION
* THE HIGHLANDER'S RETURN
RAKE WITH A FROZEN HEART

And in Mills & Boon® Historical *Undone!* eBooks:

THE CAPTAIN'S WICKED WAGER
THE HIGHLANDER AND THE SEA SIREN
BITTEN BY DESIRE
TEMPTATION IS THE NIGHT
+ CLAIMED BY THE WOLF PRINCE
+ BOUND TO THE WOLF PRINCE
+ THE HIGHLANDER AND THE WOLF PRINCESS
^ THE SHEIKH'S IMPETUOUS LOVE-SLAVE
SPELLBOUND & SEDUCED

^ linked by character
* Highland Brides
+ Legend of the Faol

AUTHOR Q&A

What is your heroine's favourite childhood memory of Castonbury Park?

As children, Kate and her siblings used to escape to the island on the big lake. They kept a chest hidden in the undergrowth there, with kindling and blankets, and would often picnic together. Both Kate and her sister Phaedra are strong swimmers and as adults go to the island with their heroes, where those younger days are specifically recalled and the contents of the chest re-used for much more adult purposes!

Which stately home inspired Castonbury Park and why?

We chose Kedleston Hall for Castonbury (http://www.nationaltrust.org.uk/kedleston-hall). This was for a number of reasons, but primarily because two of our group had visited it and so could give us some really great inside information about the layout of the place. We had a floor plan, pictures and a guidebook to work from, which was really important because the house and its grounds are vital characters in every book and we wanted to make sure that we were consistent. When we added things—such as an island into the lake, a fountain, a bath house under the fishing pavilion—we could be very clear, referring to the real house and where they were in relation to what we already knew, and when we were describing some of the key rooms—dining room, drawing room, marble hall—we could all be consistent.

Kedleston is simply beautiful. It's designed by Robert Adam, so fits perfectly into the type of house a duke would have had built, with the kind of grandeur and extensive grounds such an influential and aristocratic family would have. The grounds were important, since we needed various trysting places out of the house as so many of the relationships were scandalous, but we also wanted to have a village, a church, schools, an inn and shops, in order to give readers a whole world and a real sense of community, not just of the family.

The Dower House is taken from Luckington Court, which was used for the BBC production of *Pride and Prejudice*.

(http://www.luckingtoncourt.co.uk/index.html)

Again, because this featured across several books, we wanted somewhere with a real reference point, but we also wanted a building which was a contrast to Castonbury Park and yet at the same time in a similar Palladian style.

In *The Lady Who Broke the Rules* I also feature Maer Hall, which at the time was home to Josiah Wedgwood—son of the famous potter and head of the Wedgwood Company in 1816.

Where did you get the inspiration for Kate and Virgil?

I wanted to come up with a relationship that was outrageously scandalous, in line with the theme of social change and upheaval which we agreed would run through Castonbury Park as a series, so a freed black slave seemed like a brilliant starting point. Obviously any man who could survive the horrors of slavery and succeed on his own terms as Virgil does would have to be unbelievably strong-willed and he'd also, it seemed to me, have to have a motivation for his relentless drive to succeed which was not simply material. Virgil, I decided, would be the type of man who'd want to help others have what he'd had to fight so hard to get. Yet at the same time I thought a man like that would surely have deep-seated issues, coming from such a traumatic background. And that led me to the idea that, while Virgil was freed, he was at the same time a slave to his past.

Which led me to Kate… To be the perfect match for Virgil, my heroine had to be a very strong-willed, independent woman, willing to stand up for her beliefs and to stand apart from a society which would completely disown her once she made her choice. So she had to be a woman who was already in a sense an 'outsider'—or at least a rebel, a thinker and a woman with a social conscience too. Like Virgil, Kate is a righter of wrongs—a woman who sees imbalance and wants to correct it. And the reason Kate sees imbalance so clearly is that she too has suffered injustice and is using philanthropy to avoid dealing with some deep-seated personal issues. Both are still bound by the chains of her past.

What are you researching for your forthcoming novel?

Not for my current book, but I am reading up on the Crimean War at present and thinking about writing something which is set in and around the aftermath of this, when the social upheaval which began after the end of the Napoleonic Wars had really started to set in.

What would you most like to have been doing in Regency times?

I love to travel and I'd love to think that, despite the social and possibly financial constraints which the Regency would place on me, I would have boldly gone where no woman had gone before. I'd have been an intrepid explorer like Lady Hester Stanhope, who went off to Arabia and never came back and whom I researched for my Princes of the Desert series.

AUTHOR NOTE

The history of slavery has fascinated me. It's a complex, emotive and often controversial subject and no one except those who experienced it can know what it was really like. In writing this book I did a lot of research, but ultimately what I've written is a personal take which may or may not resemble 'reality'. What I want to share with you are some of my reasons for choosing to take on the challenge of making a freed slave a romantic hero in the first place.

The Lady Who Broke the Rules is set in 1816. In the United States the trade of slaves was abolished in the north in 1804, after which the manumission of slaves in those states gathered momentum. In the South, however, where cotton was in increasing demand (paradoxically thanks to the north's industrialisation of textile manufacture), slaves were a hugely important part of the economy and resistance to abolition was significant.

Virgil, my hero, was born into slavery in the South and freed in the north. He was one of the fortunate ones who came to true eminence and used his wealth to give others the chances he had had to make for himself. Though in reality this kind of success was rare, it was not unheard of. Robert Purvis is just one example of the black philanthropists from whom I took inspiration for Virgil, but his entrepreneurial side is an amalgamation of a whole number of black men and women who flourished in nineteenth-century Boston, renting out real estate, setting up restaurants and beauty parlours, making shoes and clothes for the mass market, taking on the establishment by training as lawyers and doctors.

Across the pond in Great Britain many aristocratic families had derived a large part of their wealth from plantations in the West Indies which relied on slavery, but their influence was on the decline. The actual trade of slaves became illegal in 1807 and, although it was not until 1833 that slavery itself was abolished, by 1816 the growing Abolitionist movement, coupled with the decline of the economic significance of the West Indies plantations, made the idea, if not the reality, of slavery much less politically and socially acceptable than it had been a decade or so before.

From the point of view of this story, what interested me most about the British abolitionists was how many of them were women. It was one of the few political causes in which it became acceptable for women to participate and in which women took a leading and influential role, so I relished the opportunity to create a heroine who could, without it seeming a historical anachronism, be active politically and philanthropically. Josiah Wedgwood's daughter, Sarah, who introduces Kate to Virgil, was just one real-life example I drew on.

There's a huge difference between perception and reality. Kate had only read about slavery. Virgil had experienced it. As a writer, I had to try and imagine myself in both sets of shoes and whether I've managed it or not—well, that's for you to decide. But ultimately this isn't a book about slavery—it's about love. And I hope you'll agree that Kate, *The Lady Who Broke the Rules*, is as perfect for Virgil as I imagined her to be.

Don't miss the next instalment of Castonbury Park—
LADY OF SHAME
by Ann Lethbridge

'You're in danger of dishonouring the family name for good!'

Lady Claire must put pride above prattle if she is to shake off the not-so-respectable reputation of her youth. Swapping rebellion for reserve, she returns to her imposing childhood home, Castonbury Park, seeking her family's help. Penniless Claire needs a sensible husband…and fast!

But when the dark gaze of head chef Monsieur André catches her eye, he's as deliciously tempting as the food he prepares. Claire knows he's *most* unsuitable…even if the chemistry between them is magnetic. Risking her reputation for André would be shameful—but losing him could be even worse!

LADY OF SHAME

Ann Lethbridge

'You risk too much.'

A band tightened around her chest. Apparently he did not feel the same way. And yet she persevered. 'If we are careful—'

His eyes found hers. A gaze filled with regret, or pity. She could not be sure.

'I cannot be that man.' He shot a look towards the door and moved closer, lowering his voice. 'I cannot be your dirty little secret, at your beck and call while you court a husband.'

The flatness of his voice when he spoke those words stung like a whip's metal point. She had never thought about what they had done in those horrid terms. She'd been too busy living only in the moment, in the joy of it. She could see what others might make of it, though. What he had made of it.

'Don't make this any harder than it is, Claire,' he murmured softly. 'I cannot be what you want. I am sorry if I let you think otherwise.'

She wanted to plead with him, but instead spun away, gazing out of the window before he could see her disappointment or the hot moisture welling in her eyes.

He had clearly made up his mind. And he was right.

Their lovemaking was risky.

Fear and relief had sent her into his arms the first time. Loneliness the second.

'Of course,' she said, keeping her voice calm. 'I beg your pardon...' Her voice cracked. 'I did not mean to insult you.'

'Claire,' he said softly. 'You know this is right.'

She turned with a bright smile, patently false but a smile nonetheless. 'The Dowager Marchioness has indicated that she will not attend our next dinner party, so our company will be smaller than usual, but I think we should not change the dishes. Are you agreed?'

'I agree. But—'

'Then there is no more to be said, Monsieur André. I bid you good day. I assume there will be no more little dramas like last time?'

His dark eyes held hers. Unreadable. His expression severe. 'No, *madame.*'

'Very good. You may go.' She sounded every bit the duke's daughter with those words, and she held her head proudly in clear dismissal.

'It is for the best,' he said, clearly trying to soften the blow.

'Close the door on your way out.' She spoke coldly, refusing to acknowledge his power to cause her pain. She turned back to the window, looking out blindly, staring at an imperfection in the glass that made the outside ebb and flow in ripples of light and shadow.

'As you wish, *madame.*'

The silent pause said he'd bowed. The whisper of sound and the click of the door echoed in her ears. She collapsed onto the sofa, the tears she'd held back hot on her cheeks.

She dashed them away. Had she so little pride? No common sense when it came to this man? This servant? Any hint of such a scandal would lead to utter ruin. For herself, she didn't care about being an outcast. She'd been that for years. But Jane's future hung in the balance. The sins of the parent would not be visited upon the child. She would not permit it.

© Michèle Ann Young 2012

So you think you can write?

It's your turn!

Mills & Boon® and Harlequin® have joined forces in a global search for new authors and now it's time for YOU to vote on the best stories.

It is our biggest contest ever—the prize is to be published by the world's leader in romance fiction.

And the most important judge of what makes a great new story?

YOU—our reader.

Read first chapters and story synopses for all our entries at
www.soyouthinkyoucanwrite.com

**Vote now at
www.soyouthinkyoucanwrite.com!**

 HARLEQUIN®
entertain, enrich, inspire™   MILLS & BOON®

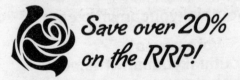